Legion.

Evil Has No Bounds

Shane Walker

Copyrights

: **Disclaimer**

This novel contains scenes and discussions that may be distressing or triggering to some
readers. It includes depictions of sexual abuse and violence. Reader discretion is advised. If you are a survivor of such experiences or find these topics deeply disturbing, please take care while reading...

ABOUT THE AUTHOR

Shane Walker is a 57-year-old author of fiction, poet, and semi-professional photographer from Spreyton; a charming suburb nestled in the picturesque state of Tasmania, Australia. His passion for writing was ignited later in life, originally inspired by his father's poetry and captivating storytelling. Over the past decade, Shane has dedicated himself to honing his skills as a poet, pouring his heart and soul onto the page to capture the intricate beauty of the world that surrounds us. Thriller and supernatural themes captivate Shane's creative spirit, fuelling his imagination to explore dark and untamed depths within these genres. His vivid storytelling paints gripping narratives that transcend the boundaries of ordinary reality, transporting readers to thrilling and mysterious realms.It is worth noting that Shane has also dedicated the past 25 years of his life as a Ship Security officer aboard the Spirit of Tasmania 2, exemplifying his unwavering commitment to ensuring the safety and well-being of those on board.

Shane Walker epitomises the essence of an artist who unceasingly strives to share his unique vision with the world.

Dedications:

To my mother Dorothy, who has a love for reading and unwavering support for my creative pursuits.

To all my crew on the ship, thank you for lending parts of your names to my characters, bringing them to life with each stroke of the pen.

To Julie Wilson, who faithfully read most mornings, eager to uncover the next page of this novel's journey.

In addition, to my own imagination, a realm both captivating and daunting, for guiding me through the depths of storytelling.

This novel is dedicated to all those who believe in the power of words and the magic of imagination.

Thank you.

S. Walker

To my mother, Dorothy, who has a love for reading and unwavering support for my creative pursuits.

To all my crew on the ship, thank you for lending parts of your names to my characters, bringing them to life with each stroke of the pen.

To Julie Wilson, who faithfully read most mornings, eager to uncover the next page of this novel's journey.

In addition, to my own imagination, a realm both captivating and daunting, for guiding me through the depths of story-telling.

This novel is dedicated to all those who believe in the power of words and the magic of imagination.

Thank you.

S.Walker

Contents

1

WHAT IS THY NAME

Jesus asked him, "What is thy name?" And he answered, saying, "My name is Legion: for we are many." And forthwith Jesus gave them leave. And the unclean spirits went out, and entered into the swine: and the herd ran violently down a steep place into the sea, and were choked in the sea."

Mark 5:1-20,Luke 8:26-39

2

LEGION

The ground trembles with the sound of thunder, while bolts of lightning light up the darkness with an electric intensity. Despite the cold weather and slippery roads, a man attempts to outrun a car as it honks its horn. Meanwhile, an elderly man exits the King Street supermarket carrying a small bag of groceries, as the store remains quiet on this overcast Wednesday night. Despite the fact that precipitation has once again started, the gloomy appearance of the sky has created a melancholic and disheartening ambience that has persisted throughout the entire day. Working at the checkout, Julie Gaffney helps one last customer purchase a box of tissues and a small bottle of Worcestershire sauce. Julie struggles to make ends meet. Julie is a single mother who works three days a week and volunteers at a care home part-time. Unfortunately, her children's father left her for a younger woman when she turned thirty-eight, leaving her to raise their three children alone. Despite feeling undesirable, Julie continues to work hard to provide for her family and gain valuable experience through volunteering.

It's 1985 and Julie is having a prosperous year, working hard both on and off duty as she studies to become a caregiver for the elderly. She is a pretty girl with wavy brown hair down to her shoulders, a lovely smile, and a slim figure that she always strives to maintain. Behind her, Julie's boss Steve struggles with his apron. He joins Julie at the checkout and suggests, "You go, Jules; I'll finish up here, it is nearly 9 o'clock. And it's starting to rain." Julie quickly grabs her purple jacket from under the counter and heads towards the store entrance. She calls out to Steve, "I'm grabbing a drink," to which he jokingly responds, "It's coming out of your wages every time you know that, right?" Julie laughs and playfully retorts, "Blah Blah Blah," as she picks up a small bottle of lemonade from the fridge. She then asks loudly, "Can I also borrow your umbrella?" Steve agrees, and Julie grabs the umbrella leaning against the window next to the doors. As she steps outside, a cold draft briefly sends shivers down her spine. Several cars drive by with their lights on, splashing water from puddles as they go. Meanwhile, an elderly woman rushes past Julie, hunched over and holding her handbag above her head. The woman's white high heels slip and slide on the wet pavement, causing her to blame the conditions for her distress.

As Julie walks down the sidewalk, she sees a child crying as her mother tries to get her into the car in the rain. The child struggles with the door but manages to squeeze inside and continues crying. Julie's car is parked more than 250 metres away in a small lot off Formby Road, next to the Saxon River in the city of Coulson. While walking, Julie avoids a large puddle and drinks from her bottle without spilling. The lightning flashes, making the night briefly turn into day. The wind and rain are intense, stinging Julie's cheeks and making her feel like Mary Poppins in a hurricane. Her umbrella flutters and is too weak to stay above her. While walking, Julie notices a homeless man sitting on the sidewalk next to a shop. He reaches for his nearly empty can and rattles it, hoping to get the attention of people passing by. Julie reaches into her pocket and takes out two coins, placing them on top of his can. The man thanks her with a toothless smile. Julie continues her walk, still concerned for the crying child and her mother.

Despite the rain, there is still activity on King Street. Pedestrians hurry to find shelter while cars speed through the street, likely on their way home to their loved ones. A biker on a blue Harley Davidson starts his engine, causing Julie to jump, as she did not notice him before. She notices rainwater rushing around his black leather boot due to the clogged drain caused by fallen leaves. Suddenly, the wind picks up and Julie turns her head to avoid the rain, almost dropping her bottle. She places it next to the building to prevent anyone from accidentally knocking it over since there is no nearby bin. Out of nowhere, a voice calls out, startling Julie and causing her to momentarily levitate. She quickly turns around to see a thin man in a grey raincoat standing at the entrance of an abandoned shop.

Julie shouts in anger, "Oh my goodness, what are you thinking? You almost gave me a heart attack!" She quickly walks away. From a distance, the skinny man shouts, "Sorry, ma'am." Julie's heart is racing, and she feels pins and needles in her arms. She even notices her throat is sore from screaming when she got startled.

She arrives at the gravel lot, and the shiny red paint of her 1976 Holden Gemini car reflects the carousel of lights. Digging in the pocket of her jacket for the car keys, she notices the rain pelting the gravel and glances at the two cars parked across from her. While searching for her keys, the snowflake on the keychain becomes hooked on the lining of her pocket. She tries to pull it off, but the lining tears, causing her frustration. She mutters, "God dammit," and yanks it off with all her strength. She closes her umbrella, unlocks the creaky door, and throws the wet umbrella onto the passenger seat before flopping down in the driver's seat. Slamming the door, she checks the mirror on the visor, wiping away the mascara that has run down her cheeks due to the rain. As she turns the key, the car fails to start and instead makes an annoying clicking sound. Julie is puzzled. Why won't the car start? She turns the key again, but still, nothing happens. However, this time she notices that no lights were glowing on the dashboard, which is strange. At last, she realises that she has a flat battery. "Oh, you've got to be kidding me," Julie says out loud to an empty car.

She needs to call her babysitter and let her know she will be a little late. She hurries her way to a pay phone down the other end of the car park. It radiates light like a beacon of hope. The phone booth door is stiff, but after she forces it open, she grabs some change from her purse and finds just enough to make one call and a button from her shirt she keeps in her purse for later to mend. She inserts her coins. She is relieved when she hears the dial tone. Then quickly dials her phone number and waits for her babysitter to answer. After a few rings, a sleepy voice answers the phone. Julie explains that she had a flat battery and will be home soon. The babysitter says it is no problem and that she will stay awake until Julie gets home. Julie thanks her and hangs up the phone.

Julie heads towards the taxi rank but realises she has no money left. Disappointed, she turns back and embarks on a long walk home under the pouring rain and flashing lightning. Her fastest route back home is to cross the park near the river and catch the railway at the end of the park.

Within minutes, the rain soaks her clothes, making them stick uncomfortably to her skin. Her hair is plastered to her head, and her mascara runs down her cheeks again. Formby Road is deserted, and she crosses it to follow a path to a gate. Julie places both hands on the cold bars of the gate, pushes it open, and walks into the park. Her attention is caught by twinkling lights on the river, flickering far down the bank next to her. Suddenly, a cracking sound startles her, and she looks up into the trees. She can barely see anything, but as she looks up, she notices something yellow moving back and forth in the wind. It flaps wildly, and she realises it's a flag moving on a flagpole, making a whipping sound.

To her left stands eerie trees whose shadowy shapes resemble the limbs of a colossal monster. As she walks along the pebble-covered path, she can't help but notice the sound of the pebbles against her shoes resembling the crunch of breakfast cereal. This realization brings a smile to her face. The rain starts to pour harder, and she urgently needs to find cover. The downpour is so intense that she can barely make out the path ahead. Completely soaked from head to toe, her shoes are filled with water, and her hands are as wrinkled as prunes from soaking in the water for too long.

Julie spots a small wooden shed in the distance, hoping it will provide shelter from the wind and rain. She runs towards it, stumbling on the wet grass. Finally, she reaches the shed and takes cover. Although the roof is slanted and water is pouring out in front of her, hardly any rain falls on her. Meanwhile, the wind howls all around her. As Julie tries to regain her composure, she notices a person approaching her on the pebbled track. The figure is silhouetted by amber lights from the surrounding parkland. She initially thinks it's foolish to be out in this weather, but then realises that the person is probably trying to get home too. The figure turns out to be a man wearing a black hoodie sweatshirt with the hood pulled over his head. He is wearing a grey tracksuit and his white sneakers are muddy from walking the rain-soaked path. As he walks past her, he pays no attention to Julie. She watches him disappear into the darkness.

She strides through the park, feeling intimidated and perplexed by the man who blatantly disregards her. Abruptly, a brilliant flash of lightning illuminates the sky, startling her. Despite thinking the storm has subsided, a deafening crack of thunder resounds overhead, causing her to scream and leap. Rattled, Julie slows her gait and strolls along the riverbank, attempting to compose herself. As she brushes away damp strands of hair from her visage, she hears footsteps trailing behind her. Glancing over her shoulder, she gasps at the sight of the same man she saw earlier in the black hoodie and tracksuit pants sauntering on the path behind her. She questions *where he has appeared from?*

As the wind gets worse, it howls loudly past the leafy trees, causing them to sway and dance in its powerful path.

Julie's work trousers are rubbing against her skin as she pushes forward on the muddy track, and she begins to move at a faster pace. She peers behind her and notes that the man in the hoodie is catching up to her. Her fear is getting the better of her now, and she starts to run.

She glances behind her over her left shoulder to see if the hooded man is chasing her; he is sprinting down the track, directly toward her. "Leave me alone," she yells, but he continues to run towards her.

Julie runs to the right, dashing down an embankment beside the sidewalk and towards a riverbank. Maybe if she gets down there, in the dark, he won't be able to find her.

Wet grass clings to Julie's shoes as she slides down onto a rock next to the river. When she tries to get back up onto her feet, her shoes slip out from under her, and she falls back down to the rocks. She gets herself up again, but slips again, this time further down the bank. She runs along the edge of the river, trying to keep her balance on the slippery rocks that are being kicked together by her feet, but she cannot keep herself from slipping. The clattering of the rocks is loud enough to give away her position, but she is too scared to stop running.

The sound of loose rocks slipping underfoot comes from behind her. She screams, hard, and she can't stop screaming; her screaming is on autopilot now. A sharp pain jolts the back of her head, and Julie falls onto the rocks. She tries to get up, but her shoes are wet and slippery. She scrambles up again. She realises that she's been hit with something hard, but she doesn't feel the pain yet. She can feel the warm wetness of blood on the back of her head as she runs in the dark. Julie yells as loud as she can, hoping someone will hear her cries. The man chasing her seems to be laughing.

Julie stops to pick up a large rock. She throws it in the direction of the man; it misses him by a few metres. She snatches up another rock, spins around, and throws it at him. The man dodges it and grabs her wrist in one swift movement. He punches her squarely on the nose, and she slaps onto the rocks on her back. She hits her head on the ground in the fall. Julie's purse falls out of her jacket pocket and empties its contents, cards and shirt button onto the rocks. The rag that he has muffles her scream as he shoves it in her mouth; she tries pushing it with her tongue to stop gagging. Her back is numb from the fall; she tries to push herself up.

She struggles with ferocity as his hands press down on her head, forcing her face onto the rocks. The sharp oyster shells seep red blood from the cuts in her cheeks.

Julie punches and claws at him, but he is too strong. He pulls out a Bowie knife that he has strapped to his forearm. With a flick of his arm, he slashes her dark blue work pants from the pocket and tears them off her leg with a tug and a single swipe. He grabs her blue panties with his free hand and tries to rip them off, but his hands are shaking with the cold, which is the only thing preventing him from shredding them. Suddenly, the rain stops as if it were turned off.

He leans down and holds her head against the rocks, keeping her head steady as he places his knife against her underwear. "I am Legion, for I am many," he whispers, trying to catch his breath. He lowers his face to her cheek, close enough for her to feel his breath on her skin as he licks a trail of rainwater off the side of her face with one big sweep of his tongue.

He then sits up and struggles with Julie's erratic movements, he cuts the skin on her pubic bone as she thrashes side to side then he slices the material so easily down between her thighs, she can feel the cold hard metal touching her skin, her vagina is now exposed to the cold freezing wind and pelting rain that has started again.

The man hits Julie with the back of the knife handle, knocking her out.

As soon as he stands up, he becomes calm, and he pulls down his wet tracksuit pants. His penis is erect. Julie's thighs part easily as he kneels between her legs, and he thrusts into her vagina with so much force that he almost falls on her. He pumps hard and fast for at least five minutes, and he orgasms. He pulls out of Julie and ejaculates over her left thigh.

At that moment Julie is waking up from her unconsciousness; she squints and turns away. She sees the river lapping on the shore beside her, illuminated by the red light of the beacon standing two metres away in the water.

She lifts her head and feels pressure on her abdomen. She tries to scream, but her mouth is full of cloth rag, and she can't get away. The man is straddling between her legs, and she kicks and tries to arch her back so he will let go of her. But he just reaches up and pins her down with his hands.

Her strength is weakening to the point of exhaustion, and she has started to breathe in through her mouth against the wishes of the attacker as the rag in her mouth is loose. The attacker leans over her and begins to squeeze her neck, cutting off her air supply. If this goes on for much longer, she will stop breathing entirely.

Julie struggles against him, trying to pull his hands away. It is too late though, her eyes continue to stare at him in silence, wide open just like the glass eyes of a doll.

Without hesitation or emotion, he grabs his Bowie knife, gripping it by the handle with his palm, and plunges the knife into her neck.

He stabs her with such force that the blade pierces her flesh and slices into her spine. He plunges the knife repeatedly into the body until it is a bloody mess. The man seems furious that she is dead. He thrusts the knife deep into her chest and begins dragging it past her stomach. It moves so hard and fast, she is cut open all the way, down to where her pantie line would be.

He starts talking to himself aloud. "This is not my fault you made me do this, I did not want to do this, you make me do bad things. Stop shouting at me, leave me alone."

It is a gruesome scene, reminiscent of a butcher's work floor. Blood has spattered onto his clothes. The blood on the rocks is illuminated a deep crimson by the red beacon flickering out in the river.

The black hooded man wipes her blood off his blade with a filthy rag that he had earlier shoved in her mouth. He returns the weapon to its clean state before turning his attention to the corpse. Grasping onto her intestines, he tugs at them and throws them on the rocky ground beside her. As if someone has told him something funny, he roars with laughter while the smell of her innards fills the air, dissipating with each passing second.

You can see the steam from the intestines billowing into the air, as the hooded man stoops over them, shielding himself from a gust of wind. With his bloody index finger, he then makes a cross on her forehead. Suddenly, without warning, he stands up and wipes his face which had been splashed with gore. Blood drips down his neck and runs under his hooded garment. He swiftly ascends the riverbank and starts to whistle Camp Town Races, before vanishing into the night.

3

WAITING NIGHT

L isa Chapman the babysitter, sits nervously on the couch, growing increasingly impatient as she waits for Julie to return. She is worried, imagining all possible scenarios, like an accident downtown or a delayed taxi due to the stormy weather, that could be preventing her from coming back.

Lisa pulls back the flowered curtains to look out into the front yard, but everything is still. She can see the yard whenever lightning flashes, illuminating the night sky. The clock on the fireplace reads 11:21 p.m. Lisa walks back to the low-lit hallway and peeks into each bedroom to check on the children, who are sound asleep.

Lisa walks towards the hallway telephone and feels uneasy. She dials the Coulson Police Station and a young police lady answers. "Hi, this is Constable Kathy Colgrave how can I help you?"

Lisa introduces herself as Mrs Gaffney's babysitter and explains that she has not returned home after her car battery died earlier in the night. The young lady on the phone confirms Mrs Gaffney's name and reassures Lisa that she may still be on her way. However, Lisa's worry grows as she points out that it has been over two hours since Mrs Gaffney last contacted her. The young lady promises to send someone over to investigate and asks for Mrs. Gaffney's last known location.

Lisa speaks hesitantly, "Her car is a red Holden Gemini. If you're driving north, you'll find it in the car park off Formby Road, just after King Street." The lady on the phone asks Lisa, "Do you know what she's wearing tonight?" Lisa replies, "When she left here, she was wearing an orange short-sleeved top and dark blue trousers. She's also carrying a purple jacket." "Okay, thanks, Lisa. Can you give me the phone number you're calling from, please?" asks the lady on the phone. Lisa reads out her phone number, and the lady says, "I'll get back to you later." Lisa places the handset down and walks back to the living room. She peeks out of the curtains again to see if anything is happening outside, but everything seems quiet.

Lisa and Julie have had a rocky relationship ever since Julie falsely accused Lisa of stealing money from her underwear drawer. Lisa believes that one of Julie's children must have taken the money, but she knows that it is impossible to convince Julie otherwise. Despite their strained relationship, Lisa doesn't wish any harm upon Julie and is anxious about her well-being. Lisa contacts her parents to explain the situation, expressing concern that she may have to spend the night if Mrs Gaffney doesn't arrive soon. Leaving abruptly is out of the question for Lisa, as it would be unreasonable and inappropriate.

She would never forgive herself if something happened to the children. Jane is six years old, and Drew is four; Lily is almost three. *"God, I hope Julie is alright!"* she thinks to herself as she slumps back onto the couch and starts biting her fingernails and continues watching the TV screen with the volume down just in case, she hears a car door shut or anything.

Wondering what the time is now, Lisa leans around to view the clock above the fireplace once again. It is 01.16 am, and still no reply from the police, Lisa can hear the rain start again on the roof of the house it is rather noisy.

Lisa jumps up out of the warm comfy couch and rushes for the telephone, which she has dialled so many times over the last few months that it now feels like an old friend. She dials the phone and waits, "Hello, Coulson Taxi Company?" The line is silent for a moment, and then a deep raspy voice responds, "Hello." "I don't want to be picked up. That's not what I'm calling for," says Lisa. The voice on the other end of the call is silent. "I have a query you might be able to help me with. Did you pick up a lady around 9.30 pm at the taxi rank on Best Street tonight?" questions Lisa. The man on the other end groans with an attitude that he can't be bothered thinking to answer her question.

"Come on sir, it's important Mrs Gaffney meant to get a taxi at that time, but she has not arrived home yet," says Lisa. The man replies, "There were two people picked up around that time" "Any to 24 Kingston Drive?" asks Lisa, "No sorry, is that it?" grumbles the man. " Yes, that's it, sorry to bother you," and Lisa slams the phone down hard annoyed he did not come up with the answer she is looking for.

She heads to the kitchen, being careful not to make any noise that will wake the children and shuts the door in the hallway on the way past. She turns on the electric kettle and grabs a mug, then puts instant coffee powder into it. As she waits for the hot water to boil, the phone begins to ring. She rushes out to the hallway grabs the handset and holds it tightly against her ear. "Did you find her?" she asks.

"Lisa?" the voice asks. "That's me," Lisa says, trying to conceal the excitement in her voice. "Did you find Mrs Gaffney?" "Not yet," the lady says, "But we will keep looking. The weather is terrible out there they called me on the radio, and they found her car, but she is not there, and they drove up to her street entrance and back and found nothing at this stage" Lisa quickly butts in, "I rang the taxi department and they said no one got a lift from them to Kingston Drive."

"Oh OK, thanks for your help," the lady says "Um, would she go anywhere else?" the police lady asks. "And has Mrs Gaffney done this before?" "No, she hasn't, she was on her way home when we spoke, and I am babysitting her three children. And she wouldn't do that to me." Lisa sounded worried, "We'll continue to search in this storm," the lady officer said. "The guys who called it in said they couldn't see anything, but they'll keep looking. And we have another shift starting at 3 a.m."

"In the meantime, hang in there and try and get some sleep if she arrives home to tell Mrs Gaffney to give us a ring, OK?" says the lady. " OK thanks," Lisa did not want to put the phone down it felt like it is the only thing that is helping to find Julie. She can hear the lady hang up on the other end.

Lisa is very worried now. "*What will happen to the children if it is really bad like someone kidnapped her?*" Lisa growls at herself as she walks back to the kitchen. She can see the flash of lightning and hear thunder off in the distance through the curtains.

A squeak of a door can be heard in the hallway Lisa goes to the hallway entrance and opens the door she finds Drew standing there, rubbing his eyes and half asleep. He is wearing his tractor pyjamas. "Go back to bed." "But I want mummy." His voice is sullen. "Your mummy is not here yet. She's running late tonight. Go back to bed," Drew keeps walking up the hallway towards Lisa, "I'm scared." Lisa picks up the young boy and walks back to his bedroom dodging all the toys on the floor.

She lays Drew back on his bed, throws the covers over him, and sits next to him on a small chair in the dim light coming in through the half-shut door of the hallway and waits for him to fall back to sleep again. The rainstorm continues to be a loud annoyance for another hour, then it dies down.

Drew is fast asleep, and she walks quietly out of the bedroom and closes the door. The rain has left the building quiet, and she returns to the living room. It is now 3:45 a.m. and still no call from the police. Lisa is exhausted now, all this worrying and not getting much sleep from the night before partying at a friend's place has taken its toll on her. She decides to go and have a nap. Lisa leaves the light on in the lounge room grabs a blanket off the armrest of the couch and lays down on the comfy couch to get some shut-eye.

4

FRACTURED DUTY

Yellow cigarette smoke stains the edges of the clock on the opposite wall, which displays the time, 08.05. "*In another hour, I gotta start work,*" Detective David Moore is thinking as he finishes his whiskey.

"Once a cop, always a cop." That's what people say, and they could be right. He remembers this as he steps off the bar stool and calls out to the bartender. The bartender doesn't respond to him over the music, so he continues out the door.

As soon as he steps outside, the sunlight hits him like a freight train. He is still feeling tipsy and has a bout of hiccups, but he pats down his new grey suit and finds his car keys in the inside pocket. As he unlocks his car door, he climbs inside. Moore pops open his glove box and fishes around for some spearmint-flavoured chewing gum. He takes two pieces out of the wrapper, puts them in his mouth, and begins to chew like crazy. He was trying to get rid of the smell of alcohol. Taking a can of aerosol deodorant out of under the front passenger seat, he sprays it all over himself, drowning out his smell. He blows his breath into his cupped hands and smelt spearmint, then drives off to work.

Moore grew up as an only child to working-class parents in Coulson. A poor area of the town, now a city. His mother a midwife died suddenly with a stroke when David was only thirteen.

His father Thomas never married again and worked overtime as much as he could at the Canning factory to provide for and raise his son on his own. David joined the police force when he was 27 years of age. His father died a year later of a heart attack. His father was proud of him, he always said so.

After parking his blue Mazda RX7 in his designated spot, Moore turns the ignition off and opens the door. He takes a few minutes to gather himself, he walks down the parking lot's aisle to a back entrance where some officers are standing outside.

The officers greet him as he walks by, and he nods and forces a smile. Many of the officers just stare at him. Moore keeps walking up the staircase to the sliding doors of the headquarters. He can feel eyes boring into his back as he walks, and it makes him uneasy.

When Moore enters the main room, his colleagues notice him. They greet him with silence as they go back to their work.

"Hello, chaps," Moore says, trying to break the awkward silence. Three men and one woman officer turn towards him. One picks up a phone and starts speaking into it.

The others go back to their work. The woman smiles and nods at him, but no one else acknowledges his greeting. Another man carries in a bag of hot muffins and walks to the far corner of the room. The scent of cinnamon wafted across from where he sits, alongside the smell of pine from a car air freshener shaped like a tree that hung from the back of the police officer's chair.

Sitting down and chucking his car keys into the right top drawer of his desk, Moore observes most of his stuff on the desk had not moved in six months—which is strange, as somebody sometimes moves his stapler or his pen holder, and they always hid his coffee mug if he was not careful.

Today, however, both the stapler and the mug are in their usual spots. Moore picks up the mug and investigates it to see a bit of coffee left, but it has grown into a black mouldy substance on the bottom sprouting fluffy things. He spots a piece of cotton string someone had carelessly tossed into it.

Moore glances out the window next to his desk and observes the sky is beginning to darken, and it is getting rather grey now. He thinks he might have a hangover, but he isn't sure. He tries to stand up, turning around so he can grab the desk for leverage, and then he stumbles out of his chair. "Hey, Moore," someone shouts from an opened office door, it's Chief Dwyer.

When Moore walks into the office and the Chief closes the door, it rattles the thin Venetian blinds on his partition wall window. "Take a seat, Moore," Chief Dwyer says. "I'll stand," says Moore.

Moore is uncomfortable, he never likes going into the Chief's office in the first place—the walls are plastered with diplomas and pictures of Chief Dwyer shaking hands with other important-looking people.

The detective knows what this means: he'll get yelled at, it's usually the case with Chief Dwyer and him.

It was like being in the headmaster's office at school, David Moore was what they called a 'nuisance' at school, always showing off and trying to get the other boys to like him; but usually, it backfired.

And he would get in trouble—and occasionally get six of the best across his open hands with a strike of the bamboo cane from the headmaster until he couldn't pick up his bag.

High school was challenging, being bullied and having to stand up for himself, there was no running to the teacher back then. Man, up or get hurt every day.

One day he was suspended for two weeks for breaking a bully's nose after he had enough of being attacked from behind every morning at school.

"Welcome back, Detective Moore," Chief Dwyer says. "It's good to have you back." Chief Dwyer has a broad Scottish accent, which somehow makes the greeting sound serious. He was a solidly built man of average height with well-placed sandy hair.

He had a bit of an indentation to his chin and a fresh scar across one eyebrow after a serious car accident on the way to work one morning two years ago that put the Chief out of action for a while. "Yeah, I feel good, sir. I just want to get back into it," says Moore.

Chief Dwyer gives Detective Moore a concerned look as he spoke. "Are you sure, Detective? We can give you more time off." Moore nods. "I'm sure, Chief. I just want to get back to work."

"I understand," the Chief replies. "You have been through a lot. As you know, we are willing to accommodate you however we can."

"I do not want you out in the field doing detective work if you are not yourself," Chief Dwyer says. "Do you understand me?" He speaks in an authoritarian voice that makes it sound like Moore is a child being reprimanded. "I completely understand, Chief," he says, "And I am ready to go out there and do what I enjoy."

"Detective! Let me know if you need more time off at any point, and I will arrange it. Oh, and I have a partner for you to work with too." Moore looks stunned, and snaps back at the Chief, "A partner? Why would I need a partner? I've worked alone for years."

"Oh, for fuck's sake." Moore slams his hands on top of the table. "This is bullshit." Moore is livid with anger. "Detective, I have had enough of your attitude," says the Chief. "You will be out of this department on your arse if you don't watch your mouth."

"Detective Moore it has been decided by the top brass, so live with it now, get out of my office."

Moore swings the door open and then slams it behind him. As he storms across the room, everyone turns to look at him. The Chief then walks up to the door swings it open and roars out, "She will be here sometime today!" Detective Moore grabs his coffee cup off his desk and shouts in reply, "Oh great! She's a woman! Just brilliant." He then starts walking to the lunch-room.

At the sink, Moore makes a cup of coffee from the charred percolator that looks like it has lived there for fifty years. Three heaping spoonfuls of sugar and a vigorous stir, and he turns around to see an empty chair waiting for him. Many of the other detectives are coming in to sit down and have a break.

Moore notices Officer Brady walking across the room towards him. Moore nods in his direction and says, "Hi, Officer Brady." "Welcome back, Detective Moore," Brady replies. He was about to continue talking when Moore shuts him down. "Brady, I don't want to talk about it. Just leave it." Brady turns around and walks out of the lunchroom.

"There is no need to be rude. He was only being polite." Moore looks over to see Constable Stubbs sitting at a table on the other side of the room with a packet of sandwiches placed in front of him. "Mind your own business," Moore shouts. "I just want to come back to work without getting pounded by pity and sorry."

Moore sits there, enjoying his coffee and being completely ignored by the rest of the officers. They were not going to talk to Moore while he was in a mood. Everybody who works in the police force here in Coulson knew or knows of him as a bit of a loner, but also a good detective. He works well with everyone, except the Chief.

Moore looks at his watch: it's 10:14, after drinking his coffee, he walks back to his desk. He grabs his keys and walks to the parking lot. He opens the door to his car and grabs the bottle of pills from inside the glove box and shakes out two pills into his palm, then tosses them into his mouth. Next, he unscrews the cap to a hidden bottle of whiskey that's half full.

Moore crouches behind his car's dashboard so no one can see him and takes a swig of the whiskey to wash down the pills. The burning sensation as the liquid makes its way down his throat gives him a screwed-up face, his lips pull back and his eyes squint. He is sick of the pain. What he wouldn't give for a moment's respite from the blinding headaches. He sits back up and gets out of the car, then saunters back to his desk.

Sitting back at his desk, he can feel the ache in his skull, the pounding behind his eyes. The pills aren't working.

Moore begins looking through paperwork on the side of his desk, and he wonders what it is.

He recognises the forms as paperwork from an old case that he had been working on before he had taken six months off. He hasn't forgotten about the case, just forgotten where the rest of his colleagues are in the investigation.

"Jenkins, who has taken over that case?" Detective Jenkins turns around on his swivel office chair, a pen jammed into his mouth, and looks up at the ceiling as if searching for an answer. "If I'm not mistaken..."

"Detective Jordan, you know the one with the limp" "Oh, the defective detective," Moore grins at Detective Jenkins. "Hey, you can't say that stuff anymore," Detective Jenkins replies in a serious voice. "The Chief is on the warpath about rude behaviour and name-calling."

"We just had a meeting on it, cleaning up the crap in the department, it's all changing mate, you cannot say things now" "What things?" says Moore.

"You know," Jenkins looks around and leans over his desk and takes the pen out of his mouth, "Tits, vagina, poofter, or bad nicknames like defective detective, the Chief says if anyone is caught they will be out of the force."

Moore is shocked his voice is sharp. "Really, so what do you talk about now?" Jenkins smiles again, "Football," he grunts. He spins back to his computer screen.

"So defective, Oh I mean Jordan is on that now," asks Moore. "Yeah," Brady says as he walks over to the filing cabinet, "Jordon caught the guy. He left the papers for you to have some light reading." "Is that so? Well, I'll have a look at them later. It's a good thing Jordon caught him," comments Detective Moore.

Chief Dwyer calls out, "Moore, come to my office." Detective Moore groans while Jenkins laughs under his breath. They both know something is up.

"What'd I do now?" Moore mutters, under his breath as he stands and walks over to the Chief's office.

Moore begins to sit down when the Chief says, "Detective, don't sit down." Moore stops mid-sit and looks confused. "Sorry, just habit, I guess. What do you want?" The Chief sits back in his chair, looking Moore up and down.

Chief Dwyer announces, "They just found a body on the shore of the river next to the parklands, not a nice one either so I've been informed" "What do you mean?" Moore asks.

"They did not say on the police radio just that it was not a nice one, anyway that's your job Detective Moore to find out, is it not?" says Chief Dwyer.

"Yes, Chief I will get straight on to it," replies Moore.

Moore walks swiftly out of the Chief's office before he gets another flacking over something. A shout comes from the Chief's office, "Your partner is not here yet, so start without her". Moore grabs his car keys out of his desk drawer and comments to the men at their desks, "See ya, boys."

Moore pulls up in his car, the day no more improved than before, and glances at his watch: 11:05 a.m. Across the road to his right, police cars are parked around a large part of the park.

Moore thinks to himself, "*I need this,*" before leaning down and retrieving a whiskey bottle from under his seat. He takes a swig, then returns it to its spot before climbing out of the car. He pops another piece of chewing gum into his dry mouth and strides across the road.

Moore sees a policeman keeping watch over the riverbank, the area off-limits to the public. A photographer is trying to get close to the crime scene, pushing the police tape with his stomach as he snaps photos with a long lens. Moore shouts at a nearby officer, "Get that guy out of here," and the policeman grabs him by the arm and pulls him back. "Move this police tape back thirty metres so no one can see," Moore orders, flashing his badge as he ducks under the tape and marches toward the scene of the crime.

Sergeant Flanagan has the challenging task of safeguarding the crime scene from contamination by rookie police and the public. Moore notices him standing in front of him, notepad in hand. Flanagan has been serving on the force for quite some time and Moore remembers seeing him when he joined the station.

"Howdy Detective Moore, welcome back to the madness," Flanagan speaks with a smirk. "Thanks, Sergeant," Moore responds sarcastically. He looks at Flanagan and asks, "So what do we have?" Flanagan replies, "We have a thirty-eight-year-old female, Julie Gaffney. She was reported missing last night around 11:30 pm by her babysitter, who said she hadn't made it home to her and the children after work." "Did someone question the babysitter?" asks Moore. "Yes, we sent someone over there a while ago," Flanagan reports. "How did they know her name was Julie Gaffney?" Moore questions again. "They found her belongings scattered around next to her body, including her driver's license which was wet and tattered, but they were able to make out the address and followed up on it," says Flanagan.

"Fantastic work, Flanagan. Is forensics here yet?" Moore continues.

"Yes, detective," Flanagan responds.

"Very good Sergeant. Carry on," Moore replies before turning his attention to the riverbank, where he spots a naked woman lying on the rocks about two metres from the edge of the water.

The abhorrent sight was one that Moore tries to shake free from his mind.

Blood is smeared across her body, and the forensic team led by Allison Lord was hard at work gathering evidence. A man in a black coat snaps photos of the crime scene as Moore slides down the riverbank and carefully stands up.

He brushes off the wet grass clippings that are on the back of his grey suit pants, complains to Allison Lord, and wipes his shoes against a nearby driftwood log.

"Just bought this fucking suit," Allison looks up at him and replies, "Better than having blood on it, hey Detective?"

"I guess you're right Allison, you usually are," says Moore.

"Welcome back, Detective Moore," states Allison.

Moore's eyes widen in horror as he surveys the young woman's body. "Oh no, what the hell happened here? Why would someone do that?" He can't look away from the disturbing sight of her intestines carelessly piled up next to her and the crabs feeding on them. He takes a deep breath to steady himself before turning away, and mutters under his breath, "I've never seen anything like that before."

Allison Lord pushes a long chemical mercury-type thermometer into the deceased woman's left nostril. "What's that for?" Moore inquires. "This will give a more reliable reading," she replies, as she extracts it and writes more notes. Moore looks over the body, noticing the odd colours that form when the blood starts to go into Hypostasis. He observes that most of her purse contents are placed in plastic bags and marked with numbered tags in the spot where they are found. "Who found her?" Moore asks.

A young male police constable walks down the riverbank to where the detective is reading from his notes. He says, "A woman walking her dog found the body around 9.50 a.m. sir." "Where is she now, constable?" inquires the detective. "She's in the ambulance, sir. She's in an awful state after making the discovery. Her pet was off its leash at the time and had already started to eat the organs when its owner ran up and took it away from the corpse." The constable went on, "The animal wouldn't come when she called it, so she had to run down to it and forcibly remove its mouth from the dead body."

"Really? Poor woman, did you get her statement of events, Constable Godfrey?" asks Moore.

"Yes sir. Sergeant Flanagan did." Moore observes that Godfrey looks ashen in the dull daylight and asks, "Is everything alright, Constable?" Before Godfrey could answer, he vomits on his shoes, making Allison shout in frustration. "Oh, for fuck's sake! Get him out of here! He's contaminating the crime scene!"

One of the forensic team grabs Constable Godfrey by the arm and yanks him up onto the riverbank. He is then released to clean up the mess on his shoes.

Moore spots a woman walking towards him at the crime scene, "Officers! Get this woman out of here! This is a crime scene, not a sightseeing tour!"

She shouts, presenting a police badge. "I'm a detective"

"Detective Moore, I'm Detective Sarah Reilly. I've been assigned to work with you. Moore grunts as his new partner introduces herself. - "Is there a problem?" asks Detective Reilly.

"No," he replies, "It's nice of you to show up," mumbles Moore.

Reilly circles the body and asks, "Why did he or she or even they, place the intestines next to her?" Allison replies without hesitation, "You don't mess around, do you? It appears to be some kind of ritual, probably with an attempt to write a cross in her own blood on her forehead. There is not much of it left though, thanks to the rain. It sounds like we're dealing with one really twisted individual or multiple people."

"Hi, I'm Allison Lord and I'm the head of the forensic team. Where are you from, Detective Reilly?"

"Hobart," says Reilly, "Stationed there for four years as a detective and five as a police constable."

Moore snaps at the two women, "Hey enough of the women's club chats - can we get on with it? What time do you think she was killed, Allison?"

Allison turns to Detective Moore and says, "Around 14 hours ago. Moore looks around the scene and states, "I remember there was pouring rain and fierce thunderstorms last night and early this morning. Whoever did this has lots of motivation."

Allison interrupts, "The rain did stop at some point because I remember waking up to close the shed door that was shaking in the winds. Oh, detective," Allison interjects, as if she has just remembered something important. "I found a piece of tracksuit material, I think until I can get it back to the lab and do a proper check.

It looks like it might have been from the knee of whoever was kneeling on these sharp rocks. Plus, there's some penetrating neck trauma, as you cannot help seeing, looks like it was done with something sharp and narrow, probably a bayonet or a hunting knife by the size of the wounds."

"Nice job," Reilly says loudly.

Allison Lord begins again, "When I checked earlier, her tongue was swollen, and she has a Petechial haemorrhage— pinpoint red spots on the surface of her eyes and eyelids — which could indicate strangulation."

Moore asks, "You mean she was strangled?"

Allison kneels at the corpse and replies, "That's what I am thinking. It looks like she also has a broken nose and a hematoma on the back of her head."

"Good work Allison," says Moore.

"Did the river tide reach her?" asks Reilly.

Allison turns and glances at Reilly, "No the river did not touch her, as you can tell since the waterline mark on the rocks is a metre away from her body. If the tide did cover her the intestines and the blood in between the rocks would have been washed away."

Moore butts in again, "I think it's likely that the rain diluted some of the blood, but there's still a noticeable amount here so I'm with Allison, — no."

Moore yells for Sergeant Flanagan to join him. When the Sergeant arrives, the Detective asks, "Is there any family?" Flanagan replies, "The babysitter said the father of the children, Sean Gaffney, left about eight years ago. There are no parents or siblings either and no current boyfriend. She kept to herself, according to the babysitter. There were no signs of ill will on his part." "Can you find out where he lives and report back to me?" says Moore.

"Oh, by the way, Flanagan, this is my partner, Detective Sarah Reilly," Sergeant Flanagan extends his hand to shake hers. "Pleased to meet you, Detective." Flanagan heads up the embankment and out of view.

Moore turns and walks towards Allison and says, "Listen; later we need the babysitter to come and confirm the identification at the morgue, Allison. Can you take care of that for me?"

Allison replies hastily, "I sure can do that for you, Detective." "Reilly, did you bring a vehicle?" Asks Moore. "Yes, I did, Detective Moore. What's the need?"

"Once Sgt Flanagan has given us the address of the ex-partner's place, we will take my car," answers the detective.

Allison stands up from the body and says, "It's now 11:35 a.m. There are no fingerprints yet unless we can find the murder weapon but the search so far has come up empty."

Moore shouts towards the embankment, "Hey Constable! Go and find your sergeant and tell him to widen the search area by another three hundred metres from where they last looked." The young police officer runs off out of sight.

Reilly peers closely at Julie Gaffney's head, "Hey Allison, do you think this cross on her forehead could be an upside-down Antichrist sign?"

"It's hard to tell with so little left of it," Allison responds.

"I wonder if this was a ritual killing and if it was a devil worshipper who did it," comments Reilly.

"That is usually the case with ritual killings," Allison says. "Though I haven't seen many of them in my eighteen years."

Flanagan rushes down the embankment to Detective Moore. "Detective, I just called the station on the radio, and they told me they rang his house, and he is not home at the moment but will be back shortly," Flanagan says.

"His girlfriend Tayla Ryan told them he got home around 3 a.m. this morning. Here's his address."

Moore glances at the paper in Flanagan's hand: Unit 1/43 Dana Court. His face lights up.

"Looks like we have a lead," he says, looking at Reilly and Allison.

5

FALSEHOOD

The roar of the engine and the smell of fuel is intimidating, and Detective Moore drives every which way. He hardly keeps his eyes on the road, and Reilly tightens up with anxiety.

She tries to act as if it's normal behaviour, but it's not.

"Apart from the smell of fuel, why does your car stink?" asks Reilly, scrunching up her nose. The detective ignores her and continues to drive. "What is it?" Reilly continues, pressing on. "What do you mean stinks?" Moore snaps back. "Can you not smell that?" retorts Reilly, rolling down her window.

"I haven't driven in a while, so the smell might be lingering from when I left fish and chips in the car, but I found them yesterday," Moore is smiling as he mentions it.

"What happened to your other partner?" asks Reilly, "I never had a partner before until now," says Moore in an irritated tone of voice.

Reilly stares at him; one eyebrow raised as she tries to figure out what Moore is talking about. "Oh, I never knew a detective to work on their own," says Reilly in confusion.

"Well now ya do," says Moore.

He squeals the tyres around another corner with Reilly hanging on for dear life, "What's the rush detective?" Moore smiles at her as he continues to drive erratically.

"So why do you need a partner now?" Reilly asks curiously, "I don't," says Moore. "They feel like I need one."

"Who's they?" asks Reilly.

Moore takes his eyes off the road and glances at Reilly and says, "The big knobs upstairs, who do you think? Father Christmas?" Reilly notices that Moore is getting agitated with the barrage of questions and decides to shut up and enjoy the rest of the drive.

Moore pulls over and parks his car halfway down the street and turns off the motor. Suddenly Reilly pivots in her seat and looks at Detective Moore with a stern expression on her face. "Detective Moore," Reilly begins, her voice steady, "I think it's important for us to understand each other better if we're going to work together effectively."

Moore leans back in his seat; his expression is guarded but attentive. "Alright, Reilly. Understand what?"

Reilly continues, "I grew up in Hobart, a city that faces its fair share of crime and challenges. From a young age, I developed a keen interest in solving puzzles and understanding the complexities of human behaviour. That's what led me to pursue a career in law enforcement."

She pauses for a moment, gathering her thoughts before delving into her past experiences. "During my time in Hobart, I worked on various cases ranging from petty theft to two homicides. I've dealt with organized crime and drug trafficking, and I was involved in bringing down a corrupt politician. Those experiences have taught me the importance of perseverance, attention to detail, and understanding the human psyche."

Reilly's eyes lock with Moore's as she continues, her voice growing more determined. "I'm also facing my fair share of challenges as a female detective in a male-dominated field. I have to work twice as hard to prove my capabilities and earn the respect of my colleagues. But I never let those obstacles define me or get in the way of my pursuit of justice."

She leans forward, her tone softening with sincerity. "Detective Moore, I know you have a wealth of experience in Coulson City, and I really believe that we can learn a lot from each other. I bring a fresh perspective, innovative ideas, and a passionate spirit to this partnership. I'm devoted to making a difference in this city, just like I did in Hobart."

Reilly finishes, awaiting Moore's response. His expression softens, and he nods thoughtfully. "OK, I understand, Reilly. I may not have shown it at first, but I value commitment and competence. Let's put our differences aside and concentrate on solving cases together. I'm willing to give this partnership an opportunity, but enough with the fucking questions," says Moore.

A sense of relief floods over Reilly, knowing she has made headway with her new partner. They still have quite a long way to go, but this conversation marks the start of their journey towards mutual respect and productive collaboration.

They both climb out of the car and walk towards the number of the street they are looking for. They both notice a young woman who is taking the mail out of the mailbox and walking back inside the unit.

"Do you think he is home yet?" asks Reilly, "I don't think so — at least, not unless he has parked out here on the street," says Moore.

Moore opens the gate to the small front yard with Reilly close behind him. Moore knocks on the door and waits, but no answer.

Reilly shouts through the door, "Hello?"

Moore knocks on the door harder than before, but again no answer. Reilly notices that a shadow is cast through the mottled glass on the side of the door, so she pushes her face against it to look inside. "We know you are home we saw you get the mail," shouts Reilly.

The shadow moves back as it notices Reilly, and she roars through the glass, "We know you're in there; please open up."

The door opens slowly, revealing a pretty young woman that they saw earlier at the mailbox standing there. Her hair is dark and curly, falling to her neck at the ends. It is glossy, shiny, and clean. Her face is pale and smooth, she has big green eyes and a cute nose. She is in her twenties and stunningly attractive. She is wearing a shiny pink shirt and a pair of denim shorts that fit her lean legs with a hint of snugness.

"Sorry I didn't answer; I thought you were the religious people going door to door bothering us again."

Moore smells a mixture of perfume, conditioner, and soap, like a bathing beauty from a cigarette commercial.

Her skin is soft looking, with a clean baby powder odour, and a hint of fresh sweat. The young woman is softly tapping her foot on the floor and her leg is bouncing with nervousness.

Moore speaks, "Hi, I'm Detective Moore and this is my colleague, Detective Reilly. We're here to talk to Sean Gaffney. Is he home?" The young woman says, "Yes, he is home." Reilly asks the next question, even though she already knows the answer. "Are you, his girlfriend?" The young woman smiles coyly and replies, "Yes, I'm Tayla Ryan."

Moore begins to walk forward until he is a few steps away from the girl. "Can we come inside Tayla and talk with Sean?"

"Yes, sure come in detectives," says Tayla as she leads them down the hallway to the living room.

The living room was very stuffy, and a smell of bleach was filling the room. The living room was a camouflage of colours, odd and disturbing, but brilliant and captivating. Moore studies Tayla as she walks around the room, picking up cushions that lay on the floor. Reilly shakes her head as she watches Moore staring at the young woman.

Tayla catches Moore staring at her, she smiles at him and says, "Would you like a coffee or tea?" Tayla turns around and starts to walk to the kitchen, and Reilly quickly says, "No thank you. We don't have time right now." Moore looks at Reilly angrily, but Reilly does not notice as she is writing something down on her notepad.

Tayla yells towards the back half-open sliding door to the small backyard where she knows her boyfriend, Sean, is working in her shed. "Hey Sean darling you are wanted in here, it's the Police."

The detectives watch Sean exit the garden shed and padlocks it. He walks into the living room through the sliding door. His sharp jawline and shaved face make him look like an exchange student with tanned skin. He has on a long-sleeved shirt and pants that are rather tight-fitting.

Sean Gaffney looks nervous as the detectives are standing in his home, but he heads for the kitchen pulls down a coffee mug for his daily coffee, and begins to brew it, glancing up at Reilly and Detective Moore to see if they are watching him.

"We just want to ask a few questions if we can," says Reilly. "Where were you around 10:30 last night?"

Sean glances at Tayla, who is sitting in a nearby armchair. "I was out with a mate having a few drinks at the local pub," says Sean. "The Roksy got home about 3:00 a.m."

Tayla butted in angrily "Yes you did, I remember looking at my alarm clock when you walked in the bedroom and woke me up getting undressed."

"What's going on?" asks Sean. Moore replies, "No, nothing happened at the Roksy. We found a body this morning on the rocks of the river."

This alarms Sean. "What does that have to do with me?"

The detective continues, "Well, we found a body on the rocks near the parklands, and it seems to be your ex-wife, Julie Gaffney." Sean drops his coffee mug on the counter so hard coffee splashes everywhere. Tayla gasps in shock and covers her mouth with her hand, "Julie? Are you sure it's Julie?" says Sean in disbelief.

"What about the children are they alright? Oh my god, you sure it's Julie?"

"Your children are fine they are being looked after by Child Welfare till things get sorted," says Reilly in a calm voice. Reilly states, "All her belongings were with her, and her driver's license was there as well. The babysitter would be down at the city morgue right now giving a proper ID of Julie I reckon."

"What the hell happened?" gasps Sean grabbing the back of his neck and pacing back and forth. Moore replies, "We cannot go into details Sean, but she was murdered, that's all we can say at the moment as the investigation is still ongoing."

Reilly butts in, "Hence that is why we are asking you about your whereabouts last night to rule you out of the investigation."

Sean points the finger at Moore and shouts, "Am I a suspect? I was with one of my mates last night, ask him." Reilly notices that Sean is nervous and stuttering a bit. Reilly asks, "Do you have a name and address, Sean, so we can verify that?"

"Neil Laycock, I will write down his address," shouts Sean.

Tayla rushes for the kitchen draw grabs a yellow pad and pen, and nervously hands them to Sean.

Reilly asks Sean while he is writing down the details, "When was the last time you saw Julie?" Sean looks at Tayla as if he is in trouble, kind of look, "I saw her only recently at the supermarket where she works about 4 days ago. I called in there for some bread and cigarettes."

Tayla snaps into a rage of anger at Sean, "You did not say you saw Julie."

Sean growls back at Tayla, "What if I did, what is your problem? Stop this jealousy shit will ya!"

Tayla runs out of the living room crying, Sean looks at the two detectives and says, "Tayla does this all the time, she needs to grow up. Just ignore her."

Reilly grabs the piece of paper off Sean and both detectives start walking to the front door.

Moore opens the door and lets Detective Reilly out to the front gate; he turns and asks Sean, "Are you working at the moment, Sean?" "No detective I am between jobs at the moment," says Sean with a grin on his face.

"OK thank you, Sean, for the information we will contact Neil and follow up on your whereabouts."

"You do that detective, see ya." And Sean closes the door in Moore's face and continues to shout at Tayla.

"Hey Reilly, what's the address for Neil Laycock on that piece of paper?"

"14 Richmond Avenue. Do you know where that is?" asks Reilly.

"Of course, I know, I've lived here my whole life," says Moore.

Getting back in Moore's RX7, they speed down the street. "It's only five blocks from here," Moore weaves between the cars as if he were in a race.

Reilly grips the dashboard and asks, "Who taught you to drive, Peter Brock?" Moore grins and says, "You keep tabs on the car racing scene, Reilly?"

"No," Reilly answers, "I just know Peter Brock is a great driver." Moore chuckles, "Well, he's definitely a better driver than me!"

Reilly replies, "I can definitely see that," holding on for dear life.

They reach 14 Richmond Avenue and as they come to a stop, Reilly nearly smashes her face against the windshield if it weren't for the seatbelt she was wearing. Reilly gets out of the vehicle and starts to make her way to the house, while Moore stretches to reach into the glove box, taking out two tablets, which he throws into his mouth. He notices Reilly's gaze on him and can't grab the whiskey bottle from beneath his seat, so he just swallows them dry.

Reilly strides back to the driver's side of the car. "What are you doing, Moore?" "Oh, just taking my vitamins," he lies, knowing full well that what he is taking is antidepressant drugs. He reaches for the glove box and locks it with his car keys before swinging open the door and getting out of the vehicle. "You okay, detective?" Reilly asks. "I'm fine," Moore says, "Nothing wrong with me."

Both detectives trudge up the pathway to the dilapidated old house, its weatherboards stripped of paint and covered in vines. The gardens were filled with weeds instead of flowers and the lawn had grown over their waists.

Moore cast a glance to his right and spots a huge Mastiff dog, hidden amongst the tall grass, ready to pounce when it notices the two detectives. Its bark was loud enough to shake the ground, and Reilly hopes its chain was strong enough; an unfed dog like this could do some serious damage if it got loose.

Moore's gaze lingers on the dog, struggling to escape its chain as he knocks on the door. He hears someone shuffling their feet across the wooden floorboards inside before the door creaks open. Neil Laycock, a scruffy individual with greasy hair and holes in his baggy jeans, stands nervously in the doorway smoking a cigarette and mumbling "Yeah what do you want?" Moore observes that he is trying to act like a tough guy but is quite fragile—the wind could have easily knocked him down.

"Hi Neil, I am Detective Moore and this is Detective Reilly, we would like to know, where you were on Wednesday night after 10:30 p.m? "I was down at the Roksy drinking with my mate Sean Gaffney," says Neil.

"What time did you two leave the bar?" asks Moore.

Neil Laycock stamps out his soggy cigarette and answers, "Around 2.30 a.m."

"How did you get back home?" asks Reilly.

He says in a slightly mocking tone, "We walked. Can't drink and drive, can we? Sean and I parted ways around 2.45 am and I got home at around 3 o'clock."

"So, you're both regulars at the Roksy?" "Yep, we play darts there every Tuesday night. We have a good team of four, the Roksy Shooters." "How long have you known Sean?" "15 years. We met at the Roksy. That all your questions? I gotta go take my dad to the doctor. Is that okay with you?" Neil said, giving Moore a stern look.

"Thanks for your help, Neil," the two detectives said as they walk back to the car and climb in. Reilly quickly rolls down her window as she can still smell the fishy scent; it seems to be growing stronger. "Do you think Neil is telling the truth about Sean's location?" Moore asks.

"It sounded true to me, why?" Reilly remarks.

"It sounded like he was expecting us like he had the answer waiting for when we got here and why did he not ask what we were questioning him for," says Moore.

"I believe him," Reilly says, struggling with her seat belt.

Moore speeds down the street and pulls up to a stop in front of Neil's house. "What are we doing here Moore?" Reilly asks. "We're going to see if Neil is going to pick up his father," says Moore.

In the car, Reilly is growing restless, "Come on, let's go, this is a waste of time," but Moore notices a shift in activity. Neil has emerged from the house and is now striding along the sidewalk toward his red Ford Escort parked on the street. Moore carefully starts his own car and quietly follows Neil's car from a safe distance.

The red Escort took a left onto Maxwell Street, in the direction of the shopping centre. Reilly, waving her hand in front of her nose, complains: "Can we use the work car instead of your car? This thing reeks!" "Stop whining, Detective Reilly," replies Moore. "It's not so bad."

Suddenly, the car veers off and pulls up to Dana Court. Moore was pleased with himself: "Ah, I love good detective work! I can tell you now, Sean Gaffney is not Neil's father."

6

THE PACT

As they drive down the main street, Moore suggests to Reilly that they make a stop at the Roksy hoping to find someone who may have seen the two guys there on the night of the crime. Their plan is to then head to the crime scene where Reilly's car is parked and meet up at the station afterwards. Upon arriving at the Roksy, they notice a few people enjoying their drinks outside while a group of intoxicated men attempt to sing along with the Eagle's song, Hotel California. The Roksy is an old stone building covered in ivy, worn down by the sea air and permeated with the scent of cigarette smoke and beer. Moore and Reilly head to the back area, where it is quieter and less crowded. The tavern smells of stale beer, cigarettes, sweat, urine, vomit, and spilled booze. They are greeted by Yvonka Kellaher, the barmaid from a side room who asks what they would like to drink. Moore declines, even though he suddenly craves a beer or two, he announces to the barmaid that he and Reilly are detectives and want to ask some questions, she nods and tells them her name while she polishes another glass and places up on the shelf behind her. Moore asks if she knows Sean

Gaffney and Neil Laycock and if they have been here any time lately. Yvonka confirms that they both were at the front bar the previous night and that Sean left at around 11:40 PM, while Neil left at around 2:30 AM after being asked to leave for being drunk and causing trouble.

Then she shouts across the bar at the other bartender Clinton, asking him if Sean had left at 11:40 PM.

"Yeah," Clinton shouts back, "He bought three bottles of beer over the bar and left saying he could not stay he had something to do." Moore looks at Reilly and then back at Yvonka the barmaid. "Thanks for the help, we might call you sometime for a proper statement if we need one," she nods, polishing another beer glass before placing it on the rack.

"Can I use your phone, Yvonka?" "You may, detective," she says. "And Yvonka, would you have Sean's phone number?" She nods and starts searching behind the counter near the cash register.

"Here it is," she says, handing the membership card with the phone number to Detective Reilly. Reilly shows it to Moore before dialling. As it rang, someone answers, "Hello? Sean speaking."

"Hi Sean, it's Detective Moore here. We need you to come down to the police station today for an interview."

"Why?" queries Sean. "We just need to ask you some more questions." says Moore "Can't you do that over the phone?" groans Sean,

"No Sean, we need you to come in for a formal statement this time. OK? And if you don't, I will have the constables come and get you personally."

Sean Gaffney goes quiet on the other end. "You still there Sean?" Moore asks.

"Yes, still here Detective, I'll be down around 4 pm."

Thanks, Sean. Bye." Moore puts the phone down with a smile towards Reilly. "He sounds annoyed, thank you Yvonka.

We might be in touch." Yvonka waves goodbye as she walks into the front room, and the two detectives leave and climb into Moore's car. Moore drives to where Reilly's vehicle is parked at the crime scene.

He pulls over and lets Reilly out. "Will catch you back at the station," says Moore as Reilly gives a small wave and heads towards her car. Moore looks over to the crime scene, which is still taped off, and sees a couple of police officers talking to each other.

As he watches Reilly drive away, he reaches under his seat and grabs the bottle of whiskey, taking a big drink before finishing it off.

It is 4:00 pm and Reilly walks into the station and into the office, where three constables are seated at their desks, gawking at her as if she is an extra-terrestrial.

Detective Reilly carries the scent of sweat and musk of a woman on the go. A hint of vanilla and spice from her perfume makes itself known over her natural scent. She smells like a regular girl, not someone in the force.

Suddenly, one of them shouts, "You right love? The department store is down the street." She gives him a stern look, growling, "Detective Reilly to you, Constable. Any more smart remarks like that and I'll shove my boot up your arse."

The embarrassed constable hurriedly resumes typing, and the other two constables keep their gaze on the floor. Detective Moore walks in and sits down at his desk, dropping his keys into the top drawer. "What a day, Reilly," he muttered. Reilly occupies her new desk, inspecting the drawers. "What's our next step, Moore?" she asked. "Allison Lord from forensics just told me that they haven't found any murder weapon or anything else that can help us in the investigation—apart from that bit of grey fabric which could be related to tracksuit pants." Moore sighs.

Reilly stands up and confidently approaches the whiteboard. She grabs the red marker and starts to write the names of Julie, Sean, and Neil Laycock. Moore smiles approvingly at her initiative.

When she is done, all the details of the investigation are displayed in clear view on the board: from names to places to little side notes. Reilly begins to talk aloud, summarizing what they know so far for the benefit of everyone in the room. "We have no prints, no murder weapon, no witness," she says. "All we have is a small piece of tracksuit material."

The constable interjected, saying they had talked to Julie Gaffney's boss at the supermarket, Mr. Steve Brattan, and he said she had been heading home at 8:55 PM.

Sergeant Flanagan stands at the doorway and adds to the discussion. "A woman walking her dog discovered the body at 9:50 AM this morning. We canvassed Formby Road and Steele Street, which go past the parklands, but we haven't found anything yet."

"Thanks, Flanagan," hollers Moore, across the room. Reilly sinks back into her seat on her swivel chair.

Officer Brady tells Moore and Reilly that Sean Gaffney and his lawyer have just arrived and have been guided to the interview room.

The two detectives make their way down the hallway to the room, when Moore opens the door at the entrance, right away; he catches Sean Gaffney picking his teeth with a makeshift toothpick.

The room was small and quite dreary in colour, with four chairs and a metal table attached to the floor, upon which rested a cassette recorder.

Sean's Lawyer is a seasoned attorney, Graeme Porter, who has been practicing for over two decades. He chiefly takes on cases for people who are out of work.

Moore and Reilly sit down opposite Sean and his lawyer at the table, "How is the family Graeme?" comments Detective Moore just to break the ice.

"Yeah good, all doing well, sorry to hear what happened."

"Thanks, Graeme," utters Moore.

Graeme Porter's voice was deep, low and monotone. He spoke slowly and with assurance, that without a doubt, he was the smartest person in the room.

Reilly looks at Moore and wonders what the lawyer is talking about. "Alright, shall we get this interview started?" Moore reaches over and presses the record button on the machine, which produces a loud buzz and a bright red light. Moore's voice was loud and clear as he says, "This is an interview with Sean Gaffney in the presence of his Lawyer Graeme Porter, I am Detective David Moore, and also present is Detective Sarah Reilly.

The time is 4:20 pm, and we are here to discuss Sean's whereabouts on Wednesday 23rd June 1985 at 10:30 pm onward." He then looks at Sean and says, "Thank you for coming in to answer some more questions. Just let the tape know that you have not been arrested and you came in here of your own accord. Sean, you are not obliged to answer any of our questions but whatever you say or do will be recorded and may be used against you as evidence in a court of law, do you understand?"

Sean nods his head, "Do you understand, for the tape?" "Yes, I understand," Sean, replies miserably. "Your statement to us earlier today was not accurate," the detective says.

"What do you mean?" Sean asks. "In Layman's terms," the detective explains, "the statement you gave me and Detective Reilly about your whereabouts is not truthful." "What!" Sean snaps. "I told you to ask Neil Laycock."

"We did ask him and he's not exactly a great liar either." "He's not lying; I was with him at the Roksy!" Sean growls. "You're the one who's lying, Detective!"

Moore raises his voice. "Just for the tape," he says, gesturing to Sean. "Sean Gaffney is pointing his finger at me, Detective Moore. What are you hiding that you had to mislead us about your whereabouts on Wednesday night?"

"I'm not lying! I'm telling you the truth; I was with Neil at the Roksy!" shouts Sean. "That part is true, Sean, but the part about staying there until 2:30 am is bullshit," says Moore angrily.

"No, it isn't," snaps Sean. "We have two bar staff who know both of you well and they told us that you left the Roksy around 11:40 pm. Neil Laycock stayed there until 2:30 a.m. was visibly intoxicated and was asked to leave. You bought three bottles of beer and left the Roksy early, Sean," growls Moore.

Sean's lawyer leans in and whispers something in his ear. Sean's leg is shaking and so are his hands. Sean rises and begins to yell at Detective Moore, "I'm not lying! They have got it wrong!" His lawyer tells him to sit back down, but Sean is too irate to hear him.

The detective remarks, "Just so that we are clear, Sean Gaffney is standing up and appearing rather agitated." Sean reluctantly sits back down, with a more nervous look on his face. "Why Sean," the detective continues, "Why did you get Neil Laycock to cover for your location? I could have him arrested for lying to a police officer and providing false information.

He must be a close friend of yours for him to take the fall for those charges, if you have nothing to hide, why not just tell me where you were?" Sean stutters out an answer about the bar staff having gotten it wrong.

Moore stands up and shouts, "Sean Gaffney I am arresting you for obstructing a murder inquiry. You do not have to say anything but anything you say...."

Sean stands up and steps back to the wall. "Okay, okay, I'll tell you where I was," "Sit down, Sean," Detective Moore shouts, "This is your final chance."

Sean drops his head into his hands and onto the table. "I was with a woman at her house," says Sean. "Another woman? Not Tayla?" Reilly shouts, looking at Detective Moore in surprise. "Yeah, another woman," Sean says sarcastically, "I've been seeing her for about three months now."

Reilly cannot help herself and comments in disgust, "No wonder Tayla is jealous and insecure; she's justified in feeling that way."

"That's enough of that, Detective Reilly!" Moore yells. Sean's lawyer barks at Reilly, "My client doesn't have to listen to you lecture him about his love life, Detective."

Reilly apologises and sits quietly in her chair like a scolded schoolgirl. Moore continues talking. "So, you mean to tell me that you and your friend Neil have been leading us on a wild goose chase because you're being unfaithful?"

"If this gets out that I've been sleeping with someone else, I'll lose my girlfriend and then I will have to find somewhere else to live," Sean says miserably. "Ugh," grunts Reilly.

"I got home around 3 a.m. and I took a taxi if that helps?" Sean was shaking now. "We need to look into this further; do you understand Sean?" Moore says sternly. "Yeah, I know," he answers quietly. "Who is she?" Moore questions. "Christine Reece lives at 49 Cameron Street with her sister Angela," Sean mumbles. Moore announces the time and states he is stopping the interview, "It's 4:35 pm now."

Moore clicks off the record button, "We are going to get you to stay here Sean until we can clarify your alibi with Christine Reece, OK? I'm not arresting you, but I need you to stay here, I can be a fuckin prick and arrest you to detain you, but I don't want the paperwork shit, OK?" Sean's lawyer looks at Sean and nods his head, Sean agrees to stay. "Can I get you a coffee, Sean?" Asks Moore. "Yeah," says Sean. "Do you want one also Graeme?" says Moore.

"Cup of tea for me," says the lawyer. Moore shouts out to the constable who is waiting out at the door "Constable" the young constable walks in, "Can you get a coffee for Sean here and a cup of tea for his lawyer please." The Constable agrees and walks back out the door. Moore and Reilly leave the room and Moore snatches the unmarked police car keys off the vehicle wall, where all the keys are numbered and stored. Then they go out of the back door to the car compound.

"What a jerk," Reilly mutters, climbing into the passenger side of the unmarked VH brown Commodore.

"Come on Reilly, people make mistakes," comments Moore. "He was talking about his girlfriend's insecurity while he was cheating on her!" growls Reilly.

"We need to get this done Reilly, I can't believe they screwed us around," Moore says, starting the car and heading out of the compound. He fumbles with the glove box and realises he is not in his own car; he needs his tablets. He reaches into his pocket and grabs a piece of chewing gum while he veers across the roadway and almost runs into a parked car. "Watch what you're doing, detective!" Reilly shouts. "Sorry, my fault," he admits, straightening up on his side of the road and squealing around a corner down an alleyway that met up with Cameron Street. "What number was it again, Reilly?" "Number 49," she answers. He swerves over to it and hits the edge of the gutter. Both detectives get out and Reilly notices that Moore has dented the wheel cap on the front passenger-side tyre and shakes her head at him. "What, Reilly?" shouts Moore. "I'm driving back to the station, Detective Moore, or I'll walk back," growls Reilly.

Reilly taps on the door of the modern house. When it opens, a woman in her thirties with red hair appears. "Hi, I'm Detective Moore and this is Detective Reilly," he says. "Are you Christine Reece?"

"No, that's my sister. I'm Angela. What's she done?"

"Oh nothing," Detective Moore replies. "We just want to ask her some questions".

Angela invites them into the stylish lounge area adorned with modern furniture, where another woman around the same age as Angela sits next to the window. She had jet-black short hair and an athletic figure.

"Hi," Detective Moore says. "You must be Christine?"

Christine smiles at them both and nods in confirmation before asking what they need to know.

"Are you seeing a man called Sean Gaffney at the moment?"

"Yes, I am," Christine, replies.

"On Wednesday night around 11.40 p.m., what were you doing?"

"I was home here watching a video and Sean arrived roughly about midnight with a pizza," Christine answers. "What time did Sean leave here that night?" queries Moore.

"He left around 2.45 a.m.; he got a taxi because he said he told his girlfriend that he would be home at 3 a.m. on the dot." Reilly interjects, "So you know he has a girlfriend?" "Yes, I do detective, it's nothing serious between us two, just having fun," Reilly looks slightly disgusted and stays quiet. Angela speaks up at the entrance of the lounge, "I came home just when he was getting into the taxi, I work the night shift at the hospital."

"OK, that's all we need to know. Thank you, girls, for your assistance," says Moore.

"Is Sean in trouble of some kind detective?" asks Christine. "No not at all, just needed to know his whereabouts, we will help ourselves out. Bye." Both Moore and Reilly depart, and Moore tosses the keys to Reilly. "Go on then you drive" Reilly laughs and gets in the driver's side and shuts the door. Moore grabs the handpiece of the police radio that is mounted underneath the dashboard and contacts the station.

"Charlie 32 to Coulson station, are you there? Over," A prompt response comes from the speaker on the side panel of the door, "Roger this is VKT Coulson Station, got you loud and clear." "Can you call the taxi service and check if they gave a ride to a man from 49 Cameron Street on Thursday morning around 2:45 a.m.? Over," says Moore.

"Okay, Roger will do. Over," says the officer on the other end.

"We will be back at the station soon. Charlie 32 over and out." Moore hangs up the handset on the dashboard. He then shouts at Reilly "No speeding!" before they head back to the station.

It is 6.15 pm and Moore and Reilly are walking back into the station. "That was the longest journey to the station I've ever had," Moore tells Reilly, who gives him a cheeky grin in response.

"Hey, Detective Moore!" The police officer manning the radio desk calls out. "I just got a call from the taxi rank. They picked up a man and sent him to number 1/43 Dana Court."

"Thank you, officer," the detectives reply in unison before heading to the interview room to find Sean Gaffney in conversation with his lawyer.

"Right then, Sean. You're free to go. Your alibi checks out with what you reported initially," Moore says. "Now get out of my police station before I change my mind and arrest you for misleading police."

Sean and his lawyer get up quickly and rush down the hall, around the corner, and out of sight.

"Well, Reilly," Moore says, "I'm going home." He walks to his desk, pulls out his keys, and heads out of the compound to his RX7 car. Reilly follows shortly afterward, only to witness Moore downing a handful of tablets before starting the engine. With spinning tyres, he zooms away out of sight.

7

ON A HIGH

The beach grass is dancing in the wind adjacent to the gravel car park at Arthur Heads, situated five miles from the outskirts of Coulson City. A popular spot for lovers and pot smokers at night, and a great surfing spot in the day when the waves are right.

The westerly winds are rather strong this evening shaking the bare tree branches surrounding the car park. The night was dark no stars can be seen. A few silver gulls are running across the gravel being helped by the gusts of wind, in the distance you can see down the coast back to Coulson City, with streetlights shimmering in the night.

A silver 1983 Nissan Bluebird arrives and turns into the far west corner of the car park. The engine is still idling, and the headlights turn off, the exhaust fumes swirl across the rear of the vehicle in red, coming from the glow of the brake lights. The engine stops and the brake lights glowing red turn to black as the driver takes their foot off the brake pedal.

The car park goes quiet again, as quiet as it can be from the wind whistling through the trees. In the vehicle behind the steering wheel sits Suzette Twiss, a short girl of nineteen years of age, she loves to come out to this area to smoke some joints before going home and avoiding her parents.

She tries to stretch the night out so when she gets home her parents are in bed.

For the past twelve months, Suzette has not got on with her parents, with too many rules and always telling her what to do, being the age of nineteen Suzette thinks they have no right to tell her how to run her life, she's a rebel.

Reaching for the lid of the console in between the car seats, Suzette pulls a broken piece of plastic from the side that is back into place, hiding behind it is a clear sandwich bag, Suzette opens it and shoves her face into the opening and smells the contents like she was smelling a fresh rose, but this smell did not smell like roses but an earthly plant smell that penetrates her senses.

She turns on the radio and searches the stations to find something suitable to go with her smoking session, she stops searching as soon as she hears The Cure playing The Caterpillar and lets it play. Suzette reaches for a packet of salt and vinegar potato crisps that she has brought with her and opens them revealing a nice smell of vinegar and cooked potato through the car.

Pulling out some rolling papers that are laying in the dashboard ashtray she starts to roll some cannabis inside the paper and licks it together to produce a fat joint.

The car is toasty and inviting, the scent of Sure Deodorant mixed with the smell of potato chips wafting through the air. Suzette lazily passes a blue Bic lighter back and forth between her fingers, occasionally glancing down at the friendship ring she received from a former flame who had broken her heart—a love she cannot let go of, hoping that one day he'll come to his senses and return regretfully.

Suzette sparks up the joint, taking in a large breath of smoke and holding it before slowly exhaling. The space quickly fills with a hazy cloud of smoke that hangs in the air like a fog.

She takes another drag, this time holding the smoke for a few seconds longer before releasing it. Suddenly, she starts to cough as the smoke overwhelms her lungs. She drops back into her seat, shaking her head and laughing to herself at the joys of smoking.

Suzette feels the effects of the drugs kick in, a dull but pleasurable tingling feeling that runs through her body. Her mouth has gone dry, and her lips feel wooden; she reaches for a can of Fanta and pops the top open before chugging from it. She sits there in a state of relaxation, looking outside her car window and watching the silver gulls scurrying about in the dark.

Suddenly, a flicker of light is reflected off her side mirror, and Suzette notices a car in the distance coming her way. Worrying that it could be the police, she frantically packs up her stash and stashes it away in a secret compartment in her car console and takes one more puff of her joint, and butts it out in the ashtray. She can't make out who it is through the rear vision mirror, so she just sits and stares at it looking for any sign of movement. Nothing appears.

The vehicle roars off again, spraying gravel and dirt as it fish-tails and spins in the car park, whipping up a thick cloud of dust from its rear tires. Suzette shakes her head in disbelief. *"What an idiot!"*, she says to herself as the driver eventually drives off in a straight line, eventually disappearing out of view. Suzette relaxes again, picking off the chipped black nail polish from her fingers. She likes being Gothic - wearing her black Ramones shirt black canvas trousers, and square buckle boots. Her parents disapprove of her "morbid" look, which she resents. She told her mom once that it beat looking churchy, but this comment was not appreciated.

Glancing at her car dashboard clock, Suzette sees that it reads 10:51 p.m. She decides to go home to her warm bed, as the cold air is starting to seep in without the heaters going. She quickly tidies up, grabbing the car ashtray and empty crisp packet and Fanta can, before stepping out of the car. As soon as the cold air hits her face and hands, she feels a burning sensation. Suzette heads over to the rubbish bin about twenty metres away from the beach side of the parking lot. She chucks in the crisp packet and Fanta can before bashing the ashtray against the side of the bin to remove any traces of joints and ash.

Suzette swings around to go back to her car and sees someone illuminated by the interior light near her driver's side door. They're dressed in a black hoodie and jeans, yet Suzette can't make out their face. It's strangely disconcerting, but her curiosity takes over and she says, "Hi, who are you? Can I help you?" No response. Suzette feels a wave of fear come over her and she nervously lies, "My boyfriend will be back in a sec; he just nipped off for a wee." The person continues walking towards her without uttering a word. She looks around; she is the only one in the entire car park with her car, *so where did this person come from?*

The hooded figure begins to race towards Suzette, and in response, she takes off running towards the exit of the parking lot, screaming for help. But her pursuer quickly closes the gap and lunges at her, stabbing her in the shoulder. "Stop, you fucking bitch!" he shouts. Suzette lets out a shrill scream and pleads, "Oh my God, help me!" Unfortunately, no one could hear her, in the middle of nowhere.

The attacker falls to the ground slipping on the gravel, giving Suzette just enough time to make her escape into the shadows of the trees. She knows if she keeps running, he will catch up to her, so instead, she looks for a place to hide. In the dim light emanating from behind her, she makes out a dark outline in front of her; it is a fallen tree and under it, is a gap - raised off the ground - Suzette takes refuge. She tries to keep quiet while breathing heavily through her nose and covers her mouth with her hand.

Struggling to get enough oxygen, she hears him walking through the scrub towards her; twigs are breaking under his feet as he approaches, and his heavy breathing grows louder. He calls out: "Where are you, ya fucking bitch? Don't bother screaming, bitch. You're just wasting your time."

The attacker's footsteps crunch against the foliage and get louder, and then they stop. He is getting closer. She must make a run for it. Suddenly, the bushes shake, and she knows he is heading in the same direction he had come from. Suzette manages to sit up, wanting to get home to her parents, feeling the warm blood trickle down her back into her trousers.

The back of her t-shirt is soaked with blood, and she begins to shake from the shock. In the distance, she can see the top of her car illuminated by the lights of Coulson City in the car park, revealing its shape. Just then, there's another crack of twigs to the right of her and she knows he is coming closer. He's only two metres away from her. She quickly drops to the ground again back beneath the fallen tree.

Suddenly, Suzette hears a cackling sound in the distance. It is a car driving down the road headed for the parking lot. She considers getting up and running to get the driver's attention, but she doesn't know where her attacker is. If she gets up, she might run right into him. She decides to wait until the car is in the parking lot before seeking help.

The headlights of the car illuminate the parking lot as it arrives. To her horror, Suzette sees a figure just to her right. *"Oh no, it's him,"* she thinks. She gets on all fours and notices that his back is to her as he watches the approaching car.

Desperate to reach safety, Suzette sprints towards the car and screams for help. The attacker quickly turns and starts chasing after her.

The vehicle starts to move faster towards the exit, but Suzette is not fast enough. She screams repeatedly, but with loud music blaring in the cab of the car, there's no way the driver can hear her.

She is not going to make it to that car. She turns around and heads back to her Bluebird. But before she can reach it, she feels a sharp blow in her lower back near her kidney as the attacker stabs her.

Suzette collapses to the ground outside her car and is hit hard in the back of her head. The attacker then drags her over the pebbly ground to the edge of the car park, where the beach sand starts. She's punched in the face until she stops fighting him.

The attacker uses his sharp bowie knife to cut her clothes off as she lies there helplessly. He mutters to himself as he works, "Leave her alone, don't touch her," as he slices her pants and pulls tight on her red polka dot panties before cutting them off.

He hits her again before roughly tearing off her shirt. He places the knife beneath the strap of her bra and slices it in two, exposing her petite breasts with hard and erect nipples from the cold air.

He leans down over her and sinks his teeth into the side of her breast. Suzette cries out in agony, and the attacker holds the knife against her face, pressing against her cheek until her skin starts to split. "Look how easily I could kill you," he says, and she begins to weep as the blood trickles from her nose and mouth. He inserts his index finger into her mouth, then pulls it out covered in blood. With a sinister smile, he draws an upside-down cross on Suzette's forehead before rolling her onto her stomach. He fishes a length of twine from his pocket and ties her up.

Blood trickles from her nose down her chin, sand spatters her face, her mouth is filled with it, and a tooth is knocked from her mouth. Her eyes are wide with terror.

Blood runs down her face and drips from her mouth as she weeps at the torment before her. Her attacker is focused on her, his face twisted in anger.

The metallic taste of blood fills her mouth, and each slow swallow brings it to the back of her throat. His hands are rough against her skin, digging into her like a vulture tearing into its prey.

Rolling Suzette back over onto her back, he bites into her breast again and she screams out in pain.

He forces Suzette's legs apart, and she lays there, still stunned and dazed from the forceful blows to her face. The assailant, still muttering to himself, pulls down his jeans and underpants and lowers himself onto her.

He covers Suzette's sobbing lips with his hand, her breathing laboured from a clotted nose. She tries to struggle, but he hushes her and says "My name is Legion, for I am many," in a low voice.

Suzette's fighting stops, and he continues his brutal thrusts not for pleasure but for pain. She lays there crying, not moving as each thrust brings her closer to her demise. Her arms are numb from being pressed against the ground; her spirit is broken. All she wants is for it to end.

If there was a Hell, she has found it.

Her face is badly swollen and distorted due to the numerous punches she has taken from the attacker, one of her eyes is closed, and a large hematoma is growing near her left temple. "Please let me go," Suzette mumbles. "Shut up, bitch," the attacker quickly snaps back. He then cries out, "Leave her alone" and starts thrusting into her again. "Please, please," she stutters before he strikes her with his fist again and tells her not to talk to him. His body begins to tremble as he reaches orgasm, and his eyes roll back in his head like a Great White shark feasting on its prey. The attacker pulls out of Suzette's vagina and lifts up his pants, zipping them up.

Suzette, still in immense pain and weeping, pleads to her attacker to leave her alone. He grins wickedly and continues mumbling to himself. He brandishes his knife in both hands, as if in a dark ritual, and brings it down hard into her neck. Blood starts to pour out, and Suzette struggles to scream, but it's no use; she is quickly drowning in her blood.

She wriggles desperately but he keeps on stabbing until there is no more movement from Suzette. The attacker pauses, watches her bleed out profusely, and then wipes the bloody blade across her left breast before standing up. He blows a kiss in Suzette's direction, grabs her torn blood-stained shirt from the ground and walks off, whistling Camp Town Races till the sound of his whistle dissipates. He leaves behind a rough-looking cross drawn with Suzette's blood on the car door.

8

THE BEACH

The car speeds down the road, the detectives sitting in silence, each lost in their own thoughts as they make their way to the crime scene on this glorious Friday morning.

Reilly wants to ask Detective Moore about the other day in the interview room when the lawyer said to him, *"Sorry about what happened,"* what did happen?

Reilly is too frightened to ask just in case she got her head bitten off. Moore is quiet; since Reilly has known him for six days, he never usually shuts up.

Moore feels like shit this morning, it is 9.45 am and the sun was already belting through the windscreen. Moore had too many antidepressants and too much whiskey last night in his hotel room. He thinks to himself, *"I am dry as a nun's nasty, I could do with a nice cold drink right now."*

"Hey, Reilly what did ya do last night anything exciting," says Moore trying to crack open a conversation. "No, not much, had a couple of wines and unpacked some boxes for the apartment, to make it more homely" "The place where I picked you up from, is that your apartment?" asks Moore "It is not mine, I am renting it," says Reilly.

"What about you Moore have you a nice place?" says Reilly trying to find out things about Moore.

"I had a nice place, Reilly, but not anymore," mumbles Moore.

"Oh really? Why not?" "Just haven't, OK?"

"Oh OK..." Reilly's comment hits another nerve and the car's cabin falls silent again. Reilly is wondering if Detective Moore had a shower this morning, as he smells rather stale, the faint smell of whiskey and sweaty armpits making her feel queasy. "Do you believe in aftershave?" questions Reilly. "I don't know what you mean, replies Moore. "It's an easy question; let me rephrase that: Do you wear aftershave or deodorant, Detective?" says Reilly. "You're saying I stink?" blasts Moore. "Yes - basically, that's what I'm saying," complains Reilly.

"I had a shower this morning, and this sun is making me perspire," explains Moore. "I can smell the whiskey coming out of your pores. You must have had a gutful last night - should you even be driving?" growls Reilly. Moore turns and glares at Reilly and blasts, "Excuse me Reilly, but what I do in my own time is my business, OK? And yes, I am fine to fucking drive. If you have a problem with me driving detective, get the fuck out and walk".

Reilly looks out the passenger side window and does not say a word; the atmosphere is intense and smelly.

Arriving at the edge of the car park Moore realises it is blocked off steers to one side and parks behind a marked police car. The two detectives exit and walk toward the area of the crime tape.

"What do we have here?" Moore looks at a group of onlookers congregating next to the police crime tape " Didn't take them long," Moore gawks at the nosy parkers, Reilly comments, "Bad news travels fast." Moore notices Sergeant Flanigan standing beside him, "Hi Sergeant Flanagan, what have we got so far?"

Sergeant Flanagan trying to catch his breath after running over from the victim's vehicle reads from his notepad "An anonymous caller called the station at 8.50 am saying he saw a body on this beach and hung up the pay phone, call taker at the station said it was a pay phone and not a house phone as he could hear some traffic in the background and a drop of a coin before the caller spoke". Moore views the body from a distance where he sees the area in its entirety while he focuses on the victim's body lying under the forensic marquee that has been erected over it from the sun. Moore and Reilly approach the body, Reilly studies the blood stains noticing the upside-down cross on her forehead "How long has she been here?" asks Moore, Allison Lord answers, "Well it's now 10.00 a.m. I estimate the girl has been here in the sand about 11 hours detective".

"We meet again Allison under horrible circumstances" states Moore. "Yes, we do detective," mumbles Allison. "Anything that helps us, Allison?" Reilly asks. "Found two pairs of footprints here on the sand, and also over there in the middle of the car park in the gravel and next to the car," comments Allison. "Murder weapon?" shouts Moore. "Not at this stage detective, they are still searching over there," says Allison pointing in the direction. Moore turns and looks over at the trees and bushes and views police officers walking amongst them "What are they doing over there?" Moore queries. Allison quickly replies, "We found blood drops over there as well, some near the car and some leading to the entrance of the car park, they are searching for a weapon."

"How many murders have you done Detective Reilly?" questions Allison "This is my third," says Reilly.

"It doesn't get any easier if that's what you're thinking?" smiles Allison as she starts writing in her notepad again. Reilly notices the stab wounds around Suzette's neck; dry stained blood has run down onto the sand from her neck to form a jelly-like substance that has set in the morning sun. Reilly comments "Same stab area as the one on the river of Julie Gaffney, and an upside-down cross on her forehead more prominent this time, the cross on the car is new and it is not painted but in fact, the blood of this girl I would say."

"Huh, Good detective work Reilly" scoffs Moore, "It's not like the murderer carries a red tin of paint around with him."

"Reilly gives Moore a mean look not liking his comment. Reilly continues to look over the body of Suzette.

Suzette's hair is all stuck together by dry blood, and she has a horrible look on her face with her eyes wide open all milky glazed and dried up from the sun, sand flies have got themselves stuck on her eyeballs and around her nose and mouth in the dark blood.

"Do we know who she is?" Allison Lord opens her notepad, "A Suzette Twiss. Her driver's license was in her purse that was in her trouser pocket, and also we got an officer to check the registration of the car it comes up with Suzette Twiss as well Detective".

"I wonder Detective Moore if the caller was the killer?" says Reilly.

"You might be right, let us get a full background of friends and her hangouts, and let's find out why she was out here and where she came from before coming here. Have you searched the vehicle yet Allison?" asks Moore.

"I had one of my guys search it, just a cigarette lighter and a small bag of cannabis hidden in the console not much else," says Allison looking at her notes.

"That probably explains why she was out here, a popular smoking hangout I heard," comments Moore. Allison kneels beside the body and states "Oh yeah Detective Moore she has been raped, just like the last one near the river nearly the same style of attack, stabs to the neck, bruising around the vagina. But this girl was not strangled, could have been interrupted, or just wasn't in the mood, you do not know sometimes with these sick bastards."

Reilly notices Moore is looking rather pale, "Alright Moore? You do not look so good," says Reilly. Moore wipes the sweat from his brow, "I could do with a drink, it is very hot out here, hey Reilly, we better go and do the horrible job of telling her parents if she has any?"

Reilly stands up from kneeling next to the body and strolls over to Moore. Allison tears a page from her notepad and passes it to Detective Moore. "Here is the address detective, and good luck, I will give you all the details and findings hopefully later today."

"Thanks, Allison, says Moore.

Moore and Reilly walk back down the road to their unmarked police car. After starting up the car and turning around, Moore passes the piece of note paper, Reilly reads it out loud "18 Wescombe Drive, that is where we are going. "OK I will do the talking," says Moore

"That's fine with me, I wouldn't know what to say. Have you done a few in your time in the police force?" asks Reilly

"Hell, yeah Reilly," snaps Moore.

Arriving at Wescombe Drive, Detective Moore drives the car slowly around looking for number 18, every house in the street is beautiful, all their gardens are manicured, and trees and bushes are trimmed to perfection.

Luscious green lawns with not a blade of grass out of place.

Reilly points her finger to the left, "Here it is number 18." Moore turns up the driveway behind a nice red sedan.

"Wow a lovely Mercedes Benz 380 there, they look good red with the black top," Moore is stunned that Reilly knows the car and the model, "Bit of a car buff Reilly?" "Not really, my uncle had one similar till he crashed it," "Ouch very costly," says Moore pulling an awkward expression on his face.

Climbing out of the unmarked police car they both headed for the front door of the house, they are in awe of this splendid structure of a home.

A two-story brick house with huge windows and a massive front door, like something from a castle. The detectives catch the sound of a vehicle pulling up at the curb out front of the house, and a tall man in a grey suit climbs out and walks in their direction, It is First-Class Constable John Rowe.

John is the family liaison officer; Moore radioed the station earlier while on the way to this house and asked for him to attend to this address.

The primary purpose of a family liaison officer is to provide support and information compassionately to families of victims of crime, and John Rowe was good at his job. "Hi Detectives, got your message at the station, I'm ready when you are."

"Nice to see you again John, It's been a long time," mumbles Moore.

"It has been a while Detective Moore, you have been off work for six months I heard," says John.

"Yes, I have, but I am back now," moaned Moore.

"Sorry to hear what happened must have been hard?" says John placing a hand on Moore's shoulder.

Moore pushes the doorbell button in an attempt to interrupt the conversation. Reilly hears that statement again "Sorry to hear what happened" "*What happened*?" Reilly says to herself, *why was he off for six months?*"

You can hear the doorbell chimes playing a soft tune inside the premises. The street was rather quiet apart from a distant lawn mower and some singing birds and Reilly kicking her shoe at the step scuffing the front of them while she is waiting for the door to open.

A sweet fragrance surrounded them at the doorstep coming from the direction of a large Daphne bush situated just beside the steps, it was a relaxing smell.

Suddenly the door opens and there stood a man with black hair and splatters of grey hair amongst it, he was wearing a shiny brown suit, "Hi sir, I'm Detective Moore this is my colleague Detective Reilly and also first-class Constable Rowe, is this the Twiss residence?"

"Yes, it is," declares the man, "And you are?"

"I am Peter Twiss, what is this all about? Is it about the tenants in Palmer Street?"

"Palmer Street?" says Moore looking confused. "I'm the real estate agent who rang the police station about the tenants that won't leave," says Mr. Twiss. "No Mr. Twiss we are not, may we come in? says Moore.

"Yeah certainly, What's going on detective?"

"Is your wife home?" asks Moore.

"Yes, she is in the lounge to your right". Moore, Reilly and Constable Rowe enter the house and stand in the hallway, noticing the shiny wooden floor and the beautiful timber walls, and the big arched doorways. Mr Twiss has a confused look on his face as he leads them into the lounge.

"Honey this is Detective Moore and his colleagues; I cannot remember your names sorry," says Mr. Twiss.

"Detective Reilly and First-Class Constable Rowe ma'am," says Reilly.

"Please do not call me ma'am, call me Karen", comments Mrs. Twiss."

"Please have a seat, Mr. Twiss," says Detective Reilly softly.

"So, what's this all about?" asks Mr. Twiss with a confused look on his face.

Moore quietly speaks, "Do you have a daughter named Suzette?"

"Yes, we do, is she in trouble again?" says Karen.

"No, she is not in trouble, I'm sorry to say we have bad news to tell you regarding Suzette," says Detective Moore.

"What do you mean?" Karen asks nervously.

"I'm sorry to tell you that your daughter was killed last night," says Moore. "Someone found her early this morning, and we confirmed her identity from her license and car registration at the scene."

The father and mother's faces just drop into a horror stare at Detective Moore, Reilly could see the happiness leave their faces.

Mrs. Twiss looks at her husband in disbelief and then again looks at Moore realizing this is not a joke she begins to scream and falls off the chair and lands hard on her knees onto the plush white carpet.

Reilly hurries over to Mrs. Twiss and helps her settle back into her chair. She is still crying and shaking from the shock.

Mr. Twiss ambles around the room, his hands on his head in despair.

Reilly looks at Moore and feels bad about the situation they have created, but to be the bearer of the terrible news about their daughter, it had to be done.

Moore says, "Suzette was murdered. We know that for sure, but who did it we do not know yet."

Mr. Twiss stands up and snaps at Moore "Who would want to murder my daughter?"

After Liaison Officer John Rowe tells Mr. Twiss to sit down and catch his breath, Moore asks a question. "It's a bad time I know to ask," he says, "but when was the last time you saw your daughter Suzette?"

The question caught Mrs. Twiss by surprise. She shakes her head and says nothing, but her husband fills in the silence. "About 3.30 pm yesterday afternoon," he answers.

"Do you know where she was going?" asks Moore. Mr. Twiss looks at him and shakes his head, as he says, "No."

"Does she have any close friends or a boyfriend?" the detective asks.

Mr. Twiss replies, "She is a loner, she didn't socialise with others that much, she did have a boyfriend a long time ago, but he moved on, and she is a Goth," "Oh OK, I kind of see what you are saying," says Moore.

"Do you know if your daughter takes drugs?" the detective asks. "I beg your pardon Detective," Mr. Twiss says angrily. "How dare you insinuate that my Suzette takes drugs?"

Meanwhile, Mrs. Twiss continues crying, her hands cupped around her face. The liaison officer kneels beside her and tries to reassure her, but she shooed him away.

Mr. Twiss says. "We were having trouble with Suzette most of the time. So, we really don't know much about her over the past twelve months.

"I'm sorry," Moore says.

He pauses for a moment, looking at the grieving parents. "Do you mind if I ask what kind of trouble Suzette was having at home?"

"She was just being a typical teenager, I suppose," Mr. Twiss explains. "She was mouthy and disrespectful, and she stayed out late without letting us know where she was going. We tried to talk to her about it, but she blew us off, it's like she didn't care about anything anymore."

It has been ninety minutes, and the Twists were growing weary of the unending interrogations. All the while, their answers were being gathered and stored away.

Reilly asks Mr. Twiss a question, "I am wondering is she a regular smoker of weed, you know cannabis?"

"My daughter does not take drugs," muffles Mrs. Twiss through her cupped hands.

"I suggest you leave now and let us grieve," Mr. Twiss growls at the Detective, with an undercurrent of menace in his voice. Mrs. Twiss starts to cry again.

"Liaison Officer Rowe will stay with you," Moore explains.

"Oh yeah Mr. Twiss, we'll need you to identify her body at some point as well.

Officer Rowe will organize that for you when it's appropriate." Mrs Twiss starts to cry heavier now after hearing Detective Moore's comment.

Reilly and Moore walk back outside to their vehicle. They climb in, shutting the door behind them, Reilly says, "That was a hard thing to do, poor parents." Moore starts the car and drives out of the driveway while answering, "Yeah, it was a difficult one. I must admit, and they never get easier."

Reilly and Moore make their way back to the station. They are both tired and frustrated, having spent the last two days searching for leads in both murder cases.

Once they reach the station, they examine the photos taken at the crime scenes for any clues they had missed. The detectives browse through the heavy stack of autopsy pictures. They utilized the rest of the day to question the woman who had stumbled upon the first victim Julie once more. As the evening approaches, Moore looks at the clock and lets out a sigh, "It's been busy. I think it's time to call it a day and come back fresh on Monday."

Reilly nods in agreement, "Yeah, I think we can all use a break." The two detectives gather their things and head out of the station.

9

VOICES OF HADES

In the dimly lit kitchen, Daniel sits calmly at the table, a woman's lifeless body sprawled on the floor before him like a macabre trophy. The sunlight flickers through the curtains, casting eerie shadows on the scene, but Daniel shows no signs of shock or remorse. Instead, he regards the body with a cold, calculating gaze.

His fingers, long and thin, trace the lines on his palms, almost as if seeking a connection to the life he has taken. There is a sinister fascination in his eyes as he studies the lifeless form before him, and a twisted sense of satisfaction fills him.

The kitchen, usually a place of warmth and nourishment, now serves as his chilling sanctuary. The sight of the woman's corpse does not repel him; rather, it becomes his dark confidante. To him, she is not a victim but an object of control, a silent listener to his darkest thoughts.

He rises from the table and stands over the body, his eyes fixated on her lifeless face. His rough hands, covered in dark hair, gently stroke her cold skin, almost caressing it with an eerie intimacy. He talks to her as if she were still alive, sharing his twisted desires, and relishing the power he holds over her now. All around him is deathly stillness as his words hang in the air.

Dirty dishes clutter the sink and half-eaten pizza lies strewn about the table. The woman's carefully arranged body represents the twisted sense of control he seeks in his deranged world.

As he speaks to the lifeless woman, his voice takes on a haunting tone - a mix of tenderness and madness. He tells her how he feels, how the voices in his head torment him, and how he revels in the darkness that surrounds him. The woman remains motionless, a silent spectator to his unravelling mind.

Sunlight continues to playfully dance through the curtains, ignorant of the horrors unfolding within the walls of the kitchen. People pass by the yard, unaware of the depravity residing behind closed doors.

Daniel finds solace in his victim. The woman's body has become more than just a casualty; she is now an extension of his own twisted psyche. As days drag on, he continues engaging her in macabre conversations, finding comfort in her unyielding silence.

The kitchen, once a place of sustenance and life, has now become a chilling chamber of death. Daniel's fascination with the woman's body grows deeper, feeding the darkness within him and spiralling him further into his own demented world.

The stench of decay fills the kitchen, a noxious blend of the decaying corpse lying on the floor and the pile of mouldy, decomposing food scattered on the table and countertops. The putrid odour hangs heavy in the air, suffocating and oppressive, yet Daniel seems almost indifferent to it as if he has grown accustomed to the morbid atmosphere.

He sits at the table, the offensive smell wrapping around him like a shroud, but he shows no signs of discomfort. Instead, he leans forward, studying the lifeless body and the festering remnants of his own negligence with an eerie stillness.

His eyes, once filled with life and energy, now hold a vacant, almost soulless look, reflecting the dismal scene in front of him. The pale sunlight streaming through the curtains is barely able to break through the overwhelming gloom in his mind. He fixates on the putrefying food as if some strange fascination lies within its decomposition, mirroring that of the woman's lifeless corpse.

The sounds of buzzing flies further enhance the morbid scene, drawn to the putrefaction like vultures to a carcass. But even the incessant buzzing seems to blend into the background noise, lost amidst the tormenting voices that plague Daniel's mind.

The thoughts are coming back again of his first kill.

He still remembers her like it was yesterday, the horrified look on her face when she saw him hiding behind her door at her home.

The demons in his head like it when they scream. There was so much blood, more than he thought there would be. She screamed and cried as she tried to get away across her clean wooden floor but, it did not take long for him to practically slice her back while she was crawling trying to get away.

The walls and ceiling were caked in blood, like a Rorschach painting: every time he looked, he thought of the inkblots his Psychiatrists made him stare at during their visits.

The sound of the knife grinding into her neck bone, he could not forget it, that's what the demons enjoyed the most. He remembers how they like him more using his knife.

At the killings, the blood left a metallic tang in his nostrils that he could not get away from. He knows he has killed people, but he cannot help it, the demons make him do it, and he has no choice they will not go away otherwise. He knows he is driven by the savage desire for blood and violence the demons in his head thrive for.

They revel in the rush of adrenaline that course through him as he commits these heinous acts, feeling powerful and invincible ad-midst all the chaos. However, even as he continues to kill repeatedly, he knows that there will be no escape from these demons that talk to him; they call themselves Legion for they are many.

They control every aspect of his life now, and there is no way to break free from their ruthless grip, he has tried, and doctors have tried to stop the voices and he has given up on their failures.

Daniel was a quiet and introverted child, growing up in a small suburban town with his parents, he was an only child.

He had a few close friends, but often felt misunderstood by his peers and struggled with feelings of isolation. Despite his struggles, he was a good student and had a passion for art and science. However, his life changed forever when he was just 15 years old when his parents were killed in a devastating car accident. Daniel was sent to a foster home and then another.

He felt alone, lost, and hopeless. He struggled to cope with the loss of his parents. He became increasingly isolated, sinking into a deep depression.

As he entered adolescence, he began to experience strange and disturbing voices in his head. He sought help from a therapist, he was then diagnosed with schizophrenia. His voices only grew louder and more persistent. As he grew older, the voices convinced him to commit acts of violence. He realised he was being held captive by what felt like unseen monsters.

Despite efforts to understand and treat his mental illness, he was never able to fully control the voices.

Daniel works part-time as an orderly at St Francis the local hospital in the middle of the city. He was studying to be a doctor and was doing rather well till the voices came again.

He did enjoy it once, but now he cannot stand it. The voices make it impossible to enjoy anything.

He seemed to keep it together at work but, the voices were beginning to get worse. A couple of months ago, he almost lost his job, he tried to force a male patient's arm, and he ended up badly bruising the man.

He could not control himself at that moment.

When he is working in the hospital, he hates the sound of the wheelchairs and mobile bed squeaking as they roll on the floor, he even has tried to oil the wheels himself, but they continue to squeak.

The water hisses through the pipes that run across the ceiling like a giant snake trying to find a way out of the building.

The patients speak in whispers, like they have some big secret, with their eyes darting from side to side as if being watched.

Today is Monday he has an afternoon shift from three to nine, pushing patients around in wheelchairs and mobile beds to their activities appointments, and treatments. In addition, he has to disinfect the facility during his shift.

The chemical smells are terrible. The patients smell like ammonia and bleach. There's also a faint smell of mildew and sickness tinged with the smell of alcohol and blood.

Most of the time the white noise of the squeaks of the wheelchairs, the announcements from the PA system, and talking in the hallways are loud enough for him to concentrate and keep doing his job without hiding in the storeroom and muffling himself with a cleaning rag while he screams at the voices in his head.

At the hospital, if the voices keep to themselves, he feels like he belongs, a normal person like his coworkers and patients. But if the voices are loud and bothersome, he feels different and out of place.

He stands up from the table and goes to the kitchen window, where he sees a mailman placing junk mail into his letterbox. He waits till the mailman walks away and then he heads outside through the front door.

After a short walk, he arrives at the hospital.

Daniel strides through the sliding doors of St Francis, passing by the myriad of staff, visitors, and patients.

Daniel can smell disinfectant, which invokes feelings of cleanliness and the smell of soap. The smell is stinging and cold, like a stab to the chest.

Daniel hears sore throats and groans, the echoing of nurse's heels, the squeaking of wheels on wheelchairs.

He takes his place next to two men at the elevator. The man to the left attempts to start a conversation with Daniel by saying, "It's been a good day so far, weather speaking."

Daniel, however, ignores him and stares at the elevator doors. The man soon realises that Daniel does not want to engage in any polite conversation and thus does not continue trying.

The elevator dings as the sliding doors separate to reveal four nurses, obviously completing their shift for the day. One of them notices Daniel and offers a friendly greeting.

Daniel ignores her and instead engages the number two button. The other two men enter and remain silent.

On floor two, the elevator opens once again, and Daniel strides out down the hallway, skirting around the hospital beds that line the wall.

Daniel enters the changing area and hangs up his coat, the changing area is white and brown, and every surface is tiled and impeccably clean. Exchanging his holy blue jeans for green hospital-issue trousers and a sweatshirt, he heads for the workstation in the corridor.

It's a large counter, round, situated perfectly in the middle of the hallway.

Warm, fluorescent lights flicker like an old 1920's silent movie. An older woman is sitting at the counter her name is Brenda. She has been here at the hospital for a long time, so someone commented when Daniel was eves dropping one day to some nurse conversation.

Brenda, with her head down and voice low, is speaking on the phone to someone privately. Then, noticing Daniel, she quickly places the call on hold and gives Daniel a clipboard with a list of tasks. Her tone is raspy from many years of cigarettes as she says, "These are the jobs you need to do today."

The list typically included duties such as keeping the wards in order, assisting patients with their physical needs like rolling them over or helping with basic personal care, and transferring patients from one place to another either with a wheelchair or a portable bed.

Once the clipboard is in Daniel's hands, Brenda resumes the phone call she has on hold, while Daniel begins scanning the list. Suddenly, he notices that the faint whispers of voices within his head have returned.

Daniel steps into one of the rooms on the list and finds a patient lying on a bed, a short and stout middle-aged woman he has yet to learn the name of. An unpleasant, distinct odour lingers in the air around her; sour, stale, and musty. Daniel lingers in the room for a few minutes trying to help.

The woman is wearing a white nightgown with a red rose in the middle. Her eyes are sunken in her head. She lies on an older model bed with a thin mattress and four wheels. The sheets covering her are creased and stained, making it obvious that she is feeling discomfort. Daniel takes note of the situation but does not speak to her; it wasn't in his plan. He has no knowledge of what medications she has been given or what her symptoms are, but it is clear that she does not have long left in this world. Gently, he shifts her position on the bed and tugs on the sheet beneath her. Her skin is pale and clammy, with bed sores on her back. The bed is hard, the sheets stiff from starch; her skin is cold and rough to the touch, her hands bony.

The hospital room is rather old-looking, having never been updated since the building was erected. The room is old and bleak. The walls are painted in a soft baby blue, with a rough-coated ceiling of white. The room is dimly lit by fluorescent lights that buzz overhead like a swarm of bees in the centre of the room. The paint is peeling from the walls and the grey floor tiles are stained and cracked in multiple places.

Daniel can hear the sharp short intakes of breath from this woman, with a liquid bubbly sound coming from her breathing also.

Daniel could hear the voices in his head shouting at him, *"Cover her face with a pillow and suffocate her. Stab her in the neck with a scalpel."*

Daniel continues to pat his head to silence them from speaking to him. The woman on the bed watches him hitting himself and asks; "Are you alright?" to which Daniel responds angrily, "Yes, I just have a headache."

The woman struggles to talk and says, "Hit your head, and your headache will not stop but get worse." He snaps at the woman, "You don't think I know that?" He hurries out of the room.

Outside of the room, Daniel can hear her shout in distress, "What about my water?" However, Daniel continues to walk away.

The voices seem to be getting louder.

He proceeds down the hallway to the next room on his list, he is familiar with the man in this room. He has been hospitalised for a few weeks now. Gerry is his name. He is an elderly individual who has just ran out of luck while driving; his reflexes are not that great anymore. Gerry ended up crashing into the back of a garbage truck and he was unable to move, this trapped him for three hours. After the accident, he has two broken legs and a fractured skull, he also has a punctured lung and blood behind the thorax, and it will take Gerry a long time to recover.

Without saying anything to Gerry, Daniel walks into the ward. Daniel receives a sidelong glance from Gerry as he inquires about his time off and whether he enjoyed it.

"Yeah good," Daniel murmurs.

Daniel ignores Gerry's disappointed inquiry, "Is that all, good?" and empties the glass water jug from the side table into the bathroom sink.

"You're not going to drink that?" Gerry asks jokingly, Daniel shakes his head, "No."

Daniel looks down at the glass water jug in his hands. He stares at it for a long moment, and then a voice growls at him in his head again, "*Smash it and ram it into his neck,*" Daniel tries to ignore the voice, he places the water jug back on the side table and walks out of the ward without saying anything else.

A loud voice shouts out, "Hey Daniel, you going to fill the water jug again or what?" It was Gerry complaining, Daniel realises what he has done and returns to the ward grabs the jug and fills it back up with water and slams it down on the side table, and splashes the water everywhere. Gerry shouts at Daniel, "What the hell is wrong with you boy?"

Daniel walks out of the room and saunters off down the hallway to the restroom.

Suddenly Daniel collides with a nurse causing him to stumble slightly before gaining his balance again quickly and continuing towards the restroom. Daniel does not say anything to the nurse who was getting herself up off the floor, the nurse shouts, "Look where you're going, you moron." Daniel does not even acknowledge her, he gazes out the side windows, even thinks to himself, the windows are pointless here since there is nothing outside only trees and grasses growing out of the concrete walls.

Daniel enters the washroom, occupies the first stall, and sits down on the hard toilet seat. The sound of a large voice is pounding his head. To the point of choking, he fills his mouth with toilet tissue. From the stall, nothing is heard when he screams.

He screams repeatedly, he notices the voices are a whisper, relieved Daniel stands up and walks to the washbasin, turns on the cold water, and splashes his face. The cold water does the trick.

Daniel steps back out into the crowded hallway, with people barely noticing him as they rush past. He has left his list of tasks in Gerry's room, so he turns and walks back in the direction of Gerry's ward. He can still make out the whispers that fill his head.

Gerry let out a laugh as he addressed Daniel. "You going to throw the jug at me now?" Daniel glances back at him, his expression is serious and slightly intimidating. Gerry's smile fades and he remains silent. Daniel reached for his clipboard of tasks and leaves the room without speaking another word.

Daniel looks at the to-do list and notices he has to take Mrs. Astley to a CT scan in a wheelchair right down the end of the hallway on this floor. It's a part of his job to do so, as an orderly. The evil voices are still present in his head, and they continue to say bad things.

He takes a deep breath and begins to walk down the hallway. He can still faintly hear the voices. He feels his chest beating and knows that if he does not keep walking, he will never make it to Mrs. Astley's room.

His heart pounding faster and faster with every step. He fights the urge to turn around, to run away from this place, to forget about Mrs. Astley and all the other patients. Nevertheless, he knows that he cannot just run away, he needs to resist.

He reaches Mrs. Astley's room, and for a moment, he just stands there. He takes a few deep breaths, trying to regain his composure. He can feel the tension in his body.

He forces himself to enter the room. The voices are telling him faintly to just kill her now in this room, but he fights the urge. Mrs. Astley smiles at him and tells him that she is ready. He takes a deep breath and begins to wheel her down the hallway.

As he pushes her wheelchair, he can still feel the tension rising.

He sees Mrs. Astley sitting in the wheelchair leaning forward. She is thin and frail and looks like she is about to fall over. He must get Mrs. Astley to the CT scan, dodging loitering staff and patients, he glides down the corridor at a reasonable speed.

He reaches the end of the hallway and Mrs. Astley smiles at him, thanking him for pushing her all the way. He just stares at her and ignores the thank you.

At the same time, the internal conflict is still present. He can hear the voices in his head, still demanding to hurt Mrs. Astley, but he knows he cannot do that.

Out front of the scan room, Daniel notices the walls are scuffed, and a rubber glove is lying next to the doorway obviously dropped by a nurse or doctor.

He takes another deep breath and enters the CT scan room. He hands the wheelchair over to an Asian man who is the radiographer, he then wheels her over to the bed of the CT scan machine and is assisted by the nurse and Daniel, they lift her out of the wheelchair and lay her onto the bed of the scanner.

Mrs. Astley looks worried in the machine, as the nurse is busy getting her ready.

Daniel takes a step back and watches. He sees Mrs. Astley's worried expression, her face illuminated by the light from the machine.

It is a strange mix of conflicting emotions - on one hand, he feels the urge to do what the voices are saying and that is to cut her throat while she is laying down, but on the other is to get her away from this place and him. He clenches his fists, feeling the temptation within him as he battles against it. Looking at the nurse and Mrs. Astley the thought of hurting them and making them bleed fills his mind.

The light surrounds Mrs. Astley, a faint red and blue glow as if they are illuminating her on the machine. Her face is pale, her eyes closed, and her mouth is slightly open.

The CT scan machine is a hulking mass of machines on rollers. It has a big round doughnut-looking device with a larger outer ring that makes loud mechanical whirring and buzzing sounds. The machine is a cyclone of whizzing noises, of plastic and metal parts spinning and clunking as the machine is prepared.

A faint smell of something metallic mixes with the antiseptic and burnt metal fumes float in the room.

No one is allowed to stay in the room of the device when it is operating, so standing in a small separate room behind thick glass Daniel and the radiology staff watch as the machine starts. A deafening buzzing sound fills the room.

The machine frightens Mrs. Astley by the absence of space between the machine and her face, making her hot and feeling claustrophobic.

Twenty excruciating minutes later the procedure is over. Daniel the whole time just stands there, trying to keep it together, and watches and listens to the voices shouting at him as the radiographer and the other staff talk to each other and press buttons and watch a screen.

After getting a relieved Mrs. Astley down off the bed and back in the wheelchair. The voices are relentless, and Daniel can feel their anger boiling inside of him.

He fights against their taunts and eventually manages to get Mrs. Astley back to the ward and settled. Without saying a word, he exits the room in haste.

Daniel knows that if he does not leave the hospital soon, someone will be the next victim. He is on the precipice, and if he does not find a way to contain the darkness within himself, there will be no turning back.

The voices bring a sour taste to his mouth. He feels like he's about to vomit and his tongue feels dry. As the voices grow louder his hands go numb, his spine hurts and his teeth ache.

Daniel can feel the skin on his face burn as if acid has been thrown onto him. He can feel his flesh blistering, the heat rising.

Sweat beads on his forehead, his underarms dripping wet, and his sweatshirt clings to his back as the dampness spreads.

He must go home, or someone will die here today from his hands.

He hurriedly walks past Brenda at the counter and says to her, "I gotta go home!"

Brenda looks confused and shouts, "But you haven't finished your shift."

Brenda's face is a blur, the hallways are a blur as he races down them. He can feel the hairs on his arms sticking to his skin. The bile rising in his throat tastes sour. The voices only grow louder as he runs, they scream at him.

The screams are so loud that he can barely hear his feet pounding against the floor. Dodging people and obstacles he shouts, "Get the fuck out of my way!" His heart beating faster with each stride.

Pushing through the doors with all his might, Daniel runs out of the hospital, fresh air hits him hard, cleansing and calming him. He stops for a moment and looks up at the sky, letting the tears fall freely.

The birds are singing in the scattered trees in the yard, a car honking its horn nearby.

Daniel can feel the evil force over him recede, and he takes a deep breath. The screams are now whispers again, and he can feel the darkness slowly fading away.

He must get home before it comes back again.

As he walks down the street towards his home, his heart settles back into a normal rhythm and his breathing becomes more even. He passes people on the way home just like any other day, but today it feels different somehow. Daniel continues home.

10

THOU SHALL FOLLOW

For two long days, the detectives scoured the city, revisiting crime scenes and searching down leads, but their efforts had yielded nothing but dead ends.

It's a Wednesday the door opens, and Reilly and Moore walk in together after meeting in the car park. The familiar hum of the police station envelopes them as they make their way to the big room where their work desks are.

After taking a few moments to gather their materials, the two make their way to the whiteboard and begin to review the data related to the murder cases. Reilly writes Wednesday 15th March 1985 Julie Gaffney and Thursday 16th March 1985 Suzette Twiss in bold black marker on the board and subsequently sticks some Polaroid pictures on the surface as well.

The pictures on the whiteboard tell a story of the two horrific crimes that have developed over the last few days. The photographs of the victims are utterly depressing. They were happy once, but now they never will be again.

The photographs of their bodies are disturbing in the way that a car crash is disturbing. It is a moment frozen in time that is agonising to look at because of the look on their faces that the victims have, they knew that they were going to die.

The detectives spend the next hour going over the notes and research that has been collected, by them and the forensic team and their police colleagues.

Moore looks at the whiteboard again, his eyes taking in all the information so far and details that he might have missed. But nothing was jumping out at him.

Reilly is feeling overwhelmed with guilt and sorrow as she stares at the images. Not only is she failing to find any suitable leads to the murderer, but she is also failing the victims, the families of the victims, and herself.

Moore notices Reilly staring at the whiteboard and her eyes are welling up. "We'll get the bastard, Reilly. We just keep digging."

Reilly is obsessed over the pictures of the victims that she has on the board. She can't look away, hoping that one of them will give her a clue, but they are just as sad and depressing as the last.

Chief Dwyer shouts across the room from his office door, "Reilly and Moore, in here now."

They look at each other and walk their way to Chief Dwyer's office, Moore sees that the Chief is not in a good mood, obviously about the murder cases. As soon as they enter his office Chief Dwyer growls, "What the hell is going on? I've been hearing that there is another woman murdered now. What are you guys doing about it?"

Reilly and Moore remain quiet, unsure of how to respond.

Reilly is nervous and can feel her heart racing while Moore is hesitant at first but then speaks, "It's true Chief, we have been having a busy time with these two murders, due to lack of evidence like fingerprints and witnesses, it's hard to pin down a suspect.

Chief Dwyer sighs and sits back in his chair, "I understand, but I want results and I expect results." Reilly and Moore look at each other and then back to the Chief.

Moore speaks again, "We've been going over what we have plus research that was collected by us and the forensic team. We've noted every detail and have been working hard on finding a suspect or a lead. We're doing our best to find the killer."

Chief Dwyer looks sternly at them and nods, "Good. I want you two to keep on it and make sure it gets done, now get out of my office."

Reilly and Moore head back with their tails between their legs to the whiteboard and start going over the notes that have been collected. Reilly starts by reviewing the timeline of events, looking for any connections between the victims, while Moore reviews the crime scene photos, trying to identify any patterns in the attacks.

Moore turns to Reilly and comments, "Both victims have a cross on their forehead, and both were stabbed several times in the neck, and raped." Reilly muses aloud, "I wonder if these crosses are a tactic to mislead us?"

Moore replies, "It could be Reilly, but mislead us to what, a cult?" Moore growls, "All we have is that material from a tracksuit pant and shoe prints, and they are fucking hopeless as evidence."

Reilly springs up and stares around the room, bellowing, "Who left this memo about a phone call on my desk under my journal?"

She passes it to Moore, and they glance around the room, trying to get anyone's attention. But no one responds. Moore reads the memo again: "It has a callback number; it is dated last fuckin Friday." Reilly snatches the paper and strides to her desk, dialling the number. The line rings on the other end, yet no one responds. Reilly redials, but it still goes unanswered. Moore remarks, "I wonder what it is about? Hopefully, something we can use."

Reilly, frustrated, comments, "It's probably nothing; whoever wrote this memo should have had the courtesy to note what it was about, stupid assholes."

Stepping out of the room, Moore makes his way to the restroom. He looks over his shoulder to make sure no one is following him and enters the restroom; the room smells faintly of urine. He reaches into his jacket pocket and pulls out a brown medicine bottle. He shakes two tablets into his hand and pops them into his mouth.

Moore senses a bitter taste seeping into his tongue. The medicine is called Atrovax, it's an anti-depressant.

Suddenly, the door of a toilet stall swings open, and Officer Harris emerges behind him. "Detective Moore," Harris queries, "Are you on tablets?" Moore responds, "Just heartburn medication mate it's a prick of a thing." Harris washes his hands, nods, and heads out the door. Moore takes a drink from the tap and swallows the pills.

Moore ventures back to Reilly sitting at her desk looking pissed off. "Any luck yet?" queries Moore.

Reilly rolls her eyes at Moore and dials again. As the phone rings on the other end, Reilly hears a click and a voice, "Hello?" Reilly sits up and snaps her fingers at Moore to get his attention. "Hello, who is this?" Reilly asks.

The voice on the other end of the line replies, "I'm Michael Casey, who is this?" Reilly replies, "This is Detective Reilly. I found a note on my desk to call you. Do you know why I had to call you?"

Michael Casey says, "I witnessed something disturbing a few nights back. Around 12:20 am Friday, I spotted a man wearing a black hoodie and blue jeans, his face and hands and jeans covered in blood, passing by my front yard."

Reilly is excited to hear the things that Michael Casey is saying. "Whereabouts do you live Michael; I want to come and see you." Michael Casey says, "33 Madden Street."

Reilly slams down the phone without even a goodbye, looks at Moore and shouts, "We have a lead and hopefully a description." Moore shouts, "About fuckin time".

Both detectives rush out of the room and head for the address.

Reilly and Moore stop in front of 33 Madden Street, eager to meet Michael Casey. A small red brick house with white trim sits there, with a wire fence lining the yard. Next door, two young boys on skateboards stop and stare as the detectives step out of their car.

Michael Casey emerges from his home and comes up to greet the detectives. Michael is wearing a blue collared shirt, long sleeves, and blue jeans.

Moore and Reilly stand there waiting for Michael to open the gate. Michael is tall with a receding hairline and an unshaven face.

"Hello detectives," Michael says, "How are you both?"

"We are doing well," Detective Moore replies, "And we hear you have something for us."

Michael smiles and says, "Depends on what you're after, took your time getting here, I called last week."

Michael opens the gate and lets the two detectives into his yard. They all stand on the concrete driveway.

Michael tells Detective Moore, "I work nightshift at the meat works, and just after clocking off at Midnight on Friday morning, I drove home. It was about 12.20 in the morning as it only takes 20 minutes to get home from work. As I pulled up in my driveway and reversed, I got out to shut the gate. When I looked up, lit up by the headlights of my car, there was a man in a black hoodie and blue jeans with white sneakers.

He had blood on his face, hands, and clothes." Reilly inquires, "Are you sure it wasn't paint?" Michael gives her a strange look and says, "I know the difference between paint and blood, detective. There was too much blood on him to be in a fistfight, looked as if it was thrown on his jeans. The man didn't even glance in my direction; he just walked away with his eyes straight ahead."

Moore then asks which way he went. Michael points down the street and explains, "That way." The street ends so I'm not sure if he went into one of the houses or cut through a footpath between them."

"What did he look like?" Moore asks Michael Casey.

Michael stoops down and tugs out a weed from the side of the concrete driveway as he describes, "His face was thin and bony, about five feet eight inches tall. I couldn't tell if his hair was black or dark brown because he had his hood up, but from what I caught a glimpse of, I think it was black."

"That's great Michael, that information definitely helps us out," Reilly smiles at Michael. "If you see this guy again, make sure to ring the station and tell them to contact Reilly and Moore immediately, okay?" Michael nods and then heads back to the house.

Reilly and Moore swing open the gate and close it behind them.

Both detectives decide to walk down to the bottom end of the street to see if there are any signs of a clue to where this guy is. They make their way down and notice how each house is a little different, how the colour of the curtains in the windows changes, how the flowers are done in pots on the porch, and the lawns are cut short. There is the earthy smell of freshly cut grass the faint smell of newly laid bitumen on the road next to them and a whiff of burnt rubber from a nearby backyard burn-off.

Standing at the end of the street they notice the footpath that goes between the two houses. One of the houses next to the path is a bit run down and has a dog, that spots them and is barking.

The other house is not much to look at either with tall grass growing in the yard and the kitchen window is covered up by a wooden board.

Moore and Reilly follow the footpath which winds its way downhill, leading to a stretch of pine trees in the distance. Ahead of them, a figure sporting a grey hoodie has emerged from the trees and is making their way up the incline.

Moore shouts for him to wait there, but to no avail—the figure immediately takes off, running towards the tree line. The detectives give chase, and Reilly closes in behind Moore as they fly down the hill. Just as Moore reaches the tree line, the hooded figure disappears from view—they have lost him. In his haste, Moore trips and tumbles onto the grassy ground, bruising his ego and his now-dirty clothing.

Groaning in pain, Moore quickly gets back on his feet; his clothing is now stained with mud and debris from his fall—a stark contrast to its pristine condition only moments ago!

Reilly takes a few steps ahead and stops at the edge of the tree line. She scans the area for the hooded figure, but nothing stirs.

"You doing okay, Moore?" she queries.

"Yeah, fuckin dandy," Moore shouts back.

Reilly cringes as Moore swears. He approaches Reilly and asks, "Did you get a good look at the guy?"

"No, he was too far away," Reilly answers.

"Just look at my fuckin suit," Moore continues, futilely brushing off the grass stains from his clothing as if they'll magically disappear.

Moore snaps, "I should have fired a shot."

Reilly retorts, "We don't even know if it was him or not."

"Why did he run then, if it wasn't him?"

"Maybe he had something else to hide," Reilly grumbles. Moore looks at Reilly and he can see the disappointment in her eyes.

"It's my fault. If only I had not shouted out, things could have been different," moans Moore.

"Don't beat yourself up about it detective," mumbles Reilly. Moore begins to hobble up the steep slope, back towards their vehicle on Madden Street. "Come on Reilly," he yelled. " Let's go across those pines and intercept him at the other end."

Moore navigates around narrow roads as they arrive near the area that is on the other side of the pine trees where they lost the hooded guy earlier.

Pulling over on the side of the road, they climb out of the unmarked police vehicle and get their bearings. It's 4.45 pm and a cold Tuesday afternoon.

The smell of pine trees surrounds them; They can hear a tractor operating amongst some sheds on a small vegetable field behind them. The pine trees are so tall and dark that they block out most of the sunlight from reaching the ground, making the whole scene dark and gloomy. The wind is whistling eerily through the trees, making them seem to sway and dance with the wind.

Three sheds are located behind them, with various farming equipment inside. Moore peers inside the first shed, but nothing seems suspicious. The next shed is much larger, and pigeons are hopping around the rafters. "Nothing here, Reilly," Moore says.

The detectives then cross the road and notice the exit from the pine forest. Beyond it is grassy pastures filled with cows, sheep, and vegetable fields. On the other side of the street is a truck depot.

"I can't tell where he was coming from, what would he be doing out here?" Moore asked.

"Might have just been a jogger that we scared off," Reilly replies.

Moore shook his head in disagreement.

Reilly walked towards the pine tree's entrance and started down the trail inside while Moore followed behind.

Reilly and Moore follow the path through the pine forest, the trees loom high above them. The trees are covered with a thick coat of moss and lichen, and the ground is covered with a green carpet of moss. Damp and soggy pine needles make it difficult for them to traverse through. The smell of nature is heavy in the air.

The forest is still and silent except for occasional twigs snapping under their feet echoing like pistol shots across the forest.

In the centre of the clearing stands an old, abandoned shed with chipped paint and broken windows. The door has been left open and there are some items strewn about inside - mostly lolly wrappers and drink cans where children have been sitting in there, probably used as a playhouse.

Moore turns back outside towards Reilly who gives him an inquisitive look with raised eyebrows and silently asks him if he found anything interesting inside. Moore shook his head in response and motioned for them to head back as they were wasting their time.

Heading back, Reilly swerves off the path; some large boulders caught her attention, and she takes a closer look. Moore continues toward the car, fifty metres away.

Reilly circles the enormous rocks that appear strange in the woods; none of this kind was seen anywhere else in sight. Moore then turns back and waves to Reilly, who returns the gesture to indicate that she has noticed him calling her. Moore continues walking.

Without warning, Reilly hears the snap of someone stepping on twigs from behind her. In an instant, a grey material arm wraps around her neck, choking her, and she is lifted off the ground. She can hear the attacker's heavy breath as they struggle. Reilly feels the attacker's hot breath on her neck. She can smell the attacker's sweaty, musty odour.

Reilly attempts to reach for her gun tucked in her side holster, but the attacker seizes her wrist and forces her down onto the ground beneath him, pressing her face against the pine needles and dirt.

Moore makes his way towards the forest's exit, glancing behind him in search of Reilly, only to find that she has vanished. Frowning, he trudges back towards the spot where he had seen her last.

Reilly fights for breath as the needles fill her mouth and throat each time she strongly inhales.

The force of a powerful blow to the back of her head causes flashes of light to burst forth behind her closed eyes. The perpetrator stands up and delivers a kick to Reilly's gut, making her double over in agony. She cries out for help, "Moore!"

Moore looks to where the shout came from to see a man cloaked in a grey hoodie looking back at him. He quickly surveys the area, his gaze falling on Reilly who lies on the ground below the hooded man.

Moore draws his gun and shouts "Freeze! You bastard!"

The attacker takes cover behind one of the boulders and darts into the forest.

Reilly, still in pain, reaches for her own gun and fires three shots in the direction of her assailant, although she cannot see him. Moore sprints toward the boulders with his pistol raised, seeking out the attacker, yet finding no trace of him.

Moore kneels beside Reilly, who is struggling to catch her breath. "Are you okay? Are you hurt?" he asks, concern etched on his face.

"I'll be fine," Reilly gasps, still trying to shake off the effects of the attack. "But we need to find that guy before he gets away."

Moore nods and helps her to her feet. Together, they begin to search the area, looking for any signs of the attacker's whereabouts. They find footprints and broken branches, but the attacker seems to have vanished. "We'll find him," Moore says to Reilly, determination in his voice. "He won't get away with this."

As the detectives make their way back to their car, they keep a watchful eye out for any sign of the attacker. They both know how dangerous the situation could have been and are relieved to have made it out relatively unscathed.

Once they're back in the car, Moore immediately picks up the police radio and calls for backup. "Charlie 32 to VKT, come in," he says, his voice tense. "My partner was just jumped here, at the

Pines on the end of Madden Street. We need to get some more officers down here to search the area for the attacker. We're on the other side of the Pines on Thomas Road."

The dispatcher acknowledges the call, promising to send a backup as soon as possible. Moore thanks them before hanging up the radio.

Turning to Reilly, he asks, "Do you need a trip to the hospital? You're hurt."

Reilly shakes her head, trying to shake off the shock of the attack. "No, I'll be okay," she says, her voice weak. "I'm more bruised in my ego than my body. I can't believe I got jumped like that."

"It happens to the best of us, Reilly," Moore says, trying to lighten the mood. Despite the gravity of the situation, he can't help but let out a small chuckle.

"We need to bring an unmarked car up here and to keep watch; if the suspect returns, he might be residing in one of these houses," states Moore.

"Why don't we get a few police up here go house to house and see if they know anything?"

"No Reilly," declares Moore, "We will scare him off and he will never show up if he does come back. We will just have a couple in an unmarked car and stick them here and see if he does. "

"That's a good idea, Moore," Reilly agrees.

***

Back at the station, the team agrees with Moore and Reilly that it's the best course of action and sets to work on organising the surveillance operation.

Reilly is given an ice pack for her injuries. As she gingerly settles into her seat, Moore looks at her with a concerned expression.

Moore gets Reilly a cup of coffee from the station's vending machine and sits it down on the desk in front of her.

Reilly takes a sip of her coffee, wincing slightly at the heat against her lips before setting it down on the desk beside her.

"Are you okay?" Moore asks. "I'll be fine," Reilly replies, trying to downplay her injuries. "Just a few bruises, nothing serious."

Moore nods but doesn't look convinced. "We need to file a report on what happened out there. Do you think you're up for it?" Reilly nods. "Yeah, I can do it. Just give me a minute to collect my thoughts."

Moore nods and gives her some space, allowing her to gather her thoughts and compose herself before beginning the report. As she begins to recount the events of the evening, Moore listens attentively, making notes and asking follow-up questions as needed. Despite her injuries, Reilly is able to provide a clear and detailed account of what happened, and Moore is impressed by her professionalism. "Thanks, Moore," Reilly says, "I appreciate it. I'll head home and get some rest. Let's touch base tomorrow." Moore agrees, and the two of them gather their things and leave the office, each heading home to process the events of the evening and try to put them behind them.

11

DOWNTIME

Moore pushes open the door to his hotel room, the stench of cigarette smoke and stale beer overwhelms him as he surveys the mess in front of him, 8:47 pm is blinking red on the alarm clock.

Moore takes his anti-depressant drugs and drinks them down with an already-opened flat beer. Moore is not coping with his mind the tablets are not working anymore, the trauma of his past is catching up to him, and having six months off work really did not help. He has bottled up his past traumas for too long and it's starting to catch up with him.

He knows that he needs help, but the thought of being stood down as a detective and losing his badge is too much to bear. He's determined to catch this serial killer and bring closure to the victim's families. He can't let them down.

As he sits on the edge of his bed, he can't shake off the feeling that his partner, Reilly, is starting to notice something off. He knows that she's a good detective, and he doesn't want her to suspect that he's struggling. He makes a mental note to be more careful and to keep his issues to himself.

Moore takes a deep breath, closes his eyes and tries to clear his mind, but the memories of the past won't go away. He knows that it's going to be a long night.

Moore gets up from his bed, feeling a sense of restlessness. He knows that he needs something stronger than beer to help him forget his troubles for a little while. He grabs his jacket and heads out of his hotel room, making his way down the street and around the corner to a bar he's been to a few times before.

As he enters the bar, he's greeted by the familiar smell of alcohol and cigarette smoke. He nods to the bartender, who greets him by name and takes a seat at the end of the bar. He orders a whiskey neat, and takes a long sip, feeling the burn of the alcohol as it goes down.

As he sits at the bar, he tries to push away his thoughts of the day's events.

He watches other people, lost in their own conversations and problems.

He orders another whiskey and lets himself get lost in the noise and chatter of the bar. For now, he's able to forget his problems, but he knows that they'll be waiting for him when he leaves. He'll deal with them tomorrow, for tonight, he just wants to forget.

It is 1.00 a.m. and Moore is being a nuisance. Intoxicated now and wanting another whiskey he shouts at the bartender.

The bartender growls at him to leave the premises or he will call the police, Moore tells him he is the police, and the bartender quickly snaps back at Moore telling him he will get sober ones, and it won't look good for your bosses. Moore slides off the bar stool and staggers to the door, he finds himself feeling mixed emotions - anger, embarrassment, and disappointment. He knows that he has let himself get out of control and that his behaviour is unbecoming of a police officer. He takes a deep breath and begins to walk home.

As Moore continues to walk down the street, he trips over his own feet and falls hard on the concrete, splitting his chin open. He groans in pain as he tries to get up, but he finds that he's too dizzy and disoriented to stand. He looks around, but there's no one around to help him.

He starts to feel a sense of panic rising in his chest as he lays there on the pavement, bleeding and alone. He realises that he's hit rock bottom.

Moore knows that he needs to get up and get back to his hotel before someone calls the police. He knows that if he's found in this state, it could mean the end of his career as a detective.

He takes a deep breath and tries to steady himself. He's in a lot of pain, but he knows that he needs to get back to his hotel before someone sees him. He uses the wall of a building to help him get back on his feet, and he starts to make his way back to his hotel, he can feel the warm sensation of the blood running from his chin making its way down his neck and under his shirt to his chest.

It's a slow and painful journey, but he finally makes it back to his hotel room. He's covered in blood and dirt, and he knows that he looks a mess. He's relieved that he's made it back without being seen, but he's also filled with a sense of shame and disgust at his behaviour. But he knows he continues to do this most nights, but tonight is worse.

He falls into bed, exhausted and in pain, but at least he's back in the safety of his hotel room.

He curls up on his bed, tears streaming down his face as he calls out for Kate, the person he loves.

He feels a deep sense of guilt and regret for the person he has become, for the mistakes he's made and for the people he's hurt. He wishes that he could go back and change things, but he knows that he can't.

***

It is 2.17 a.m. on a Thursday morning, and the street outside Reilly's apartment is still and quiet. Lying in bed, Reilly takes a sip of her wine and releases a heavy sigh.

She's still reeling from the attack that occurred earlier yesterday while she was on duty. She reaches for a biscuit and takes a bite, letting the sweet taste distract her from the pain in her stomach.

She closes her eyes and lets her mind drift, trying to forget about the events of yesterday and focus on getting some rest.

Reilly tries to focus on the face of the attacker but it's all a blur. She can remember bits and pieces, but it's hard to put them all together. She can remember his eyes, cold and calculating, and his voice, deep and menacing. But she can't remember the specific details of his face like his nose, mouth, or even his hair. Reilly starts to feel frustrated and a little defeated. She's a seasoned detective and she's never had trouble remembering the details of someone's face before. She starts to wonder if the attack has affected her more than she thought.

Reilly's thoughts start to spiral as she becomes more and more curious about Moore's behaviour also. *Why is Detective Moore living in a hotel room? Has he split up with his wife or girlfriend?*

She can't shake off the feeling that something is not right, and she wants to know what it is.

She takes another sip of wine and eats another biscuit, she knows that it's important to rest and recover, but she also knows that she can't give up until the attacker or the killer that she is looking for is caught and brought to justice.

12

THE SEARCH

Detective Moore stumbles through the precinct doors, his scruffy appearance and bruises sparking murmurs of shock and awe among his colleagues as they stare at him in surprise.

"Alright, if any of you are wondering what happened, I tripped over my shoelaces," he announces gruffly.

Moore slumps down into his chair, muttering to himself. *"I hope they bought that story; the last thing I need is for them to discover I was staggering around like a drunkard."*

Reilly enters the room and is taken aback by Moore's appearance--his chin was swollen with a fresh gash that looked like it needed stitches. "What the hell, who got into you?" says Reilly.

Moore looks up at her and quietly says, "I fell over my shoelaces and landed on the sidewalk when going to my hotel room that is all."

Reilly sits down in her chair and notices a faint waft of booze coming from Moore. She also smells a sickly sweet aroma of body odour coming from him as well. She stares at him for a few moments before asking if he needs any medical attention.

Moore shakes his head and says that he'll be alright. He then takes out a handkerchief and begins to wipe away the sweat from his forehead.

The two detectives sit in silence for a moment before Reilly asks Moore, "Do you think our suspect is living in one of the houses we were at yesterday?"

Moore grunts as he tries to get comfortable in his chair, "It's possible. We can go door-to-door to ask questions."

"Alright. Let's do that, but won't that scare the suspect off if he is there and sees us?" Reilly says as she stands up.

Moore gets out of his chair and says, "We don't really have a choice now do we, if we want to catch this guy. I need to go to the restroom."

Moore grins and walks out of the room, calling out, "I'll meet you at the car!"

Moore enters the restroom he sees the white tiles covering the floor leading to the urinal. He tries to look at his reflection in the mirror, but he can only see a blur. He stops for a moment and tries to focus his eyes. He finally is able to focus and sees a man worse for wear.

He fishes a small bottle of white capsules out of his pocket and pops them into his mouth, washing them down with a mouth full of water from the basin tap.

The alcohol from last night still leaves his head pounding. Looking back at the mirror he notices his chin is bleeding, so he grabs a piece of paper towel from the dispenser and wipes away the blood. He holds it firmly against his wound as he steps out of the restroom into the hallway. Despite the pain, he keeps up pressure applied to his chin with the paper towel.

Moore and Reilly set off to search the street, hoping they will find some clues that would help them locate the criminal. Is it possible that the killer lives here, or did he only pass through on his way to someplace else?" Moore knocks loudly on the first house they come across.

A middle-aged woman answers the door, and the detectives introduce themselves and ask if she has seen or heard anything suspicious in the area recently. The woman thinks for a moment and then tells the detectives that she had seen a strange man walking around the neighbourhood late at night a few days ago. She described the man as tall and thin and a hooded sweatshirt. Reilly asks her, "What direction was he heading?"

"Towards the path down there that leads to the pines," pointing as the woman speaks.

Moore buts in on the conversation, "What was strange about him?"

The woman replies, "He was talking to himself out loud while I was standing on my porch, it was like he was arguing with himself."

Moore gives her a card with a phone number on it, "Please call this number next time you see him please, and ask for me, Detective David Moore."

The woman nods and walks back into her home and closes the door.

Both detectives retreat to the sidewalk and move on.

At the next house, they speak with an elderly man who has lived in the neighbourhood for over 50 years. He tells the detectives that he hasn't seen or heard anything out of the ordinary, but he does mention that there has been several burglaries in the area recently.

The detectives took note of this information and continue with their search. As they go from house to house, they speak with several other residents who provide them with a variety of information, but nothing that seems to connect to the crime they are investigating.

The detectives take notes of this information and continue again.

At the next house, they come to, an old fragile man opens the door, Detective Moore proceeds to ask him, "Hi sir, we are detectives doing a search in the area for any info and any strange activities going on around in the street lately?" The old man says, " Not that I know of, it's a quiet street, not much happens here." Reilly asks the old man "Do you know most people at the end of this street?" The old man replies, "I know most but there are three houses near the sidewalk that exits the street down the hill to the pines, I don't know them.

I see a young man walk past a few times wearing a black hoodie and he usually has the hood over his head even when it's hot, I don't understand the young kids of today, especially since their outfits of choice are disgraceful." Moore asks the old man, "Which house is he in? The old man shrugs his shoulders as a sign he did not know. Moore nods, understanding the old man's confusion. He thanks the man for his time.

Moore and Reilly walk back to the sidewalk looking at the three houses at the end of the street.

Reilly looks at Moore and queries, "Do you think the murderer could be in one of these residences?"

"I'm not positive, Reilly. Let's discover the answer," Moore says.

The two of them walk to the first house and Moore pounds his knuckles against the solid wooden door.

The door opens slowly to reveal a female in her late thirties clutching a baby. Moore explains that he is asking around the area for any information regarding the recent murder and attack on his partner yesterday. The woman, who identifies herself as Karen, is clearly disturbed by this news. She tells them that she's lived at the house for quite some time now and nothing out of the ordinary has occurred. The street is usually pretty quiet.

The detectives thanked Karen for her help and moved on to the next house.

This house is run down badly, not much care is given to this place. Reilly takes her turn knocking on the door.

They wait for the door to open but nothing, Moore tries to peak through the living room window next to the door and quietly says, "Don't think anyone is home, let's try the last one,"

They both head round to the fence of the next house.

They climb the steps to the patio and Reilly knocks hard again on the door. Moore observes the yard, the grass is high that high you could hide a pony in it. Reilly knocks again, Moore peers around the side of the house, and he notices some of the windows are all boarded shut.

"Well, I guess we'll have to come back later when the owner is home that's if anybody lives here," Moore says.

Leaving the third house, the detectives are starting to feel discouraged, but they know that they can't give up. The two detectives wait for the surveillance guys to show up to watch the street and then they head back to the station.

When back at the station Moore places his notepad on his desk slumps down into his chair and sighs. Reilly is just about to sit down when from across the room Chief Dwyer shouts, "Hey Moore, Reilly in my office." Moore mumbles under his breath, "What now?"

Reilly and Moore cautiously enter the Chief's office, both feeling the tension that is hanging in the air.

The Chief closes the door behind them, his features drawn in an expression of the utmost seriousness.

Moore's eyes are filled with concern. There is a sheen of sweat on his forehead as if he has been running.

Moore is standing at attention, not an inch moving while the Chief takes up his usual spot behind his desk. Chief Dwyer has the unmistakable scent of cigars; people say that he smells like a ship's captain.

"What bloody day is it today?" "It's Thursday Chief," says Reilly.

"What's the update on the case? Any leads yet? Is this the individual who attacked you, Reilly? Is he, our killer?" growls Chief Dwyer.

"It is possible, sir," answers Reilly. "A few locals have reported seeing him in the area, but we haven't been able to confirm if he lives there or not. We have officers looking for him all around, but so far, no luck."

The Chief lets out a long sigh. "We need to get this man before he strikes again. How are your injuries doing Reilly?"

"Fine, Chief. Nothing serious," replies Reilly. "We have people watching the street, but nothing yet."

"And how are you holding up Moore? If you need time away then just say so," mumbles Chief Dwyer.

Reilly was taken aback. *"Why is he asking Moore about time off? It was me who was attacked. What is going on?"*

Reilly couldn't understand why the Chief seemed more concerned about Moore's welfare than hers. She had been working just as hard, if not harder, on the case. She couldn't shake the feeling that something was off.

"Ok continue on finding this sick bastard, now get out of my office," shouts Chief Dwyer.

Both detectives exit the Chief's office and head back to their desks, Moore turns to Reilly, "I will be back in a sec, gotta go to the restroom," and he walks out of the room.

Reilly sits down in her chair and huffs like a child not getting what she wants, her anger intense. She cannot believe that the Chief is more concerned about Moore's health than hers. She knows something is not right, but she can't quite put her finger on it. She sits there, her mind racing with questions.

"What's wrong?" asks Officer Paterson, watching her from his desk.

"Nothing," Reilly snaps. "Just some bullshit with the Chief and Moore."

Paterson raises an eyebrow. "What kind of bullshit?"

Reilly sighs. "I don't know. He is more worried about Moore's health than mine, I'm the one that was attacked."

Paterson nods sympathetically. "Yeah, I know Moore's been off for six months. I heard a rumour he had some kind of personal issue."

Reilly's ears perk up. "What kind of personal issue?"

Paterson shrugs. "I don't know."

Reilly's mind races as she tries to piece together the puzzle. *Why would the Chief be so concerned about Moore's health? Why has he been off work for six months?*

Reilly leans forward, eager for any information that could help her understand the situation better. "Do you know anything else about Moore's absence?" she asks Paterson.

"I'm rather new here so I don't have much insight into the situation. I haven't had much interaction with Moore. I'm sorry I can't be any more help," complains Paterson.

Reilly and Paterson quickly straighten up as Moore approaches them.

"What's going on?" Moore asks. "Nothing, just catching up," Reilly says, trying to sound casual. Moore gives them a suspicious look but doesn't press the issue. "Alright then," he says, turning his attention to his own work.

Reilly and Paterson exchange a quick look, both relieved that they weren't caught discussing the sensitive information. They return to their work, but both are now on edge, aware of Moore's presence and the need to be more careful with what they say.

13

THE HIDDEN

Daniel sits against the crumbling wall under the Victoria Bridge, the putrid scent of the black and sluggish Saxon River overpowers his senses.

He is rocking back and forth, his head in his hands, trying to think, but the evil voices are strong. He is bleeding from a wound on his hand, where he had fallen on some branches in the pine forest while being chased by the detective. Daniel is wearing an old grey hoodie, faded by the sun and splintered with pine needles. His hair is matted and dirty.

Further up next to him against the wall, some homeless people are huddled together, keeping their distance but clearly aware of Daniel's presence. They talk among themselves, glancing over at him every now and then as if he is an alien from outer space. Daniel seems oblivious to their presence, lost in his own internal dialogue, constantly talking and shouting at himself.

As Daniel sits there, the sun begins to set, painting the sky in hues of pink and orange. The homeless people grow quiet and contemplative, looking for a place in the shadows for the night.

Then, all at once, as if on cue, they begin to disperse, leaving Daniel alone with his voices.

He stays in that spot, he can hear the water of the river lapping up against the concrete edge echoing around him under the bridge. The voices are angry with him, and they repeat in his head.

He can't shake the ones that tell him he is a failure, that he will never amount to anything. He tries to push them away, to focus on the soothing sound of the water, but they only grow louder.

As dusk settles, Daniel is aware that he needs to find somewhere to rest for the night He cannot stay here any longer, it's too cold.

He rises from his spot by the river and starts to wander away, his mind laden with evil thoughts. His mental state is besieged by dark musings as he strolls the side streets and the voices inside him keep getting louder, goading him to act on his wicked intentions.

They remind him of an elderly woman he has been keeping an eye on these past few days, and how effortless it would be to erase her life and stay in her home. He exerts himself to ignore them and focus on something else, but they are too powerful. He has to act and find refuge where he can revive himself. A burning rage is filling up inside of him as he walks. Deep down he knows what he is going to do is wrong, but he cannot stop.

He has taken note of her routine over the last few days, she is alone- with no one going in or out except for her.

As Daniel walks to the end of the vacant block adjacent to the old woman's home, Daniel stands still, watching her house as the wind picks up. The cold night air carries the familiar odour of chimney smoke and wet soil.

One by one the lights go out in the old woman's house.

One hour later, Daniel finally takes a step forward and slowly makes his way towards the woman's home. He walks cautiously across her yard, keeping an eye out for any signs of movement or activity within her house. He is careful not to make too much noise as he steps on the grass, but it crunches underneath his feet anyway.

The air is silent with only the faint sound of a distant dog barking in the night. There are no other sounds, not even a passing vehicle or someone walking their dog. The bushes around him rustle and sway, but Daniel is focused on his task and does not let anything distract him from it.

He reaches the back door of the old lady's house and stops to take a deep breath before reaching for the handle. The door is locked, Daniel elbows the small square plate of glass above the door handle and breaks it with a crack hoping not to wake the old woman up, he pokes away at the glass and slides his hand through. He reaches for the door handle, his heart racing in anticipation as he turns it and pushes open the door, stepping inside carefully.

He enters a small hallway that leads towards a kitchen - all still dark as there are no lights on inside the house.

Quietly he works his way down another hallway, he can't focus, the voices are screaming at him from inside of his head telling him to hurry up and kill her, rip her apart, destroy her.

He stops, the pain in his head is getting too much for him, he falls to his knees in the middle of the hallway and begins to hold his head in his hands. Daniel stays on his knees rocking back and forth for a few minutes, enough time to pull himself together the voices soften a bit, and he stands back up and continues to do what he come here to do.

He reaches the old woman's bedroom door, and it is not shut, almost closed he reaches his hand in and pushes it slowly open more, revealing the old lady asleep in the bed.

The old lady is outlined by the light of the moon coming in through the window, her mouth is open in a deep snore and her head rests at an odd angle. The air in the room tastes like fresh laundry and flowers.

The blankets covering her move, lifting and falling with her breath.

Daniel creeps closer to the bed, his heart pounding and a chill running through his body. His mind is screaming. The silence in the room makes it easier for him to focus on what he has come here to do.

He stands by her bedside, he pauses for a moment, gathering himself before reaching forward with both hands and then he grabs her around the neck.

The shocked old woman has no time to cry out, She reaches for his hands trying to peel them off her neck, but she is not strong enough, her eyes beading him, a look as if her eyes are going to pop out of their sockets.

Daniel stares in shock at what he is doing, unable to move or think clearly due to the sheer terror coursing through his veins.

She starts to kick her legs and is waving her arms trying to scratch him but to no avail; his strength is just too much. The creaking bed frame overpowers the silence.

With every squeeze of his hands, her neck makes a cracking noise. He hisses into her ear, "I am Legion, fear me!" She stares at the ceiling. Her face is expressionless, and her eyes are wide and red, the blood vessels stand out like worms. Her mouth is open in a silent scream.

Eventually, he breaks his hands away from her neck and retreats into the shadow beside the bed. All that is left is the woman's lifeless body on the mattress.

His legs feel like jelly as he slowly backs away from her lifeless body, his mind racing with thoughts of what has just happened.

He slowly makes his way back into the hallway and barely registers that his fingers are cramped.

He shakes himself out of it enough to take another step forward, then another until eventually he reaches the kitchen and sits himself down at the table. The voices are fading to silence. The kitchen was deathly still, Daniel could almost feel the silence whispers in his head.

Daniel glances at the clock on the wall, noticing that it is nearly 10 p.m.

He shuffles over to the kitchen sink grabs a tumbler from the shelf and fills it with water from the tap. The water soothes his dry throat as he gulps it down in one go and places the empty glass on the counter.

In a rush, he strides back to the hallway and the old woman's bedroom. Daniel throws the comforter off the bed and onto the floor and rolls the woman to the edge of the bed, letting her fall out with a loud thump. He notices she has soiled herself, the heavy stench of urine wafting in the air. He grabs her side and starts rolling her up in the comforter like a makeshift cocoon.

She is all wrapped up in the blanket with only her head poking out. Her face was still a mottle of surprise and fear. But her eyes were dull and lifeless.

She smells of lavender and urine. It was so strong that he feels nauseous. He fights the urge to gasp for air as he pulls her from the bedroom and rushes to the back door. With a twist of the knob, he flings open the door and searches around for any movement in the darkness of the yard. He drags her lifeless body across the dirt path until they reach the weathered shed in the corner.

He swings the door wide drags her into the shed and drops her unceremoniously beside the lawn mower. He returns to the house, shutting the door back inside. He crosses the hallway into the living area.

He sees the edge of the TV and the hulking shape of a couch in the darkness. His hands grip the edges of these objects to ground himself, to help him in the right direction to the drapes covering the window.

Daniel peeks out the window, his gaze darting up and down the street. Everything is quiet and still. He can now find refuge from the police in this house. He walks into the kitchen, stops at the refrigerator, and opens it. There is no light inside, but he can just barely make out a tin can sitting on the shelf.

He stretches out his hand and takes the can from the shelf, holding it up to get a better look. It's half-full of baked beans, which he scoops out with a spoon that was already sitting in it. The beans are cold and bland and have a light metallic flavour. The can is cool in his grasp.

Daniel places the can down and looks around the kitchen for something to fix his hand that had been cut open after he tumbled in the pines. His blood stains the floor as he searches for bandages. He works his way down to the bathroom and looks in the vanity for some. He finds a packet on the top shelf sitting in a plastic lunch box container. He grabs them and gets to work on his hand, wrapping it in several thick layers of gauze. It's painful, but he knows it needs to be done if he wants to avoid infection.

He returns to the kitchen and takes his seat in the chair, noticing an elderly woman occupying the chair opposite his. The room is silent, and the darkness swallows up what little light there is.

Daniel notices it's the old woman that he just strangled to death earlier. She stares at him; he continues to eat what is left in the can.

"Why are you eating my beans?" she mumbles, still eyes fixed on him. Daniel continues to eat the beans, not allowing the old woman's presence to distract him.

With a mouthful of beans, Daniel replies to her in a cold voice, "You don't need them... You're dead." The old woman does not say anything after that and continues staring at him with no attempt to blink.

The room feels heavy with the weight of death looming over them both like a foggy blanket.

He scrapes the tin with the spoon collecting what is left of the sauce of the baked beans.

Still, she sits there staring at him.

He stands up and walks to the kitchen sink and places the can on the sink top. He turns back around and heads for the living room observing the old woman has gone.

Daniel enters the living room and opens the drapes a little to let some streetlight in and he finds the large sofa and lays down on it.

The living room seems like any other home. A suede sofa and coffee table and an old TV unit. An oil painting of a countryside landscape is hanging on the back wall.

Daniel lays on his side looking at the dark room his eyes adjusting.

In the corner of the room, the dead old woman stands still, silently watching him.

The silence is deafening, aside from the occasional tap of a tree limb against the window.

Daniel can smell the old house, and as he lays on his side with his right shoulder close to the floor, it smells musty. Daniel notices all of a sudden, the old woman has gone.

He grabs one of the cushions that is under him and uses it as a pillow, resting his head down again he closes his eyes.

The old woman is back, her cold breath in his ear, her gaunt frame pressed against his body.

Daniel's eyes snap open, suddenly aware of her presence.

"What do you want from me?" Daniel whispers.

The old woman doesn't answer, just a cold breath in his ear.

"I know why you are here, to remind me of what I have just done."

Still no sound from the old woman.

He peers over to the door and spots her leaving the room. The silence was thick he could almost taste it on his tongue.

For an hour, he lays there on the sofa, his eyes glued to the ceiling as he mumbles to himself. Eventually, his ramblings lull him into slumber.

14

THE VISITOR

A beam of light stabs through the parted curtains, cutting through the shadows of the living room and striking the arm of the sofa like a beacon. Daniel wakes from his nightmare, his eyes adjusting to the warm light that has broken him from his fitful slumber.

He stands up and stretches, feeling his bones crack and loosen.

He strides into the kitchen, the sun's rays casting a sickly yellow hue across the empty table. He takes a glass from the cabinet and slams it onto the counter, quickly filling it with a cool stream of water before gulping it down. He sits at the table and a wave of nausea passes over him as hunger roars in his stomach. He notices that the voices are back, whispering urgently in his mind.

Daniel spends his day locked away in the house, trying to ignore the relentless whispers that fill his head. He paces the floor, punching the walls, anything to try and drown out the sinister messages that urge him to follow through with the voices of murderous desires.

Everywhere he looks he's being haunted by the faces of his victims, as if they are mocking him for his transgressions. Yet despite all this, the voices still remain, growing louder and louder with each passing hour and making it almost impossible for Daniel to resist the urge to kill again. Daniel is sweating profusely from the anxiety of the voices, and the smell of his stress is thick in the air. Daniel eats nothing, too sick with himself to want to consume food.

Daniel's pacing fills up the silence in the house with the steady thud of his footsteps and shouting.

Daniel's hands are red and raw from punching the walls, his knuckles swollen. He has opened the wound on his hand that was bandaged, it is now bleeding again and dripping everywhere he paces, making the wooden floors slippery.

He clutches his bleeding hand. He knows that he has to find a way to overcome the voices, but he didn't know how. The only way he knows is to kill again, to keep them happy.

Just then, there was a knock at the door. Daniel froze, unsure of who it could be or what they want.

Peering through the curtain he sees a man dressed in overalls, a pick-up truck is parked in the driveway. On the side of the pick-up truck, Daniel notices a sign, this guy was the old woman's gardener and maintenance man.

Daniel keeps quiet as the gardener knocks again. Daniel decides to stay quiet and not answer the door.

The gardener continues to knock at the door. He knew that if the gardener went to the shed, he would find the body he had dumped there.

After a few moments of contemplation, Daniel resolves to act and approaches the door, feeling his heart racing. He opens the door, trying to remain composed and doing all he can to hide his bloody hand.

The gardener is startled to see Daniel standing before him instead of the old woman, who normally opens the door.

"Hi there," says the gardener, "I'm Danny Adams; I'm here to do Faye's lawns and garden. Is she home?"

Daniel's heart is beating, his head is pounding, and he tries to hide his anger and pain by talking.

Daniel responds immediately: "No, she's away for a week. I'm looking after her house. There's no need for you to do the yard at this time; I can mow the lawns myself."

"Oh, okay," the gardener mutters in confusion; he usually does the job for Faye. The gardener can see the blood seeping from Daniel's hand, which he tries to hide from view.

"Ouch, I would get that seen to mate looks like it's bleeding a bit."

Daniel hides his hand behind his back, "Yes I will thanks."

Daniel stares at the gardener while he walks down the driveway and gets back into his pick-up truck. The pick-up truck starts and reverses out of the driveway and disappears down the road.

Daniel looks around and goes back inside and closes the door.

The hours until sunset felt like an eternity as he struggled to keep his anger in check. The destruction is all around him, like a painting of sorrow.

The walls are scarred with holes, the floorboards are marred with carved names, and his own blood is smeared across the counters and walls. Even the sofa is not spared, bearing stains of his blood. He stands in a mix of anger and pain, wanting to do something to take away the pain, but all he can do is take in the destruction. The voices in his head are taxing, demanding him to kill.

The wind howls down the deserted street as rain pounds the pavement, creating a symphony of fury. Lightning illuminates the dark sky, casting an eerie glow over the houses and parked cars. The storm rages on, unrelenting as if the heavens are unleashing their anger upon the world below.

The pain was unbearable, a constant reminder of his inability to control himself, and his own thoughts. He was a prisoner to the darkness within, and the stormy night was a fitting backdrop for the horrors that were about to unfold for him and his victim.

Daniel steps out of the old woman's house and into the raging storm.

The howling winds and pounding rain assault his senses, but he barely notices, his mind is already the victim. He stumbles through the rain-soaked streets, searching for a victim to appease the relentless demands of the voices in his head. The voices urging him on, giving him the strength to kill.

Rounding a corner, he spots a lone woman, huddled under a small bus stop awning, trying to protect herself from the storm.

The woman was young, in her early twenties, with long, curly blonde hair that was matted to her face from the rain. Her eyes were large and expressive. Despite the cold, she wore a light summer dress that clung to her curves, and sandals that offered little protection from the rain. She was a stranger to the city, just passing through on her way to visit a friend, unaware of the dangers that lurk in the darkness. She had no idea that a killer was closing in on her, or that this bus stop would be the last place she would ever see.

Out of the darkness, Daniel sprints out towards her onto the road, and she notices him running.

The woman at the bus stop gasps as the car roars towards Daniel, and she yells out.

But Daniel could not hear her shout over the noise of the rain, he was caught in the middle of the road. The speeding car hits him with a sickening thud, sending him flying through the air. He hit the ground hard, his body crumpled in a broken heap. The woman screams a high-pitched sound that was lost in the crack of the thunder as it exploded across the night sky and following it, a bright flash of lightning that lit up the street and the mayhem.

The driver of the car quickly exits and hastens to Daniel lying near the edge of the street.

The driver kneels checking for a pulse and trying to revive him. The woman approaches cautiously, watching as the driver frantically performs CPR on the unresponsive body. The rain continues to pour down, drenching them as they desperately try to save Daniel's life.

A man in a house across the street hears the commotion and runs outside. He quickly realises what has happened and rushes back inside to call for an ambulance. The woman and the driver continue to work on reviving Daniel.

The woman feels a sense of hopelessness wash over her, as she realises the severity of the situation and the possible outcome. She can only wait and pray that help will arrive in time.

The sight of Daniel's body crumpled in a heap on the ground, illuminated by a flash of lightning, and the frantic efforts of the driver to revive him, has the woman in a panic, her hand trembles as she reaches out to touch Daniel's arm, her heart breaking at the sight of his lifeless body.

The driver frantically continues CPR, his hands pressing firmly against Daniel's chest as he heaves for breath.

A faint sound in the distance breaks through the sound of the rain. The woman at the bus stop and the driver looks up, realizing that the ambulance has arrived. They both feel a sense of relief, knowing that help is on the way. The man in the house across the street rushes back outside, flagging down the ambulance as it pulls up to the scene. The paramedics jump out and rush over to the still form of Daniel. The paramedics assess the situation and quickly realise the severity of Daniel's injuries. His body is covered in cuts and bruises.

The sound of another siren pierces the air. The woman and the driver look up to see a police car pull up to the scene, its flashing lights illuminating the dark street. A police officer steps out, quickly assessing the situation and taking control. The rain continues to pour down, the flashing lights reflecting off the puddles as the officer works to piece together what happened. Another police car arrives, two police officers exit the vehicle as well. One of them asks the woman what she saw, taking notes and asking questions as they gather information. The rain continues to pour down, the flashing lights reflecting off the puddles as the officer works to piece together what happened.

The woman struggles to remember the details, her mind still trying to process the events.

The driver tells the police officer that Daniel had run out in front of the car and that he didn't have time to stop in the wet conditions. The officer nods, taking down the statement as they continue to assess the scene. The driver continues to speak with the officer, explaining that he had been driving at the speed limit and that there was nothing he could have done to avoid hitting Daniel.

The driver and the woman exchange a worried look, both unsure of what the outcome of the investigation will be.

The paramedics lift Daniel onto a stretcher, the rain pouring down on them as they work to save his life. They load him into the ambulance, climbing in after him, and closing the door. The sound of the siren pierces the air as the ambulance speeds off into the night, rushing Daniel to the hospital and the hope of medical care. A police car follows them to the hospital with the sirens wailing.

15

THE ABODE

The drizzle of the rain was just beginning to dampen the pavement as the detectives pull up to the end of Madden Street. The sound of the raindrops hitting the roof of the car provides a gentle background noise to the start of their investigation.

Moore turns to Reilly as they get out of the vehicle. "Luckily, we come at a time like this," he remarks. "The rain's keeping everyone inside. We may get the people in both houses this time, last time we visited they were empty, remember Reilly."

Reilly nods in agreement, adding, "Let's hope it doesn't turn into a downpour, we don't want to be caught in a deluge while we're out here."

As the detectives approach the first house, they can see a woman peering out the window, her expression curious. They knock on the door and the woman opens it.

"Good afternoon, ma'am. We're detectives and we're here to ask you a few questions," says Reilly.

The middle-aged woman's expression turns wary. "What kind of questions?"

"We just have a few questions OK," Moore interjects.

Reilly jumps in, "What other people live in the house with you?"

The woman answers, "Just my husband, but he's away on a cargo ship for a month."

Reilly inquires, "How long has he been away?"

"About 15 days so far," she answers.

Moore starts to make his way off the porch and says, "Thank you for your help. That should be all we need."

Reilly offers the woman a smile before following Moore, back to the sidewalk.

"Hey Moore," she shouts, "You in a hurry?"

"No Reilly, I'm starting to think this guy is not in this street unless one of these people we've talked to lately is harbouring him," Moore remarks, his brow creasing with concern. "The people seem pretty convincing to me that they don't know him or his whereabouts."

"We still have this house to go," Reilly comments. Moore grumbles and gestures down the path to the sidewalk ahead. "You go knock; this is the one with the boarded-up windows. I don't think anybody lives there."

Reilly climbs up the steps to the patio and raps on the badly weathered door. She glances back at Moore waiting patiently below with his hands in his pockets like a schoolboy waiting for his mum to come out of the shop. Reilly raises her knuckles to knock once more, but her knuckles sting when she connects with the door again. No answer came. Taking a deep breath, she peers through the window and squints through the slit in the dusty curtains. She can see items on the kitchen table—empty tins of spaghetti and a few empty beer bottles— and she calls over her shoulder: "Hey Moore, I think someone is living here. There are empty tins of food and beer bottles on the table." "Are you sure?" Moore asks, joining her at the window. He peers through the same slit, confirming what she had seen. They step back from the window and confer quietly. Moore looks to Reilly and says, "We must get back to the car and get in touch with the station. Ask them for the details of who owns this building and get them down here."

They hurriedly go back to the squad car and Moore takes the radio mouthpiece. He informs the station of the issue and requests that they look up the owner's location, job, etc. They wait a little over twenty minutes until they finally hear back from the dispatcher on the police radio, telling them they have found out who owns the building; his name is Jack Tueon, he lives somewhere else, and they managed to get his contact number from one of the other people they had called. He's on his way now.

Reilly and Moore wait patiently for another fifteen minutes as the rain gradually turns into more of an annoying mist. The car is stuffy and humid, the windows completely fogged up from the heat inside. Moore hears a car engine behind them, and he peers out the door, it's the owner of the house. Both detectives climb back out of the car and greet Mr. Tueon. "Hi, you must be Jack Tueon," asks Moore.

"That's right, I'm the owner of the house you're asking about, it is empty for renovation, what is the problem?" questions Mr. Tueon.

"We were just there and saw signs of someone living there," says Reilly.

Mr. Tueon's face fell. "That can't be. The house is empty for renovation. No one should be living there."

They quickly filled Mr. Tueon in on what they had seen, and he agreed to unlock the house so the detectives can look inside.

Reilly and Moore stand outside the decrepit, abandoned house, their breaths visible in the chill air. Mr. Tueon pulls out a set of keys. He inserts one of them into the keyhole, and the detectives can't help but notice how the old lock resists, as if reluctant to reveal the secrets hidden within.

Reilly's hand rests on her holster, ready to draw her weapon at a moment's notice, while Moore stands beside her, his expression taut and determined.

With a creak, the door opens slightly, and a wave of nauseating stench hits them like a hammer, causing both detectives to grimace and step back involuntarily.

Moore curses, raising a hand to cover his nose and mouth.

Reilly's eyes water as she takes a sharp breath through her mouth, trying desperately to ignore the pungent smell. The scent of death and rot is like nothing she has experienced before, even during her nine years in the force. It's almost as if the house itself emanates malice, forewarning them of the terrors that await inside.

"We need to proceed carefully," Moore says, his voice slightly muffled by his hand.

Mr. Tueon, standing a few steps away, looks visibly uncomfortable.

Slowly, they push the door wide open, and the full force of the fetid air slams into them like a wall. It's as if the stench has been festering within the house, growing stronger with every passing second.

Moore steps forward, his handgun held high, as he enters the kitchen first. Reilly follows closely behind just stopping inside the entrance, keeping a vigilant eye on their surroundings. The smell is overpowering, making it difficult to focus, but they know they must do their job.

Moore rushes through the house, examining each room for any signs of life or danger. Reilly remains close to the door in the hallway, her gaze scanning the area. Every noise inside the house seems to boom in their ears as if amplifying their alertness. After what feels like hours, Moore rejoins Reilly and says, "It's all clear, however, there is a decaying body in the kitchen." Reilly clenches her jaw, steeling herself against the chill that runs through her. "Let's call for backup and contact Forensics," she states firmly. "We have to preserve everything." As they both enter the kitchen Reilly points to the wall while her other hand covers her nose and mouth.

Moore follows her gaze and at her pointed her finger and gasps at the sight of the huge red upside-down cross painted in blood and the word **Legion** next to it...

They approach the wall, carefully examining the symbol. It was clear that someone had taken great care in making the cross, each stroke precise and intentional. "It's the same as the one at the murders but this one has not been rushed but this word is new," says Reilly.

Moore's eyes widen in recognition. "You're right." He notices the walls had been damaged, with holes from punches and marks from a knife or something sharp.

"My apologies, Mr. Tueon, but we'll need to cordon off this area for our investigation," Moore says.

Moore thanks Mr. Tueon for his cooperation before sending him off with strict instructions not to enter the house again until the investigation was complete.

Once he was gone, Moore gets into the squad car and contacts the station to send out forensics to give the house a thorough inspection. He didn't want to leave anything to chance since this could be their only lead.

As they wait for backup to arrive, Reilly and Moore remain near the entrance, keeping an eye on the house and the surrounding area. Backup comes shortly, accompanied by the crime scene forensic unit, and Reilly quickly briefs them on the situation. The house is immediately cordoned off with yellow crime scene tape as investigators scour the area, meticulously documenting and collecting any evidence that could be of use.

Reilly and Moore answer questions from their colleagues, recounting the initial discovery and their first impressions of the crime scene. The nauseating stench hangs in the air, a constant reminder of the tragedy they've stumbled upon.

As the investigation continues to unfold, the detectives tirelessly comb through the house, looking for any clues or leads that might shed light on the victim's identity and the circumstances surrounding her death. Each room holds its secrets, and Reilly feels the weight of responsibility on her shoulders as she strives to piece together the puzzle.

Wearing white protective suits and latex gloves, the forensic team brush the surfaces with black powder and take photographs as they go. "Hopefully this person has been in trouble
before and we can get him on fingerprints," says Moore.

Standing in the kitchen, Moore and Reilly were both deep in
thought. The strange word 'Legion' written next to the cross
had them stumped. They had seen this cross before, at both
crime scenes, but they had never encountered the word 'Legion.'

"What could it mean?" Reilly wondered aloud.

"I'm not sure, has it to do with the Romans" Moore replies,

"Romans, what do you mean?" asks Reilly looking confused.

"Roman Legion the largest military unit of the Roman army
back in history," replies Moore.

Reilly smiles and says, "Bit of a history buff, are we?"

Moore gives Reilly a mad look and ignores her.

Moore and Reilly leave the crime scene and head back to the
police station, still puzzling over the meaning of 'Legion.' They
discuss possible connections to biblical and demonic references,
but neither of them is sure what it represents.

As they drive, they brainstorm ideas and theories, trying to
make sense of this new lead. When they arrive at the station,
they head straight to their desks and start researching the term
'Legion' in hopes of uncovering its true significance.

"What do you think, Reilly? Does this 'Legion' thing have anything to do with the murders?" Moore asks while looking at his computer screen.

"I'm not sure, but I have a feeling it's connected," Reilly replies, typing away on her keyboard. "I just found a reference to it in some biblical texts."

"Really?" Moore asks, raising an eyebrow. "That's interesting."

"Yeah, it is," Reilly, agrees. "But we must keep an open mind. Let's not jump to any conclusions until we have more clues."

They continue their research, both deep in thought.

"I think I found something," Moore says suddenly. "Listen to this: "Legion is a term used in the Bible to refer to a group of demons."

"Demons?" Reilly repeats a look of surprise on her face.

"Yeah," Moore says, nodding. "It's a term that's been used to describe a large number of evil spirits in the Bible."

Moore reads aloud, "For he said unto him, Come out of the man, thou unclean spirit. And he asked him, what is thy name? And he answered, saying, my name is Legion: for we are many (Mark 5:6–9) exorcisms of the Gerasene demoniac, an account in the New Testament of an incident in which Jesus performs an exorcism."

Reilly looks confused again and says, "Are we after a devil worshipper?"

"Could be," replies Moore. Reilly looks at Moore and says, "This is getting weird now."

Reilly says, "Hey, what's with all the holes in the wall and knife marks back at the house? Does the perp have anger issues or something?"

Moore leans back in his chair and thinks for a moment before responding. "The holes and knife marks could be a sign of rage."

"Hey, if the guy is into devil worship, he must have some serious issues, right?"

Moore nods and says, "That's a possibility. But we need to be careful not to jump to conclusions. Just because someone is involved in satanic worship, doesn't automatically mean they are a loony."

"Does in my book," snaps Reilly.

A member of the forensic team Gabe Gibson enters the room and approaches Moore and Reilly.

"Detectives, we've finished at the abandoned house," Gabe says. "We've collected fingerprints and are just getting the photos developed. That's all we could get."

Moore nods and says, "Thanks for the update, Gabe. What do the fingerprints tell us so far?" Gabe Gibson shakes his head. "It's too early to say. We need to look through the fingerprint card database to see if there's a match. We'll let you know as soon as we have more information. Also, the body in the kitchen is the woman who went missing a month ago, Miss Fran Parsons, a thirty-two-year-old school teacher's aide here in Coulson City. Remember they had that big search at the parkland and along the river."

"I remember seeing it on the television," comments Moore.

The two detectives thank Gabe before turning back to their work.

Moore excuses himself and heads to the restroom feeling nauseous. Once inside he leans over the sink, drinking from the tap. He takes a moment to catch his breath and collect himself.

With a deep sigh, Moore straightens up and takes one last look in the mirror, he sees a woman looking back at him, but as he blinks, she suddenly disappears. He quickly checks over his shoulder but there is no one there. Confused and slightly unsettled, Moore shakes his head and tries to rationalise what he just saw.

He is unable to hold back his emotions. He dashes into the cubicle and shuts the door. He leans against the wall and slides down until he is sitting on the floor, hugging his knees next to the toilet bowl. He lets out a loud cry into his hands, letting all his pain and stress escape. He feels like he's carrying a heavy burden and it's finally breaking him. He doesn't know how much longer he can keep it together. He stays there for a few minutes until his sobs turn into quiet sniffles. He takes a deep breath, gets up leaves the cubicle and washes his face, trying to compose himself before going back to work. He knows he needs to be strong and focus on the case, but it's a constant battle.

He tells himself that it was just his mind playing tricks on him, a symptom of the stress and pressure he's been under lately.

He tries to compose himself, wiping his tears and straightening his tie. He takes a deep breath and heads back to his desk, putting on a professional facade. Moore acts as if nothing happened, trying to hide his emotions and struggles from his colleague.

"You alright?" asks Reilly.

Moore nods and does not say anything, instead, he puts his head down and starts reading.

"Have you been crying?" asks Reilly as she leans over to look at him.

"No, I haven't, I just have bloody sore eyes reading all this shit," growls Moore.

16

THE REPAIR

As the ambulance arrives at the hospital, it pulls up to the emergency ward, its siren piercing the air. The paramedics jump out, rushing Daniel into the hospital and towards the waiting medical team.

The medical team springs into action, working quickly to stabilise Daniel and assess the extent of his injuries. The hospital is a flurry of activity as the medical team works to revive Daniel, administering first aid and hooking him up to machines that monitor his vital signs.

Police officers stand near the hospital bed where Daniel lies, in condition critical. They ask the medical staff if they have any identification on him, but the staff shakes their heads. The police officers nod, understanding the urgency of the situation.

The police officers are abruptly told to leave the room by the medical staff, who are focused on saving Daniel's life. The officers reluctantly step out, understanding that their presence is hindering the efforts of the medical team. They stand in the hallway, their expressions tense as they listen to the sound of the machines beeping in the background. Their faces are sombre as they take in the scene of the chaos unfolding inside.

In the Trauma ward, a faint antiseptic smell lingers in the air around them, a reminder that this is a place where miracles can happen, and lives can end.

The beeping of the machines in the background is punctuated by the urgent shouts from the medical team as they work to save Daniel's life.

As the team works on Daniel, his heart suddenly flatlines. The room falls silent as the medical staff quickly springs into action. They reach for the defibrillator, their movements quick and precise.

The police officers stand by, their expressions tense as they watch the medical staff. The sound of the defibrillator charging fills the room, and an ALL CLEAR bellows across the room, followed by the sharp jolt as they use it to shock Daniel's heart. After a few tense moments, they start to see a change in Daniel's condition. His heart starts to beat again, a steady rhythm filling the room. The medical staff continues their efforts, monitoring Daniel's vital signs closely as they try to stabilise him. Slowly but surely, Daniel begins to show signs of improvement and the beeping of the machines becomes less frantic.

They quickly rush him into surgery to repair the damage, a team of skilled surgeons working tirelessly to save his life. The extent of Daniel's injuries becomes clear as the surgeon's work. In addition to the internal bleeding from his leaky spleen, they discover that he has severe bruising and deep lacerations to his chest and right leg, including a fractured skull. The medical staff works tirelessly, stabilising Daniel's condition. After what feels like an eternity, the surgeons finally emerge from the operating room, their faces tired but relieved.

Daniel is expected to make a full recovery, although it will take time.

Meanwhile, back in the trauma ward, a nurse searches through Daniel's pockets but finds no identification or wallet just a dirty rag. She shakes her head and informs the police officer there is nothing on him to identify him. The officer makes a note of this and informs his colleague, who is in the waiting area. They begin to search for any leads on the identity of this "John Doe" and hope someone will come forward with information.

As the weeks pass, Daniel begins to come out of his coma, he starts to remember fragments of his past. The voices in his head that had been silent for so long start to return, and with them, the memories of the violent acts he had committed. Despite his attempts to push the thoughts away, the memories come flooding back. He recalls the face of the woman he was about to harm at the bus stop.

As Daniel starts to regain consciousness, his body reacts instinctively to the foreign object in his throat. He starts to gag and reach for the endotracheal tube (ETT), trying to remove it. The nurse who was near his bed checking his vital signs quickly notices and rushes to his side.

She gently holds his hand and speaks to him in a calm, reassuring tone. "Try to relax. That tube is helping you breathe, but I understand it's uncomfortable. Let's see if we can get it out now that you're waking up."

She carefully assesses his condition and, with the help of the medical team, slowly begins to remove the ETT.

Daniel struggles at first, his body still trying to reject the foreign object. But with the nurse's gentle encouragement, he eventually calms down and the ETT is removed successfully.

Daniel takes his first breaths without the tube, feeling a sense of relief as he inhales the fresh air. The nurse smiles at him, happy to see that he is starting to recover. "Good job. You're going to be just fine," she says as she checks his vital signs and updates his chart.

Daniel lies there, feeling exhausted but relieved as he tries to make sense of the jumbled memories in his mind.

The voices in his head grow louder screaming at him with abuse, urging him to act out. He feels like he's losing his grip on reality, and the fear begins to turn into desperation. Daniel starts to struggle against the tubes and wires that connect him to the machines.

The panic begins to reach a fever pitch, and he starts to scream and thrash in the bed. The hospital staff rush to his bedside, trying to calm him and subdue him. They finally manage to sedate him, and he slips back into unconsciousness.

As the days pass, Daniel's condition stabilises. The hospital staff started to wean him off the sedatives and bring him out of the coma. He begins to regain consciousness, but the memories and the voices remain within his head. As the day progresses, Daniel begins to feel more alert and awake. He starts to become aware of his surroundings and the events that have led to him being in the hospital. Police arrive at his room, and they introduce themselves.

They explain that they are trying to identify him and find out how he ended up in the hospital. Daniel is wary of speaking to the police, knowing that he has a dark past that he wants to keep hidden. The officers begin their questioning, he slowly speaks and tells them he was crossing the road and did not see the car. He tells them his name is Daniel Nash.

As the Detectives ask more questions, the voices in his head start to get louder, and Daniel begins to feel overwhelmed. He closes his eyes and tries to focus, but it's no use. The voices are too loud, and he can't think clearly. The officers sense that something is wrong, and they try to get Daniel to calm down, Daniel nods and takes a deep breath, trying to regain control. He answers their questions as best he can.

As the police officers leave Daniel's room, they assure the nurse that they might be back later with more questions.

The nurse walks over to Daniel and grabs a plastic cup fills it with cold water and passes it to Daniel, he struggles to swallow with his sore throat caused by the endotracheal tube.

Carol Maddison, one of the nurses at St. Francis Hospital, is taking care of Daniel.

Despite being a nurse for 7 years, Carol is feeling uneasy around Daniel, as he does not speak much and often mumbles to himself.

Nurse Maddison hears Daniel mumbling all the time, but she doesn't understand what he's saying. She is a bit scared of him and tries to keep her distance, but she is also curious about what he is mumbling about. Based on her medical training and experience, she suspects that Daniel might have a touch of schizophrenia, which could explain his strange behaviour. Despite her concerns, Nurse Maddison continues to care for Daniel, determined to provide the best possible care for him.

Daniel has a piercing gaze that seems to watch her every move when he's awake. It's as if he is looking right through her, which makes Nurse Maddison feel uncomfortable and on edge. She finds herself constantly looking over her shoulder.

She is medium height and slender, with bright blue eyes that always seem to be searching for a way to help those around her. Her hair is black and is usually pulled back into a neat bun, and her uniform is always perfectly pressed and starched.

Nurse Maddison carries the faint scent of lavender, which Daniel reminded of the old woman that he strangled a while back. Nurse Maddison speaks in a soothing voice, but it is sometimes tinged with a hint of worry and fatigue.

Daniel struggles with the urge to act on the violent impulses in his head. He closes his eyes, trying to block out the thoughts, but they persist. He opens his eyes and sees Nurse Maddison, busily scribbling notes in his chart. He tries to think of anything else, anything to distract himself from the dark thoughts that keep creeping into his mind. But it's no use. The more he tries to push them away, the stronger they become.

As Daniel lies in the hospital bed, he is fixated on Nurse Maddison.

Her jet-black hair is fastened in a perfect bun of control. His gaze kept drifting to her lips, imagining how it might feel on his own.

The voices in his head command him to do unmentionable things, a delirious craving he cannot resist. His heart races as he glances at the beautiful woman's, velvety skin. He licks his lips, imagining the pleasure of tracing his tongue across her naked body as he takes her life. He shivers in excitement as the voices in his head whisper menacing things of what they want to do to her. His groin tightens as he imagines himself in a frenzy of lust.

Hiding under his covers is a raging erection.

Nurse Maddison continues to tend to Daniel, feeling an ever-increasing sense of unease as she looks into his eyes. She could feel something dark lurking in the depths of his gaze, and it made her skin crawl.

As she goes about her duties, she notices that Daniel is becoming increasingly agitated. He is fidgeting and mumbling more than usual. Daniel snaps out of it and stares directly at Nurse Maddison with a look of rage in his eyes. Nurse Maddison feels uneasy and walks out of the room.

A couple of hours have passed, and Daniel jolts awake as he hears voices in the room. He lifts his head out of his pillow and blinks at the shadows, his vision slowly focusing to reveal the same police officers as before standing in the corner. Dread immediately overwhelms him as he realises they have returned.

Daniel is tense and on edge as the officers approach him.

The officers question Daniel about his home, but he shakes his head. "I can't remember," he says, his voice tight with fear. "The accident must have damaged my memory."

He feels a deep sense of panic rising in his chest, and he clutches the bedsheets in a death grip as he tries to keep his composure.

"Do you remember anything else?" the other officer asks his tone cold and unyielding.

Daniel shakes his head and it hurts him to do so.

The officers exchange a look before the other one speaks. "Can you tell us anything about yourself? Any family members, friends, or past employment?"

"I-I don't remember," Daniel stammers. "Everything is a bit blurry for me right now."

He is fully aware of who he is and what he is, but they do not need to know.

"One good thing, you don't show up on our records," says the police officer smiling.

The other police officer speaks, "Well if we find any more info, we will return, OK?"

Daniel nods.

"Bye Mr. Nash", one of the police officers says and they both walk out of the room.

Daniel relaxes, he is tired.

Laying in his hospital bed, Daniel counts down the days, each one bringing him closer to an uncertain future as he battles the voices in his head and tries to hold on to what little control he has left.

Daniel's quietness and lack of communication with Nurse Maddison only heightens her fear of him. Despite his best efforts to control his thoughts and desires, he finds himself consumed by fantasies of killing her and being with her at the same time.

Daniel's mind throbs as he dreams of Nurse Maddison, the nurse laying in front of him, her body fully exposed and trembling in anticipation of his touch. His hands move over her body with a light, tantalising caress, sending shivers through her skin. He brings the sharp blade of his knife to her flesh, parting it delicately, and unleashes a cascade of blood that spills out of her body in an erotic ribbon of crimson.

It is 5 p.m., and with a loud bang, Nurse Maddison hits the table against the bed that Daniel is in, waking him up from his dream.

He gives her a stern look.

Daniel then notices he is in another room; he looks around in surprise. Nurse Maddison realises his surprise and tells him they moved him out of the ICU area and placed him here in the close observation room.

Nurse Maddison can sense that something is off about Daniel, but she is not sure what it is. She tries to stay professional and not let her fear show.

The voices in Daniel's head are relentless and demand obedience, promising him a sense of power and control over his life. They urge him to carry out acts of violence, convincing him that it is necessary in order to bring him peace and satisfaction.

"Do it. Kill her. She is in your way. You need to rid yourself of the weakness she represents. Only then will you be strong," the voices whisper to him.

"You are in charge. You are the one with the power. Don't let anyone take that away from you. Kill them before they can hurt you," the voices urge him on.

Nurse Maddison takes Daniel's temperature by placing the thermometer between his dry lips. He tries to resist the urge to grab her, focusing on the feeling of the cold glass against his lips instead. His mind races with carnal desires, but he knows he can't give in to them. He fights to keep his breathing steady, squeezing his eyes shut and willing himself to focus on anything but the alluring nurse pressed against him. He can't risk giving in to his urges, not now, not here.

Her perky breasts were accentuated by the fabric of her clothing, her nipples embossed through the material and begging to be touched. He feels himself hardening in anticipation as he gazes at her soft skin, and he has to take a deep breath to calm himself.

Nurse Maddison glances at the thermometer, then saunters to the foot of the bed and grasps the chart. She starts taking notes. Daniel is calm again.

Daniel spent the next six hours sleeping.

It's 10:30 p.m. when he wakes the hospital is quiet. No one is at the nurse's station. He lies in bed, listening to the soft beeping of a heart monitor close by and the occasional distant echo of footsteps. He knows he shouldn't get up with his injuries, but he can't resist the restless feeling that has taken hold of him.

As an orderly part-time at the hospital and with his medical background, he knows the layout and has a good understanding of the inner workings of the facility. He slowly slides out of bed, wincing as his injured right leg protests with sharp pain. He takes a deep breath and steadies himself, trying to ignore the ache in his limbs. The last thing he wants is to make any noise that would draw attention to himself. He uses his knowledge of the hospital to avoid making any noise, sneaking past the sleeping patients, and avoiding any areas that might alert the nurses.

Daniel walks into the ward, his limp still causing him pain with each step. The room is quiet, with only the sound of the occasional beep from a monitor breaking the silence. He approaches the bed where a female patient lays, her chest rising and falling steadily in sleep.

Daniel's eyes are focused on the patient as he looks down at her with a mixture of emotions; fascination, fear, and a need to stay in control.

He stands still for a moment, the voices in his head start to whisper, urging him to do something.

He leans down close to her face; he smells her and then raises up straight again. He knows what the voices want, but he doesn't want to give in to the darkness that threatens to consume him. He backs away from the bed, feeling a bead of sweat roll down his forehead. He knows he needs to leave, to get out of this place before he does something he will regret. He turns and quickly exits the ward, his thoughts in turmoil. He returns to his bed.

But as Daniel lay in his bed, he can't shake off the image of the sleeping woman in the ward. He tosses and turns, trying to calm his racing heart and quiet the voices in his head. He coughs loudly, wiping his mouth he notices he has been coughing a lot lately.

Despite his best efforts, the urges are too strong, and he finds himself slipping out of bed and making his way back to the ward. He approaches the woman, standing over her and gazing at her peaceful face. The demon voices urge him to act, but a part of Daniel still resists. He's torn between his instincts and his desire to resist the evil urges that have controlled him for far too long. As he stands there, struggling with his inner demons, the sound of a nurse's footsteps echoing down the hall snaps him back to reality. With a start, Daniel rushes back to his bed, lying down and pretending to be asleep, his heart pounding with excitement and his leg throbbing in pain.

The nurse's heavy footsteps reverberate past Daniel's room as she moves further down the hallway. He grunts in agony as he slips out of bed, coughing and holding his side in pain. He shuffles forward, passing through the ward until he arrives at the woman's bedside. He stands beside her before slowly leaning over her and perusing her chart. He reads the words Amanda Fabris "bowel cancer" and a treatment plan written there. Daniel grabs a pillow off the chair and stands beside her and presses the pillow into her face with an unrelenting force. Daniel grips the pillow tightly, his knuckles turning white from the intensity of his grip as he presses it against Amanda's face. His fingers curl inwards, sinking into the fabric of the pillow as he holds with strength and determination that is almost inhuman. Amanda's panic gasps are muffled by the pillow as she struggles to break free of Daniel's grip. With each passing second, her struggle becomes more and more desperate until eventually, she falls limp. Daniel peels the pillow away and sees the fear in Amanda's eyes, stark and deep like an abyss staring up at the ceiling. He stares into them for a few moments before reluctantly tearing his gaze away and retreating to his room.

Daniel does not feel any guilt for taking Amanda's life. Instead, he focuses on maintaining his facade of normality and avoiding detection. He is determined to keep his secret, carefully controlling his behaviour and avoiding any suspicious activity.

For taking another life, he finally manages to quell the harsh discordant mixture of voices and falls into a fitful sleep.

***

It is 6.40 a.m. and Daniel slowly opens his eyes and lets out a loud cough, he notices Nurse Maddison, standing next to his bed with her back towards him. He immediately tenses, the memories of earlier this morning are coming back.

He cautiously sits up in bed and watches Nurse Maddison, wondering what she is doing and if she suspects anything. Suddenly, Nurse Maddison turns around and greets him with a warm smile. "Good morning, Daniel. How are you feeling today?" she asks in a cheerful tone holding a plastic cup and some tablets in the other hand. "And how is your head, Daniel? It's time to replace the bandage on your head."

Daniel tries to compose himself and put on a normal face, he mumbles quietly, "Alright".

Nurse Maddison nods and passes the cup of water and the tablets to him to swallow making small talk about his health and the weather.

Daniel throws the tablets into his dry and pasty mouth and drinks them down. Nurse Maddison begins to unravel the bandage off his head and then checks the side of his head where it is shaved and covered in a circle of stitches. "It is coming along nicely Daniel," says Nurse Maddison. "We will leave the bandage off now I think," comments Nurse Maddison.

A commotion of shouting comes from the hallway; Nurse Maddison leaves the room to investigate.

Daniel can hear people shouting. He strains to listen, trying to make out what they're saying.

Nurse Maddison enters the room and starts straightening his bed. "A patient passed away just down the hallway last night. Apparently, she died of complications from her cancer. It is a real shame. She was a young woman with so much life ahead of her," says Nurse Maddison.

Daniel is pleased to hear that the hospital staff do not suspect a thing and believe that Amanda passed away due to complications. Nurse Maddison walks up to the side of Daniel and places a hand on Daniel's forehead.

Daniel is confused about what she is doing.

"You are looking rather pale than yesterday, Daniel, are you feeling alright?" asks Nurse Maddison.

"I think I will let the doctor know," comments Nurse Maddison as she walks out of the room.

15 minutes had passed and Nurse Maddison walks into the room with the doctor in tow.

"Hello Mr. Nash, I'm Dr. Stott, Let me just check you over." The doctor reads his chart at the end of his bed.

He examines Daniel's chest and listens to his lungs with a stethoscope. "I see that your ribs are slowly healing, and I'm afraid you have a serious chest infection on top of that," the doctor says, poking Daniel around the rib area. Despite the broken ribs and leaky spleen, he has been trying to ignore the physical pain, but now the pain is too much to ignore.

"We'll need to keep you here longer to monitor your condition and make sure the antibiotics we will give you take effect, not that you are leaving soon anyway with that leaky spleen," the doctor continues. "In the meantime, I'll schedule some tests to see if there's anything else going on that could be contributing to your health problems Mr. Nash."

Another hour later, Daniel is taken for tests regarding his spleen and internal organs. He privately struggles with the voices in his head telling him to do bad things to the medical staff. The urge to hurt them grows stronger with each passing moment, and he can barely focus on the tests being performed on him. The doctors and nurses seem oblivious to the danger that he poses, and he wonders if he should act on his urges or try to resist them.

As the tests come to an end, Daniel is left alone with his thoughts. He feels trapped and helpless, unable to control the dark impulses that threaten to consume him. The voices in his head continue to whisper to him, urging him to act on his desires, and he struggles to resist their pull.

As the medical staff returns to his room, Daniel tries to appear calm and collected, but his mind is in turmoil. He can feel the pressure building inside him, threatening to explode at any moment. He wonders how much longer he can keep up this charade, how much longer he can fight the voices in his head before they finally win.

17

FINDING FAYE

Detective Reilly and Moore navigate the busy city streets in their unmarked car, the sound of their sirens cutting through the bustling afternoon traffic as they make their way to the latest murder scene.

Reilly is deep in thought. They have been working on this case for a lot of weeks and the pressure is starting to take its toll. Moore tries to lighten the mood by making a joke, but it falls flat.

Reilly and Moore have been working tirelessly on the case for over 9 weeks, but despite their efforts, they haven't been able to make any progress. The investigation has hit a dead end, and they have no new leads or clues since they found where he was living.

When they finally arrive at the scene, they are met with a chaotic and frantic atmosphere, with police everywhere.

The detectives make their way down the driveway to the garden shed where they are met by the forensic team. Reilly and Moore approach Allison Lord, the head of the forensic team, for more information about the victim's condition.

Allison uncovers the victim to reveal the body to the two detectives, Allison starts talking through her mask, "The victim is in her late 70s. She is wearing a simple night dress."

Allison continues, "It's another strangling, just like the others but no stabbing this time. The elderly woman has been lying in the garden shed for roughly three weeks."

Moore holding his nose trying to block the smell: "What's the condition of the scene?"

Allison comments, "My team has already started collecting evidence. We found broken glass belonging to a square tile of glass out of the back door, indicating that the killer might have done this to reach in and unlock the door. The comforter she has been wrapped in has grass stains on it, suggesting she was killed inside and then dragged into the shed. Her bed has been used and the comforter is probably from that bed, and someone has soiled that bed, I would say it was her.

The body is in an advanced stage of decomposition. We've got bloat, discolouration, and rigour mortis."

The strong odour of decay is making it difficult to work in the area. Both detectives cover their nose and mouth with their handkerchiefs. Allison points and says, "Grab some masks off that bag, use them."

Reilly reaches for the masks and hands one to Moore.

Reilly starts the questions, "What about the evidence? Have you found anything that could lead us to the killer?"

"We've just started processing the scene, and so far, we haven't found anything that stands out. But we'll keep looking and see if we can turn up anything useful," says Allison.

The detectives observe the victim's condition and are filled with sadness and a sense of determination to bring the killer to justice.

Reilly asks, "Who found the body?"

"A gardener, Danny Adams, discovered the body while looking in the shed. He immediately called the police."

Moore jumps in with a question, "We'll need to talk to Mr. Adams. Do you know where we can find him?"

"Yes, I believe he's still on the property. He's shaken up, but he's agreed to speak with you," says Allison.

Reilly says "Thanks, Allison. We'll go talk to him now."

With that, the detectives make their way to speak with Danny Adams, hoping that he can provide them with some valuable information that could help.

Moore queries the police officer looming nearby, asking where they could locate Mr. Adams. The police officer gestures in the direction of a man in overalls sitting on the steps of the front entrance. Moore and Reilly proceed over, introducing themselves to the individual.

Reilly asks him to explain how he had discovered her.

The gardener speaks and shakes "I pulled into her driveway at 1 PM like I always do. But when I knocked on the front door, there was no answer. I called out her name Faye, but still no response. That's when I remembered the man who said he was taking care of the house the last time I was here. So, I decided to look around the back of the house to see if he or Faye might be working in the garden."

He took a deep breath, still visibly shaken by the events that had transpired. "I called out her name again, but still no answer. I made my way to the shed, and that's when I saw her. The body, I mean. It was wrapped in a comforter next to the lawn mower and it was obvious that she had been murdered."

The gardener swallows hard, trying to steady himself. "I was so shocked and scared that I immediately called the police. The police arrived soon after and now here I am, telling you what I saw."

The detectives listened intently, taking notes as the gardener spoke. They asked a few follow-up questions, trying to piece together the events of the day.

"What is Faye's last name?" queries Reilly adjusting her hair over her left ear.

The gardener replies, "Campbell is her last name."

"Do you know what the man's name is?" asks Moore.

"No," says the gardener, "He just told me that he was looking after the house for a week while she was away, and he told me he would do the lawns and garden."

The detectives exchange a quick look, and then Moore asks, "Can you describe this man? What did he look like?"

The gardener thinks for a moment before answering. "He is in his mid-30s. He was of average height and build. He had short, dark hair and was clean-shaven. He was dressed in casual clothes, jeans and a grey hoodie. I can't really remember anything else about him, it was just a quick interaction."

The detectives nod, jotting down notes. "Did he say anything else to you? Did he seem suspicious or out of place in any way?" says Reilly.

The gardener nods, "Yes, now that you mention it, he did have a cut on his hand. It was quite serious; I remember seeing a bandage wrapped around his hand blood was dripping from it. I just assumed that he had injured himself or something. I did tell him that he should get that cut seen too before it got infected, but he did seem to try and hide it from me when I mentioned it. He put it behind his back like he didn't want me to see it."

The detectives exchange a quick look, and then one of them asks, "Did he say anything else, or did he seem to react in any way when you mentioned the cut?" asks Moore.

The gardener thinks for a moment before answering. "No, he just thanked me and said he would get it looked at. He didn't seem overly concerned or react in any way that I remember. But now that I think about it, the way he tried to hide it does seem odd."

The detectives nod, jotting down more notes. "Thank you for mentioning this," says Reilly.

Moore speaks up, "You may be asked to come down to the station at some point to give a more detailed account of the situation. Thank you, that will do for now."

As the two detectives walk away, Reilly glances back and sees the gardener bury his head in his hands, seemingly overwhelmed. Reilly can't help but feel sympathy for him.

As the detectives make their way inside the house, they can't help but feel a sense of unease. They knew that this was where the killer had struck again. The house was quiet, but the detectives could feel the weight of the recent tragedy hanging in the air. They move from room to room, searching for anything that might shed light on the events of the crime. In the living room, they find an old photo album on the coffee table, filled with pictures of the victim and her family.

Reilly looks at the holes in the wall, her mind racing. "This level of violence and rage...it's not normal. This guy's got some serious issues."

Moore nods. "Yeah, and I bet he's getting more and more unstable with each kill.

So, the killer was able to get in by breaking a glass slat from the backdoor window and reaching through to unlock the back door," Moore says, piecing together the information they have.

Reilly nods, "It looks that way."

The two detectives step into the elderly woman's bedroom they observe the bed. It was clear she had been asleep there, though the telltale urine stain says it all, this is where she was strangled to death. The room was strangely still and dreary.

Moore stares at the old woman's bed, a knot forming in his stomach. He felt a sharp pain in his chest.

"What do you see, Moore?" Reilly asks, breaking into his thoughts.

"Nothing," Moore replies, his voice tight. He cannot tell Reilly about the hallucinations, or the apparitions of his wife that he has been having the past few weeks.

They continue to search the house, their footsteps echoing in the empty rooms.

Moore's mind is racing, he notices his wife's ghostly presence standing at the end of the hallway. He shakes his head, trying to clear his thoughts and then he notices she has gone again.

Reilly looks at Moore, his hand is shaking. She notices that her partner has been acting strange lately, and she was starting to get worried.

While standing in the kitchen Reilly decides to ask the question that's been eating at her for a while now.

"So, Moore," she says casually "What were you up to while you were off work for those six months?"

Moore stiffens, and his hand stops shaking. "What do you mean?"

"I mean, you were off work for half a year. That's a long time. What did you do? Did you do something bad and got stood down?" Reilly asks.

"I took some time off to deal with some personal issues," says Moore as he begins to walk towards the back door.

"Like what?" Reilly asks.

"It's none of your business," Moore snaps, his voice tight.

"Keep your mind on the case Reilly and not in my business, OK?" growls Moore.

"Understood, but I'm here for you if you need anything," says Reilly.

Moore turns sharply and looks sternly at Reilly, "I'm fine Reilly, get off my fucking back."

Moore and Reilly walk out of the old woman's house and onto the driveway in silence. They both feel the tension in the air, and neither one of them seems eager to break it.

As they walk to their car, Reilly can't help but steal glances at Moore.

Reilly can tell that he is holding something back. The tension between them is palpable as they drive off and head back to the station. Moore's eyes are fixed on the road ahead and Reilly is looking out of the passenger side window.

The air between Moore and Reilly is thick with the scent of unspoken words and the tension of unresolved issues. The sound of silence is almost deafening, the only sound being the hum of the car engine and the occasional rattle of the car caused by the bumps on the road.

They arrive at the station, and they both walk to their separate desks, still feeling the weight of their unspoken conversation.

Allison walks into the room, a file in her hand. Laying the file down in front of Reilly on her desk.

"I have something for you guys," she says, catching her breath. "The blood results from the old woman's house. They don't match anything in our database."

Moore and Reilly perk up, eager to hear more. "What does that mean?" asks Reilly.

Allison shrugs. "It can mean a lot of things," she says. "But most likely, it means that the killer is someone who has never been in our database before. A first-time offender, so to speak."

The detectives look at each other, both feeling the weight of the case settling heavily on their shoulders.

"That's right; we've got very little to go on, just the fingerprints we found at the abandoned house. They match the ones we found at the scene of the old woman's murder," says Allison.

Detective Moore and Reilly exchange a look. "So, we're looking for someone who's left their fingerprints at two crime scenes?" asked Reilly.

"That's the theory," says Allison. "But it's not much to go on, I know. We're still trying to find more evidence, but so far, this is all we've got."

The detectives sit back in their chairs, both deep in thought. With only a set of fingerprints to go on, they know that the investigation is going to be a long and challenging one. But they also know that they must keep pushing, no matter how difficult it is, if they want to bring the killer to justice.

Reilly sits at her desk, staring at the file in front of her. Faye Campbell, the old woman who had been murdered, has no next of kin. It is a fact that weighs heavy on her heart.

She thinks about how lonely it must have been for Faye in her final years, with no family or friends to check in on her. Now, in death, she is completely alone, with no one to mourn her passing.

Reilly sighs, feeling a deep sadness for the old woman. She makes a promise to herself that she will do everything in her power to bring Faye's killer to justice, even if she has no family to see it.

She looks up at Moore, who is sitting across from her, deep in thought. Despite the tension between them, Reilly cannot help but feel grateful for his partnership. They are both united in their goal to solve this case and give victims the justice they deserve.

18

IT'S PERSONAL

Detective Moore stands up from his desk and headed towards the restroom. His hands are shaking, and he could feel the familiar urge to drink creeping up on him. He knew that he has a flask of whiskey stashed in the inside pocket of his coat, and the thought of taking a swig was almost too much to resist.

He tried to focus on his breathing, telling himself that he could make it through this. He had made a promise to himself that he would stay sober, at least while he was on the job. But the guilt and the stress of the past is making him break that promise.

As he reaches the restroom, he hesitates at the door. He can hear Reilly's voice in the back of his mind, asking him what was going on. He cannot let her know about his problem, but he also can't keep lying to her.

With a deep sigh, Moore pushes open the door and walks inside.

While Moore is away from the desk Reilly walks to the Chief's office, her heart racing. She knows that she's about to ask some tough questions, but she feels like she has to do it.

She knocks on the door, and Chief Dwyer calls out, "Come in."

Reilly takes a deep breath and enters the office. "Chief," she says, "I need to talk to you about Detective Moore."

Chief Dwyer raises an eyebrow. "What about him?" he asks.

"I just have a few questions about his past," Reilly says. "Why was he off work for six months?"

Chief Dwyer leans back in his chair and steeples his fingers. "Detective Moore had some personal issues to deal with," he says. "He took some time off to work through them." The Chief gives her a stern look and tells her that it is not her place to ask about Moore's personal life and that he trusts Moore to do his job. Reilly apologises and leaves the Chief's office.

Reilly was determined to find out why Moore was off for six months, she searched the room, who would know?

She spots Sgt Flanagan over in the corner of the room reading some letters.

Reilly approaches Flanagan, "Hey Flanagan do you know why Detective Moore was off work for six months?"

Flanagan looks around the room, making sure, no one else is listening, and then he replies, "I don't know the whole story, but I know that his wife committed suicide after she found out he was having an affair."

Reilly's eyes widen in shock.

Reilly took a step back, the weight of Flanagan's words hitting her hard. "I had no idea," she whispered, her voice full of shock and sympathy.

"That's why he's been off work for so long," says Flanagan.

Flanagan looks up to notice Moore entering the room. Moore's eyes dart between Flanagan and Reilly, and he can sense that something is going on. "What's going on here?" he asks his tone wary.

Reilly hesitates, not wanting to reveal what she had learned. Flanagan, however, speaks up. "Nothing much, just catching up about the case Reilly and you are on," he says, smiling.

"It is a pain in the arse Flanagan, that's what it is," growls Moore.

Moore's tone makes it clear that he's not happy with Flanagan's casual attitude. Reilly is still in shock from what she had just learned about Moore's personal life. She knows that she needs to keep a clear head and focus on the job, despite the personal information she has just received.

Chief Dwyer stands over Moore and Reilly's desks, his arms crossed in frustration. "Why haven't we caught this guy yet?" he demands. "We've got four murdered victims and no leads. What's going on here?"

Moore and Reilly look up at their boss, feeling the weight of his disappointment. "We're doing everything we can, Chief,"

Moore replies, trying to keep his voice steady. "But this case is unlike any other. The lack of witnesses and evidence is making it difficult to progress."

Chief Dwyer sighs, running a hand through his hair. "I understand that, but we can't afford to waste any more time. We've got the press breathing down our necks, and the public is getting anxious. We need a break in this case, and we need it now. Keep me updated on your progress. And both of you," he adds, looking at Moore and Reilly. "Take care of yourselves. This case is taking a toll on everyone." Chief Dwyer walks back to his office and shuts his door.

Moore and Reilly look at each other, they are feeling frustrated by the lack of progress in the case. The killer has struck four times, leaving no evidence at the scene of the crime only fingerprints that don't match anything on their database. The latest murder of Faye Campbell, the elderly woman, has left the detectives stumped.

As they pour over the case files, they can't help but wonder why the killer didn't leave anything behind this time. Did he make a mistake? Was he scared off? Why did he leave?

"This doesn't make sense," Moore says, throwing down the file in frustration. "The killer was so meticulous in the first three murders, leaving behind an upside down cross on their foreheads and by leaving a big upside down cross and the word

Legion at the place he was staying. But this time, there's nothing."

"Maybe we're missing something," Reilly says, scanning the photos on the whiteboard. "Let's go back over the evidence from the first two scenes and compare it to this one."

The two detectives spend the next hour pouring over the evidence, comparing the details from each crime scene.

"Wait a minute," Moore says, pointing to the whiteboard. "Look here. The first two victims were killed outdoors, Reilly nods. "Yes, that's right. But Faye was killed in her home why? Why did he change his pattern with Faye? Was he getting sloppy, or was there something different about Faye that made him choose to kill her indoors?"

Moore ponders and mutters, "Did he kill Faye for a place to stay, somewhere to hide from our surveillance? He could have known that the abandoned house we had was under surveillance, so he needed another place. But what made him leave her house?"

Reilly nods, considering Moore's theory. "That could be it. He needed a hideout, why not stay at Faye's house for a while?"

Moore shrugs. "Maybe he was scared someone would come looking for Faye like the gardener did. Or maybe he realised that killing her in her own home was a mistake and he needed to get out of there before he was caught or was he coming back?"

Another hour passes, and Moore is feeling uncomfortable. The shakes are getting worse, and he's struggling to keep his hands still. He knows that he needs a drink, but he doesn't want to let Reilly see.

"Are you okay?" Reilly asks, looking up from her desk. "You look a little pale."

"I'm fine," Moore says, trying to hide his shaking hands in his pockets. "Just a little tired, that's all."

The two detectives continue to work, but Moore is finding it harder and harder to concentrate. He's sweating profusely and he's having trouble breathing. He knows that he can't hold out much longer.

Finally, he can't take it anymore. He excuses himself and heads to the restroom. Once he's alone, he pulls out a flask and takes a long drink. The alcohol steadies his nerves and calms him down. He knows that he shouldn't be drinking on the job, but he doesn't know what else to do.

When he gets back to the desk, Reilly is waiting for him. "Are you sure you're, okay?" she asks. "You're sweating a lot."

"I'm fine," Moore says, wiping his forehead with a handkerchief. "Just a little overheated, that's all."

"I'm starving," Reilly says as she stretches her arms. "Let's go grab a bite at the cafe down the road."

Moore looks up from his desk and rubs his temples. "I don't know."

"Come on," Reilly urges him. "We could both use a break. And who knows, maybe a change of scenery will do us some good."

Moore hesitates for a moment before reluctantly standing up. "Okay, sure. Let's go." Moore stumbles as they begin to leave the room. As they make their way out of the station and to the cafe, Reilly can't shake the feeling that something is off with Moore.

***

Sitting at the booth in the cafe, Reilly looks at Moore with a furrowed brow, noticing his unsteadiness.

The cafe is thick with the smell of bacon and eggs and fried hash browns. Grease hangs in the air, saturated like a sponge. The booths are smooth, molded red plastic and hard.

"Look, I know about your wife," Reilly says, keeping her voice low. "And I heard about the affair. I'm not here to judge, I just want to make sure you're okay."

Moore stiffens, clearly uncomfortable with the straightforward remark. "I'm fine," he says shortly. "Really?" Reilly presses. "Because you've been acting strange lately." Moore avoids her gaze, staring down at the menu. "I said I'm fine," he repeats. "Let's just order and get back to the station."

"You can talk to me, Moore," Reilly says, her tone softening.

"I loved her, Reilly. I loved her more than anything in this world," he says, his voice breaking. "But I was weak. I made a mistake and it cost me everything." Reilly can see the pain and regret in his eyes, and she feels for him.

"She forgave me, Reilly," murmurs Moore.

"And then she tried to take her own life," Moore adds sadly.

Reilly is startled, "But I thought she succeeded?"

"No, she ingested a bottle of sleeping pills in an attempt to end it all, but while she was unconscious, apparently a log fell out of the fireplace in our living room and set the house alight." Moore's voice shakes as tears well up in his eyes. Reilly is stunned.

"Fortunately, a neighbour managed to get in and rescue her, but she suffered severe burns that required her to be placed on life support for four days before finally passing away."

Reilly is overwhelmed with disbelief.

The waiter comes to take their order, breaking the moment.

Reilly and Moore place their orders, but the conversation between them is stilted and awkward. Moore's admission about his late wife's suicide attempt and subsequent death has left both feeling uneasy.

The waiter leaves, and the silence between them stretches on. Reilly can see that Moore is still deeply affected by what happened to his wife, and she feels a pang of guilt for pushing him to open up.

When their food arrives, they eat in silence, both lost in their own thoughts. Reilly can't help but think about the serial killer that they are trying to catch. Four murders and no leads – it's a case that is weighing heavily on both of them. They finish their meal and make their way back to the station. As they walk, Reilly can't shake the feeling that Moore's guilt is controlling him. He seems distant and preoccupied, and she knows that he is still struggling with what he told her over lunch.

Back at their desks, Reilly lets out a frustrated sigh. "We need something, anything. We can't let this killer keep getting away with it."

Just then, Chief Dwyer walks over to them, his thick Scottish accent filling the room. "What's the holdup, you two?" he booms. "I need progress on this case, and I need it now."

Moore looks up at him, the weight of his guilt and stress apparent on his face. "We're doing everything we can, Chief," he says.

"Well, it's not enough," Chief Dwyer snaps. "If you don't have something for me soon, I'll have to give the case to someone else."

Reilly's heart sinks at the thought of losing the case. "We're working as hard as we can, Chief," she says, trying to keep the desperation out of her voice.

Chief Dwyer fixes her with a stern look. "I don't want excuses, I want results. Get your heads in the game and figure this out."

Chief Dwyer glances at his watch, "You have until the end of the week to make progress on this case. After that, I'll have no choice but to hand it over to another team."

Moore and Reilly exchange a worried glance. They know they need a break in the case soon, or they'll be off the case and all their hard work would be wasted. Reilly speaks, "Chief, there is nothing to go on, no leads, he is smart, but he will make a mistake and when he does, we will be there."

"Alright, you have one more week. If you can show me some real progress, I'll give you more time."

With a renewed sense of determination, Moore and Reilly get to work. They spend long hours at the station, pouring over files and interviewing the gardener again, to see if anything can jog his mind to give the two detectives something to go on, but still nothing that really helps.

Over the next few days, tensions between Moore and Reilly get high. They barely speak to each other, and when they do, it's only to exchange words about the case. Moore continues to drink and take pills at every chance he can get.

One evening, as they are leaving the station, Reilly takes a deep breath and decides to try again. "Moore, wait up," she calls out.

Moore turns to her, his expression guarded. "What?"

Reilly takes a step closer, her voice softening. "I know this case is getting to us, and I know your personal life is taking a toll on you also, but I just want to help."

Moore walks off to his car, "I don't need your help Reilly, I'm fine."

Reilly stands there and watches Moore drive off squealing his tyres out of the car park and speeding up the road.

19

BAD FOR YOUR HEALTH

Daniel lays in his hospital bed, in the close observation room watching people come and go past his room. As the evening draws nearer, a buzzing noise is emitted over the PA system, alerting visitors that it is time to leave.

Daniel stares out the window, watching the sunset. The sky is red, like blood. The room is white, the walls are white, the bed is white, the sheets are white, the pillows are white, and the curtains are white. Only the lights are coloured, and that's only because Daniel's eyes need something to focus on. A bluish-white with a blue glow, so much like a fish tank.

The hospital hums with a muted stillness as the bright lights flicker above him. His head throbs with the cacophony of abusive, threatening voices that he has become all too familiar with. He knows the only way to fix them is to succumb to their demands and his body tenses in preparation.

There are no more people walking past his room, It's been 4 hours since the visitors left, and Daniel pushes himself up. He swings his legs over the side of the bed and stands up, feeling the cold tiles beneath his feet.

He inhales deeply, then limps towards the doorway. He steps into the corridor. No one is around; Daniel creeps along the hallway to a doorway that leads up a staircase.

He heads upwards, cautiously climbing the steps while trying to ignore the pain in his stomach. The railing was cold, hard and smooth. It felt like a bar of soap.

Daniel tightens his hand around the railing as he drags himself up the steps. Daniel had spotted his next target the previous night while he was in a wheelchair waiting to go in for an x-ray. He notices an elderly man across from him with kind eyes and a gentle smile that he is sharing with his family members, including probably his grandchildren.

His hair was thinning, and his moustache is kept neatly trimmed, wearing a blue and white striped hospital gown. Although his family seemed concerned about his health, he appeared to be content as they shared stories and laughter.

The voices in Daniel's head spoke louder than ever, telling him what he must do. As he was wheeled away from the scene, Daniel knew it was time once again.

Daniel's ascent up the stairs is slow and arduous, his body wracked with pain from the injuries. Every step feels like a struggle, and he has to stop frequently to catch his breath. But he knows that he must keep going, that his demons are urging him on to complete his grisly task.

Finally, he reaches the floor where the old man's room is located. He pauses for a moment to catch his breath and listens for signs of movement. He hears nothing but the sound of his own ragged breathing.

Daniel starts to move down the hallway, his steps slow and careful. He tries to keep his body close to the wall, to avoid being seen by any of the night staff or other patients who might be awake.

As he approaches the old man's room, he can feel his heart pounding in his chest. He hesitates for a moment, wondering if he should turn back, but then the voices in his head grow louder and more insistent, urging him on.

He takes a deep breath and pushes open the door to the old man's room. The hinges creak softly, but there is no response from the occupant of the bed. Daniel moves silently to the side of the bed, where the old man is sleeping. The room is dimly lit by a night light in the corner, but Daniel can see the outline of the old man's body under the blankets.

Daniel's hand trembles as he reaches for the pillow off the table. He knows what he must do, but he cannot bring himself to look at the old man lying in the bed before him. The room is silent except for the sound of his own breathing. Closing his eyes, he presses the pillow down over the patient's face, feeling the resistance of their struggle beneath him.

Daniel opens his eyes, he observes the patient struggling for breath, his body wriggling on the bed. He presses the pillow harder against the old man's face, feeling the resistance of his feeble attempts to fight back.

He can hear the demons scream in his head, cheering him on. His grip tightens, and a surge of power runs through him. He feels the patient's body weaken under his control.

Finally, the old man goes limp.

Daniel removes the pillow from the man's face and views that he is no longer breathing. He can see the fear and pain etched on the old man's face, even in death. Daniel knows that he has taken another life. And that he will never be able to undo what he has done.

As he carefully places the pillow back on the table and smooths out the sheets, he wonders if anyone will suspect foul play. He knows that he has to be careful, that he cannot afford to get caught. But deep down, he also knows that he can never escape the demons inside of him, the voices that drive him to commit such heinous acts. Turning and limping out of the room, his body shaking with a mix of adrenaline and pain. He quietly heads back to his own bed on the next flight below. The corridors are eerily quiet, the only sound being the soft hum of the overhead lights and coughing coming from one of the rooms.

Daniel walks with purpose, his breath shallow and ragged from the exertion of the murder.

He is careful to avoid any staff members who may be on night shift, his footsteps silent as he tiptoes down the hallway. The occasional beep of a monitor breaks the silence.

As he descends the stairs, he feels a sharp pain in his abdomen. His injury is causing him pain, however, for now, he focuses on getting back to his own bed undetected.

He is safely back in the room, he slips into bed, feeling a sense of satisfaction wash over him and the voices are silent again.

A rattle at the window from a gust of wind wakes Daniel. He slowly opens his eyes and takes in the sterile hospital room around him.

The bright lights above him are almost blinding, and the sound of medical equipment beeping and buzzing fills his ears. He groans as he tries to sit up, but it hurts too much to do so. He thinks to himself he has strained himself too much last night. Feeling a dull ache in his side from his leaky spleen.

Nurse Maddison enters the room. She smiles at him kindly and asks how he is feeling.

Daniel forces a nod, not wanting to draw attention to himself. He knows that he needs to act normal and blend in, or else he might raise some red flags.

As Nurse Maddison checks his vital signs and adjusts his bandages, he stares up at the ceiling trying not to make eye contact. Nurse Maddison notices the bandages on his side are spotted with blood seeping through to the outside.

"What have you been doing?" asks Nurse Maddison curiously.

Daniel just lays there looking at the ceiling. Nurse Maddison growls at him and says she must change his bandage again.

He cannot shake the feeling of guilt that washes over him every time he gives in to the demons. He knows he should not enjoy taking lives, but the rush it gives him is undeniable. It is not him doing it, he tells himself, it is the demons. Nevertheless, he cannot ignore the nagging voice in the back of his head that tells him he is responsible for his actions.

Nurse Maddison begins to remove the bandages; Daniel winces as she touches the wound.

As she places a fresh bandage, Nurse Maddison notices something odd about Daniel's feet. She glances down and sees that the bottom of his feet are dirty as if he has been walking around.

"What?" Daniel asks, noticing her hesitation. Nurse Maddison quickly looks up and composes herself, "Everything is fine with your bandage. I just noticed that the bottom of your feet are dirty. Have you been walking around?"

Daniel shakes his head, "No, I haven't, must have been from when the orderlies were moving me around earlier in the chair, probably dragging my feet. You know I can hardly walk about 2 metres without getting winded."

Nurse Maddison nods, understandingly. "Yes, I know. Just wanted to make sure everything was okay." As she leaves the room, she cannot shake off the feeling there is something is not quite right with Daniel.

A few hours later, Nurse Maddison returns to Daniel's room she is holding a newspaper, places it on the table next to Daniel's bed, and tells him, "Here is something to read if you want, I found it left out on a seat in the hallway."

"Daniel, I am sorry to tell you this, but the hospital has decided to move you to another ward. They need the space in this one," Nurse Maddison says, her voice sympathetic.

Daniel's heart sinks. He has grown used to this room and the routines of the staff. "Will I be put in a room with other patients?" Daniel asks.

Nurse Maddison hesitates for a moment before answering. "Yes, there will be one other patient in the room with you. But do not worry, he is very quiet and keeps to himself."

Daniel nods and tries to appear calm, but his mind is racing with fear and uncertainty. He has always preferred to be alone and the thought of sharing a room with a stranger makes him uneasy. Suddenly the voices ignite in his head.

"Daniel?" Nurse Maddison's voice breaks through his thoughts. "Are you okay?"

Daniel blinks, trying to regain his composure. He nods to her. "Hopefully, it will be only for a short while, till you all better and you can go home," says Nurse Maddison. As Nurse Maddison leaves the room, Daniel is nervous the voices are growing stronger, urging him to act.

Daniel cannot sleep, his mind is consumed with the thought of sharing a room. He tries to distract himself by grabbing the newspaper from the bedside table and start reading. He scans the front page; his heart skips a beat.

The headline reads, "KILLER ON RAMPAGE." Four women were found brutally murdered in Coulson.

The details of the article are eerily like his own grisly attacks before he was brought into the hospital. Daniel felt a wave of panic wash over him. *What if they found out it was he?* He tried to push the thought out of his mind, but it kept creeping back in.

Daniel reads on, his heart races and his hands shake. "*Why is it only coming out now?*" He thinks to himself. The article states that it was leaked out of the police station, which has been keeping it concealed so as not to panic the public, they have been working on the case for a while now. Daniel's mind races with possibilities. *Could someone have found out about him and tipped off the police? Could they be coming for him now?*

He tries to calm himself down, reminding himself that he is in the hospital, he has seen police walk past earlier and they did not arrest him, he needs to calm down.

He spends the rest of the day tossing and turning, unable to sleep, his head consumed with thoughts of the article.

Just then, Nurse Maddison walks into the room and hands Daniel his tablets, he swallows them with the water that she also gives him. She takes his blood pressure; she notices it is higher than usual. "Your blood pressure is high 145/105, are you feeling, okay?" she asks, concerned.

Daniel nods.

"I am sure the new ward will be just fine. And speaking of worrying, have you seen the headlines in the newspaper?" she asks, picking up the newspaper from the table.

Daniel's heart races once again when he sees the headline again. He nods again to Nurse Maddison, trying to remain calm.

"It is just awful," Nurse Maddison continues, shaking her head. "What kind of sick person could do such a thing?" Daniel does not reply, he is consumed with guilt and fear. He knows all too well what kind of a person could commit such heinous acts.

Nurse Maddison finishes taking Daniel's blood pressure and sets down the equipment, "You know Daniel, reading that news about the killer on the loose has really made me uneasy," she says looking at him with a worried expression. "I have to walk to my car alone tonight and I cannot help but think about what if he is out there waiting." Daniel nods, but his mind is elsewhere, he is preoccupied with the thought of his own crimes being exposed and he cannot help but feel a sense of paranoia creeping in.

He knows he is the one responsible for her unease and he cannot shake off the feeling of guilt that washes over him.

Nurse Maddison says goodbye, and she leaves the room. Daniel is left alone with his thoughts and his demons. The newspaper headlines continue to gnaw at him. But as the day nearly comes to an end his fear and anxiety grow, and he wonders how long he can keep up the facade of normalcy before he gives in once again.

***

The next morning Daniel is lying in bed looking at the doorway watching people walk past, some look in at him as if he is an exhibit in a zoo. Daniel is still reeling over the newspaper article.

His thoughts are interrupted by the sound of footsteps approaching the room. He notices a nurse he has not seen before entering the room. Nurse Johnston is a 37-year-old nurse with long, blonde hair that falls in soft waves around her shoulders. Her eyes are a bright, piercing blue, and her skin is tanned and smooth, with just a hint of freckles across her nose. She has a warm, friendly smile that puts patients at ease and makes them feel safe and cared for.

Nurse Shelley Johnston grew up in a small town on the West Coast, the youngest of four children. Her parents were both teachers.

Shelley Johnston attended nursing school and graduated at the top of her class. She worked in a busy ER for several years before moving to a quieter hospital in the suburbs. There, she quickly gained a reputation as a compassionate and skilled nurse, someone who went above and beyond to ensure her patients received the best care possible.

"Hello Daniel, I am Nurse Johnston, I'm here to help you get ready for your move to the new ward."

"Where is Nurse Maddison?" Daniel asks, "It's her day off today, she will be back tomorrow, but because you're moving to another ward, you won't be seeing her now, it will be mostly me," comments Shelley.

Daniel is shocked and angry, she never said anything to him about leaving him, not showing Nurse Johnston his emotions, but he is boiling furious inside.

Nurse Johnston begins to assist him in getting him in his dressing gown. As she helps him, Daniel cannot help but wonder about the man he will be sharing with and how angry he is about Nurse Maddison the bitch.

As they make their way down the hallway, with Nurse Johnston pushing him in a wheelchair, Daniel can feel his anxiety building; he can hear the voices in his head returning and growing louder cursing Nurse Maddison for leaving him.

Finally, they reach the new ward and enter the room, where Daniel's new roommate is already waiting.

The roommate glances up at Daniel before returning to his book. Hoping to peek at the title, Daniel squints to read the words, but they are too small from this distance.

"Your new roommate has arrived," Nurse Johnston announces while nodding toward Mr. Dorta.

"Thanks," he mumbles without looking away from his book.

Daniel sighs with relief that this man seems uninterested in conversing with him and hopes he will be able to stay out of any conflicts. He shifts his gaze around the room which was barely furnished with two beds, a table, and a closet; painted with an uninspiring beige colour, and no natural light. The only source of illumination came from a dim lamp resting on the table and a dull wall light.

As soon as Nurse Johnston leaves, Daniel settles into his bed, trying to make himself as small and inconspicuous as possible. He can feel Mr. Dorta's eyes on him, but he tries to ignore it and focus on his breathing. The room is quiet, he listens to the sound of the man turning the pages of his book and wonders what he could be reading. He glances over at the man and notices that he's wearing a hospital gown and has an anchor tattoo on his arm. Feeling curious, Daniel clears his throat. "Excuse me," he says softly. "What are you reading?"

The man looks up at him, his expression neutral. "It's a book about a soldier in the Civil War," he says in a low voice.

Daniel nods, trying to think of something else to say. He feels awkward and out of place like he doesn't belong in this room with this man. He wishes he could be back in his old room, where he felt safe and familiar with Nurse Maddison his anger fumes again about her.

An orderly enters, pushing a wheelchair. "Good evening," he says brightly. "I'm here to take Mr. Dorta down for his MRI." The man closes his book and sets it aside before getting up from the bed. He nods to Daniel as he leaves the room with the orderly.

Left alone in the room, Daniel's mind starts to race again. He can hear the voices getting louder, urging him to act, to defend himself from the unknown. He tries to push them away, but they're relentless. As Daniel settles into his new bed, he can't help but feel a sense of discomfort. The stranger seems harmless enough, but the voices in his head are telling him otherwise.

An hour had passed. Daniel notices a magazine on the bedside table. He picks it up, hoping to distract himself from his anxious thoughts. It is a sports magazine, filled with articles about football, basketball, and swimming. Daniel has never been interested in sports, but he starts flipping through the pages anyway.

Daniel looks up from the sports magazine as Nurse Johnston wheels Mr. Dorta back into the room. They both seem quite chatty with each other, Daniel didn't want to intrude on their conversation, so he continues to read the magazine, pretending not to notice their presence.

Finally, Nurse Johnston and Mr. Dorta stop their chatty conversation. "George, would you like some water or juice?" she asks, gesturing to the pitcher and glass on the bedside table. Mr. Dorta nods gratefully, and Nurse Johnston pours him a glass of water. She then turns to Daniel. "Would you like something to drink as well?" she asks kindly.

Daniel hesitates for a moment before shaking his head and tossing the magazine back on the table. Nurse Johnston smiles at him before checking Mr. Dorta's vital signs and making some notes on his chart. She then turns to Daniel. "How are you feeling, Daniel?" she asks, her voice gentle. Daniel shrugs.

"I know this room is not as good as the other Daniel, but they really needed the other one for something else, Nurse Maddison is probably missing you also, but you never know she might come to visit, she will be working tomorrow till midnight apparently," says Shelley as she straightens up Mr Dorta's covers on his bed.

Daniel just lays there looking at the doorway.

The next day, Daniel's rage has been simmering and he is rather agitated about how Nurse Maddison is avoiding him. She has not shown up at all yet. Laying there watching the doorway for her but she fails to appear.

Nurse Johnston walks in with Daniel's medication in a cup. "Here you go Daniel, it is that time again," says the nurse. Daniel sits up and takes the cup and Nurse Johnston fills it half up with water, Daniel throws the tablets in his mouth takes a big gulp of water and washes them down.

Mr. Dorta is sitting in a chair next to his bed, dressed in a white hospital tunic, his hands shaking as he clings to the pages of his book.

The room is deathly silent, only punctuated by the ticking of the clock. Nurse Johnston walks over to Mr. Dorta, her shoes clacking on the tile floor. She stops at his side and places one hand on his shoulder. "Are you ready for your pacemaker operation George?" she asks gently. Mr. Dorta looks up at her, nervousness evident in his eyes. He gives a small nod and lowers his head. Nurse Johnston wheels him out of the ward in the wheelchair, but not before Mr. Dorta gives one last glance back at Daniel. Without looking up, Daniel ignores him.

After a few hours, Mr. Dorta returns, heavy-lidded from the anesthesia, eased into the ward by Nurse Johnston who carefully settles him against his pillows and slips him a dose of painkillers.

Daniel watches as she moves about with practiced proficiency and then smiles at Daniel and leaves.

He knows Nurse Maddison will leave the hospital at midnight, Nurse Johnston said so, probably taking the underground car park.

Daniel needs to get out before it is too late, he will never get to see Nurse Maddison again otherwise. Ticking off the minutes until midnight in his head. Daniel lies motionless on the bed, the voices in his head growing louder and more adamant until he can no longer contain them.

Finally, he hears footsteps outside the room, the nurse comes to check on old Mr. Dorta on her rounds, and Daniel knows that this is his chance. He waits until the room is silent the only sound is the soft hum of the machine next to Mr. Dorta. He also waits until he hears the nurse's footsteps recede down the hallway, before getting up from his bed and moving quietly towards the door.

When he reaches the doorway, he peers into the hallway. His heart is pounding in his chest, and he can feel every beat also as if it is a hammer driving nails into his side. He steps out into the dimly lit corridor, pain jabbing his side with each step, yet still moves at an urgent pace. He knows that taking this risk is dangerous but seeing her again is more important than anything. His eyes dart around him like a hawk looking for prey. He can hear voices in his head urging him on, telling him what to do, but he already knows what he is going to do.

Finally, he reaches the exit to the stairs leading down to the underground car park and pushes it open, feeling the cool night air rush over him.

As he makes his way to the car park, his heart pounds with excitement and anticipation. He reaches the car park entrance and hides behind a pillar, watching as the nurses file out one by one, their faces weary and lined with fatigue.

And then he sees her - Nurse Maddison, wearing her white uniform and carrying her bag. She looks tired, but determined, as if she has a purpose that he can't fathom. Daniel waits for the other nurses to walk out of view. He steps out from behind the pillar and calls her name.

At first, she doesn't seem to hear him. She continues walking towards her car, her head down, her shoulders hunched. But as he gets closer, she turns and sees him, her eyes widening in shock and fear.

"What are you doing here, Daniel?" backing away from him. "You should not be out of bed in your condition, how did you get down here?" she asks looking around.

"I walked down here, I want to know why you abandoned me," he says, his voice low and menacing. "Why did you leave me, I thought you liked me?"

Nurse Maddison shakes her head, her eyes darting around the empty car park. "I didn't abandon you, Daniel. I'm still here; I am just doing my job."

"You think you can just walk away from me? You think you can ignore me, treat me like dirt, and get away with it?" he growls.

He advances on her, his fists clenched, his heart pounding in his chest. He can feel the blood rushing to his head, his voices screaming at him for vengeance, his vision blurring with rage. He wants to hurt her, to make her suffer, to show her the true meaning of fear.

And then something snaps inside him. He feels a surge of power, a rush of adrenaline, a wave of pure ecstasy. He lunges at Nurse Maddison, his fingers curling into claws, his teeth bared in a snarl.

Seizing her and smashing her against the side of the car. Nurse Maddison attempts to scream, but Daniel clamps his hand over her mouth so tightly it cuts her lip and makes her eyes water.

He hurls her onto the cold concrete surface with such force knocking the wind out of her and she can feel instant pain and its coldness against the skin on her legs.

The slime and car oil muck has her wriggling, sliding, and slipping against the cold floor, unable to gain a foothold or get any grab on the surface. On top of her now, he swings his fist viciously towards her face, the impact making a sharp crack as it connects with bone. She cries out in pain and fear, begging for mercy. But he silences her again, this time by pushing her head into the ground until she is dazed and groggy. Adrenaline fuels him the voices yell abuse at him as he slides his hand under her dress, ripping down her panties without mercy. He swivels his head back and forth, checking for any signs of life in the underground car park - no one around to hear her scream, no one there to help. With that he rips the hospital dress thats against her petite body, exposing her body and her curves to his lust and hate. He straddles her, his hands pinning her, his knees pinning her legs. Nurse Maddison can feel him against her, his erection hard and ready, his breath laboured. He grips her shoulders, pinning her down, smashing her body into the concrete, breathing hard and fast. Daniel is lost in his own fury. It's not enough. He can't do it to her, can't do it to himself. He wants her to see him, to see what he is, to know what he is, to see what he's got for her.

He growls at her, "Look at me you bitch, fucking look at me!" He lets go of her shoulders grabs her face, forces her face in his direction and slides his other hand down her body, over her breasts, and down to her crutch, rough and ready to take her. He leans over her and says, "I am Legion for I am many".

He penetrates her vagina, she starts sobbing and shaking, he thrusts inside of her with force, harder each time, he lays on top of her breathing in her ear then biting her earlobe till it bleeds.

Suddenly she lashes at the side of his cheek. He begins to thrash her with his fists till she is unconscious. He begins to arch with orgasm and then he grabs her by the throat and strangles her till she is not breathing. His body aches from the adrenaline surging through his veins, his long-dormant muscles tightening painfully. He stands up stiffly, surveying his surroundings. His hospital pyjamas hang limply on his gaunt frame as he grasps her bag and frantically searches for the car keys. Upon finding them, he lurches over to the trunk of the car and scoops up Nurse Maddison in an ungentle embrace, throwing her into the trunk not before looking at her, her face disfigured and bruised like a prizefighter.

Daniel slams the trunk lid shut with a reverberating thud. Clutching the keys in his hand, he carves an upside-down cross on the trunk while he mumbles to himself. He stumbles back towards the stairs leading back to his room, the pain in his side, very noticeable now.

Daniel's heart is pounding more than ever, he hurries back to his ward. He can hear the sound of his footsteps echoing through the quiet corridors and he knows that he must move quickly before anyone discovers what he has just done.

Daniel finds a rubbish bin in a nearby waiting area and drops Nurse Maddison's car keys in the bin. Then as he approaches the doorway to his room, he slows down and tries to compose himself. He takes a deep breath and holding his side, he puts on a calm, collected demeanour, hoping that no one will suspect a thing.

When he enters the ward, he is relieved to find that it is empty apart from his roommate is still sound asleep, snoring loudly, and there is no sign of any nurses or doctors yet.

He walks over to his bed and sits down, his hands shaking with adrenaline. He cannot believe what he has just done, but he knows that he must keep his cool and act as though nothing has happened.

Daniel realises that his hospital pyjamas are covered in oil and muck from his attack on Nurse Maddison. He quickly rushes to the closet and grabs a pair of clean pyjamas folded nicely on the shelf, he begins to change, grabbing the stained pyjamas he darts across the doorway and looks down both ways of the corridor, and rushes over to a dirty linen trolley sitting at the side of the elevator. He throws them in there and buries them underneath the sheets.

Speeding back to his bed he climbs in and lays there reeling over a constant replay in his mind.

20

THE MISSING

As the fluorescent lights buzz overhead, casting a sterile glow throughout the hospital corridors, Nurse Maddison's boyfriend, Mark, paces anxiously near the reception desk. His eyes dart around, searching for any familiar faces as he clutches a small bouquet of her favourite flowers in his trembling hands. Approaching the receptionist, who wears a sympathetic expression, Mark musters up the courage to speak.

"Excuse me, I am Mark O'Shannessey. I am looking for Nurse Carol Maddison, I am her boyfriend she's a nurse here, and she never came home yesterday morning. We had a bit of an intense argument before she left for work the other day, and now I'm desperate to apologise and reconcile. I have a feeling she's been hiding here, working tirelessly and avoiding me." The receptionist offers a gentle smile, understanding the gravity of the situation. "I'm sorry to hear that. Let me see if I can find any information for you." She quickly checks the staff roster and notices Nurse Maddison's name listed. "Yes, Nurse Maddison works here. Let me contact the nurse's station on her floor and see if anyone has seen her today."

Mark's heart pounds in his chest as he anxiously waits for the receptionist to make the call. Each passing second feels like an eternity, his worry for Nurse Maddison growing with every breath. He thinks to himself, *"She must be angry to avoid him this long."* He clutches the bouquet tighter, seeking comfort in the familiar scent of her favourite flowers.

After what feels like an eternity, the receptionist returns, her expression a mix of concern and confusion. "I'm sorry, sir," she begins, her voice filled with empathy. "But it seems that no one has seen Nurse Maddison today. The last time her colleagues saw her was the other early morning she was on her way home."

Mark's anxiety surges, a knot forming in the pit of his stomach. "But she must be here," he insists, his voice tinged with desperation. "Please, can you check again?"

The receptionist nods sympathetically, understanding the depth of Mark's worry. She makes another round of calls, hoping for a different outcome. After a few minutes, she turns back to Mark, her eyes filled with genuine concern. "I'm sorry, sir," she said softly. "We still haven't been able to locate Nurse Maddison. Her colleagues said it is unusual for her to be absent without any notice. She is rostered to be here today, but no one has seen her."

A wave of panic washes over Mark, threatening to engulf him. Thoughts race through his mind, contemplating the worst-case scenarios.

Mark's mind races with worry, his determination pushing him forward. He makes a resolute decision to descend to the underground car park, hoping to see if her car is there and some clue about Carol's whereabouts.

As he steps into the dimly lit garage, the sound of his own footsteps echoes in the emptiness. His eyes scan the rows of parked cars, searching for any sign of Carol's vehicle. Finally, he spots her Mazda and rushes over, his heart pounding with a mix of anticipation and fear.

Mark quickly peers through the car windows, hoping to find any trace of Carol or any clue that could lead him to her. It's at that moment that his eyes fall upon the strange upside-down cross carved into the paintwork of the trunk.

Shock and curiosity grip Mark as he takes in the eerie symbol. His mind races, trying to comprehend why someone would deface Carol's car in such a manner. The sight of the inverted cross sends chills down his spine, raising unsettling questions about the motive behind this act.

Mark's concern escalates further, his mind racing with the need for immediate action. He hurries back to the hospital reception, a sense of urgency propelling him forward. Approaching the receptionist, he pleads, "Please, I need to use the phone to call the police. Something is seriously wrong."

The receptionist, sensing Mark's distress, nods empathetically and gestures toward the nearby phone. "Of course, go ahead," she says, her voice filled with genuine concern.

Mark dials the emergency number with trembling hands, his heart pounding in his chest. As he waits for the call to connect, fear and hope swirl within him. He knows that contacting the police is a crucial step toward unravelling the mystery surrounding Carol's disappearance and the ominous symbol carved onto her car.

With each passing second, the ringing of the phone amplifies Mark's anxiety. He can only hope that the authorities will respond swiftly and take his concerns seriously. As the call finally connects, he takes a deep breath, preparing himself to recount the unsettling events and seek the help that he so desperately needs.

A hello echoes from the other end of the phone, and Mark takes a deep breath before launching into his urgent explanation. "Hello, I need your help. My girlfriend, Carol Maddison, has gone missing. She never came home yesterday, and I found her car in the underground car park at the hospital where she works. There's this strange cross carved into the trunk's paintwork. I'm worried. Something isn't right."

The operator listens attentively, their voice calm and reassuring. "I understand your concern, sir. We'll do everything we can to assist you. Can you provide me with your girlfriend's full name, description, and any other relevant details?"

Mark shares the necessary information. "Her name is Carol Maddison she is a nurse. She's 28 years of age and is about 5"7" with long black hair she mostly has it up in a bun and she has blue eyes. Please, you must find her. I'm terrified something terrible has happened."

The operator reassures Mark, their tone steady and compassionate. "We're dispatching officers to the hospital right away."

Mark relinquishes the phone to the receptionist, grateful for her assistance. As he takes a few steps away, his legs feel weak, and he seeks solace in the nearby seats lined up against the wall. He sinks into one of the chairs, his mind consumed by worry and uncertainty. The weight of the situation settles heavily upon him, and he anxiously awaits any updates from the police. Thoughts of Carol and the bizarre cross etched onto her car replay in his mind, fuelling his determination to find answers and bring her back safely.

***

Meanwhile, at the police station, Moore sits on the toilet in the men's restroom. He takes a swig from his flask, the liquid burning his throat as it goes down. In his other hand, he throws a couple of tablets into his mouth, hoping they will provide some temporary relief. Just moments ago, a chilling sight unfolded before his eyes. Standing next to his car in the car park, he sees the apparition of his deceased wife. Shock and disbelief wash over him, causing his heart to skip a beat. He rubs his eyes, questioning his own sanity, but the figure remains steadfast, a haunting reminder of his past.

Moore takes a moment to collect himself, his breathing steadying as he tucks the flask back into his pocket. The weight of it serves as a reminder, a comfort, in the face of the challenges ahead. He adjusts his jacket, ensuring the flask remains concealed from prying eyes.

As Moore walks back down the corridor toward the car park, an officer at the phone desk shouts out to him. "Detective, we just got a call from the hospital. A nurse is missing," the officer reports. "But what caught my attention was the upside-down cross on her car trunk. I thought you should know."

Moore's eyes widen with surprise and concern at the mention of the symbol. "Thanks for letting me know," he says, his mind racing with the implications of the mysterious cross. "I'll head over to the hospital right away."

Moore returns to his desk, a sense of urgency propelling his steps. He spots Reilly engrossed in paperwork and approaches her with a determined expression. "Reilly, we have a breakthrough, "Someone at the hospital just reported a missing nurse, and there's an upside-down cross on her car," Moore announces.

Reilly looks up in response to Moore's words. "Missing nurse and an upside-down cross?" she echoes, her interest awakens. "That's not something you hear every day."

The two detectives quickly gather their gear, preparing to delve into this new lead. As they make their way to the hospital, their minds buzz with anticipation, knowing that this could be a significant break in their investigation.

Moore and Reilly arrive at the hospital, their footsteps echoing through the bustling corridors. They navigate through the maze of hallways, their eyes scanning the surroundings for any signs of things out of the ordinary or clues related to the disturbing symbol carved on her car.

As they approach the reception desk, they notice a distressed man, Mark, standing nearby. Mark's eyes are red and puffy, his anxiety palpable. Moore and Reilly exchange a brief glance before approaching him.

"Excuse me, sir," Moore begins his tone compassionate. "We're detectives Moore and Reilly. We've been informed about a missing nurse called in by her boyfriend. Are you Mark, the nurse's boyfriend?"

Mark nods, his voice trembling as he replies, "Yes, that's me. I reported her missing, and I found this upside-down cross carved on her car."

Reilly leans in, her expression serious. "We're here to help. Can you tell us anything else about the situation? Did Nurse Maddison mention anything unusual happening recently?"

Moore places a reassuring hand on Mark's shoulder. "We're going to do everything we can to find Nurse Maddison. Do you mind accompanying us to the car so we can get a closer look and gather more information?"

Mark nods, grateful for the support. "Of course, I'll do anything to help find her."

Moore, Reilly, and Mark make their way to the underground car park, the air growing colder as they descend. The dimly lit space feels eerie, casting long shadows on the concrete walls. They stop in front of Carol Maddison's car, the upside-down cross still visible on the trunk.

Moore takes out a flashlight and carefully inspects the carving, his eyes narrowing. "This is no ordinary vandalism," he remarks, his voice low and serious. "It's deliberate, symbolic."

Reilly, her gaze scanning the surroundings, adds, "We need to treat this as a potential threat. Mark, did Carol mention anyone who might want to harm her or had any enemies?"

Mark hesitates for a moment, recalling their conversations. "No, nothing like that. Carol was always focused on her work, and helping others. I can't think of anyone who would want to harm her."

While Reilly is peering in the passenger side window, Moore's mind races with a sense of dread as Mark denies knowledge of any potential enemies.

Moore's stomach churns as he contemplates the possibility of Nurse Maddison being trapped within the trunk. A cold shiver runs down his spine, and his instincts scream that something is terribly wrong. His eyes scan the car, and that's when he notices it—a splatter of blood on the rear bumper bar.

His heart pounds in his chest as his mind races, connecting the dots and fuelling his growing concern. With a sense of urgency, he turns to Reilly, his voice laced with unease. "Reilly, we need to act quickly. There is blood on the rear bumper, right here. We can't waste any more time. We have to find a way to access that trunk."

Moore's concern for Mark's well-being takes precedence as he recognises the distress the situation is causing him. He approaches Mark, his voice filled with empathy and authority. "Mark, I understand this is a difficult time for you, but we need you to step away from the car. This area is now a crime scene, and it's important for us to preserve any potential evidence. Please, trust us to handle this."

Reilly, reacting swiftly, spots a fire extinguisher hanging on a nearby wall. She grabs it without hesitation, her mind focused on gaining access to the car's interior. Carrying the fire extinguisher, she rushes back to the car, swinging it with force into the driver's side window, shattering it. Reilly takes a moment to retrieve a pair of rubber gloves from her pocket. She methodically puts them on, ensuring her hands are protected from any potential hazards and disturbing the scene with fingerprints. With the gloves in place, she carefully navigates through the shattered glass, reaching into the car to open the door. The door creaks open.

Reilly then leans forward, stretching her arm toward the lever that opens the trunk. As she pulls it, she can hear the distinct sound of the trunk unlocking. The anticipation in the air grows thicker, and a knot tightens in her stomach.

Just as the trunk pops open, a sharp cry escapes Mark O'Shannessey's lips. "Oh my god, oh my god!" his voice echoes through the car park, filled with a mixture of shock and horror. Reilly's heart skips a beat, realising the gravity of the situation that lies before them.

Moore's face falls as he sees the woman's lifeless body in the trunk. He quickly checks for a pulse but finds none. "She's dead," he says, his voice hollow.

Mark collapses to the ground, sobbing uncontrollably. Reilly places a hand on his shoulder, trying to offer some comfort. "We need to call for backup," she says, her voice calm and steady.

Moore nods, his mind racing. "And forensics," he adds, "We need to secure this scene and gather any evidence." Reilly guides Mark away from the distressing sight, leading him back to the hospital reception to ensure he receives the necessary support and medical assistance.

Reilly approaches the receptionist with urgency, explaining the critical need to make an important call to the police station. The receptionist, understanding the gravity of the situation, points Reilly towards a nearby office where she can use the phone in privacy.

With a sense of purpose, Reilly enters the office and picks up the receiver. She dials the local police station, her voice steady as she relays the distressing details of the crime scene and the discovery of the woman's lifeless body in the trunk of the car. She emphasises the urgency of the situation, requesting immediate backup and forensic assistance.

Meanwhile, Moore remains at the crime scene, ensuring the area is secure and undisturbed. He keeps a watchful eye, pre-

venting any curious onlookers from getting too close and po-
tentially tampering with the evidence. As he stands guard at the
crime scene, his gaze constantly scanning the area, he occasionally retreats to a secluded corner of the car park. There, hidden
in the shadows, he retrieves his flask and takes a quick, clan-
destine sip of whiskey. The potent liquid offers a momentary
respite from the harrowing reality he faces. Aware of the need
to remain composed and focused, Moore takes measured sips,
careful not to let his personal struggles interfere with his duty.
The alcohol provides a brief, temporary escape, allowing him
to momentarily dull the sharp edges of his emotions and the
haunting memories that have plagued him.

The flask finds its way back into his pocket, concealed from
view. Moore returns to his post, reaffirming his commitment
to protecting the crime scene and ensuring the integrity of the
investigation. Though burdened by his own inner demons, he
remains steadfast.

Allison, the leader of the forensic team that accompanies her,
joins Detective Reilly as they make their way down to the underground car park. The two of them exchange glances. They
step into the dimly lit space, where Detective Moore stands, his
eyes fixed on the crime scene.

Allison quickly assesses the situation, taking in the details of
the car, the lifeless body in the trunk, and the surrounding area.

The forensic team arrive, and under Allison's guidance, begins their meticulous work. They set up their equipment.

They document the crime scene using film cameras, capturing each angle and detail with precision. They dust for fingerprints, carefully lifting any potential prints using adhesive tape. Every surface is examined for trace evidence such as fibres, hairs, or bloodstains, which are collected using swabs and paper bindles. Allison sees the upside-down cross carved into the trunk, and she takes photographs of it from multiple angles, capturing every detail.

The underground car park becomes a hub of activity.

Allison engrossed in her examination of the crime scene, turns to Moore and shares her thoughts about the upside-down cross on the trunk of the car. "It's important to note that the information about the upside-down cross at the other murder scene on the car door and at the abandoned house was known only to the police officers involved in the investigations. It's unlikely that a copycat killer would have access to such specific details without being directly involved or having access to confidential information and I doubt that, I think this is our guy."

Moore realises the weight of Allison's comment.

Allison says, "By just looking at her, I can see bruising around her neck and quite a few hematomas around the face." Lifting up the nurse's eyelid, she comments again, "The bruising and

Petechial haemorrhage suggest that Maddison was forcefully suffocated, asphyxiation due to strangulation. Also, I am noticing her with no lower clothing which could be a sign of a sexual attack, but I won't be exactly sure till I get her back to the lab. A violent attack and strangulation, a lot like the killer your after isn't it Detective Moore?

Moore's expression darkens as he considers Allison's words. He knows that the similarities between Nurse Maddison's murder and the previous cases. "I think we are dealing with the same killer. It's disturbingly like the other cases we've been investigating. The signs of strangulation and the violence inflicted upon the nurse are consistent with the killer we have been chasing."

Moore and Reilly make their way back upstairs to the hospital reception. They approach the receptionist, who looks up with concern.

"Excuse me," Reilly begins, her tone polite yet authoritative. "We're investigating the murder of the nurse whose car was found in the underground car park. We would like to ask some questions to the staff who worked with her. Can you provide us with a list of names?"

The receptionist nods, her expression serious. "Of course, detectives but I will need to ring for permission from management. Give me a moment." The receptionist picks up the phone and presses a button, silently she talks with her back at the detectives, she puts down the handpiece and turns back to them both. She quickly retrieves a roster from her desk and hands it over to Moore. "Management says it's fine, here is the list of the staff who were on duty with Nurse Maddison. Let me know if there's anything else I can do to assist you."

"Thank you," Moore replies, his voice appreciative. "We might have further questions, so we'll let you know if we need any more information."

As they speak to the staff, a sense of tension hangs in the air. The hospital employees, already shaken by the news of their colleague's murder, provide earnest and cooperative answers. The detectives remain vigilant, their questions probing yet respectful, as they piece together a clearer picture of Nurse Maddison's professional and personal life.

Moore steps through the gloomy hallway with Reilly, gathering information on the nurse.

An unsettling sensation clings to him like a thick blanket. He stops in his tracks as he sees a shape ahead, shrouded in shadows and illuminated by faintly flickering lights. It's his late wife, Kate, her frail form draped in hospital wires and tubes.

"Why did you do it, David? Wasn't I good enough for you? You did this to me," she moans plaintively, her voice brimming with anguish and accusation.

Moore's breath catches in his throat, his heart pounding in his chest. He can't believe what he is seeing. He blinks, hoping the apparition will vanish, but Kate remains there, a haunting image from his past.

Tears well up in his eyes as he takes a step closer, his hand outstretched, yearning for the connection he had lost. But the moment he reaches out, the figure flickers and disappears, leaving him standing alone in the dim hallway.

Moore stands there, trying to comprehend the vision of his deceased wife when Reilly's concern breaks the silence. "Moore, what's wrong with you? Are you alright?"

Moore takes a deep breath, his voice strained as he responds, "I... I'm feeling a bit dizzy. It's nothing, just need a moment to collect myself."

Reilly looks sceptical but decides not to push further, respecting Moore's need for privacy. "Okay, take your time," she says, stepping back slightly.

As he moves away from her, Moore's heart thuds in his chest. He knows he can't hide the truth from her, but the thought of sharing the haunting encounter and his emotional turmoil unnerves him. He needs a moment alone to process everything.

"Restroom," he mumbles as an excuse, barely managing to maintain his composure. Moore hastens to the nearest restroom, his steps faltering as he enters the dimly lit space.

Moore locks the door, and his emotions surge through him. His legs tremble as he slides down the wall, tears pressing against the back of his eyelids. The haunting vision of his wife flooding his mind, her tragic death still fresh in his memory, creates an unbearable weight on his shoulders.

Unable to fight it any longer, Moore breaks down, tears cascading down his cheeks as he struggles to gasp for air. His chest tightens and his heart races as the anxiety takes over. Moore cries and talks to himself saying, "I'm sorry Kate it was a mistake, I'm sorry."

Moore wipes away his tears, taking slow and steady breaths as the storm of emotions ebbs away.

Moore steps out of the restroom, his eyes red and puffy, but an unbreakable resolve etched into his features. He strides up to Reilly, who watches him with concern.

"Reilly, let's keep going," Moore demands, his voice unwavering yet laced with fragility. He chooses not to recount the harrowing vision he had just experienced, knowing it would only weigh down his companion with unnecessary specifics.

They resume their investigation, but Moore's mind keeps drifting back to the haunting image he had seen. It is challenging for him to focus, but he pushes himself to stay attentive to the case. "Excuse me, I'm Detective Moore, and this is Detective Reilly. We are investigating the murder of Nurse Carol Maddison. We understand that you were on duty with her. Can we ask you a few questions?" says Moore trying to compose himself.

"Sure, detectives. I'm Jess Shelverton, and I worked with Carol Maddison on her last shift. What do you need to know?" says Jess.

"Thank you, Jess. Can you tell us about your interactions with Carol on the day of her disappearance? Did anything seem out of the ordinary?" questions Reilly.

"Well, Carol was her usual self that day. We had a shift together in the morning, and she seemed fine. We chatted about work and some personal stuff during breaks. Nothing stood out as unusual," comments Jess.

"Did she mention having any conflicts or disagreements with anyone recently?" asks Moore.

Jess looks hard at Detective Moore in thought, "Not that I'm aware of, Carol was well-liked by everyone, and she had good relationships with her colleagues. I can't imagine anyone wanting to harm her."

Reilly jumps in with the question, "Did she express any concerns about her safety or mention any fears to you or anyone else?"

"No, she didn't say anything like that. We mostly discussed patient care and shared some weekend plans. Carol seemed like her usual self, and there were no indications that she was worried about anything," says Jess.

"Thank you, Jess. If you remember anything else that could help our investigation, please don't hesitate to reach out to us," states Moore.

"Absolutely, detectives. I hope you catch the person responsible for this. Nurse Maddison was a kind-hearted person who didn't deserve any of this," sobs Jess.

The detectives continue their questioning, speaking to each staff member individually.

"Oh detective," shouts Jess. "She did say that she had a disagreement with her boyfriend Mark before she left for work, and she was really unhappy about how things had been between them lately."

"Did she mention the nature of the argument or what it was about?" asks Reilly.

"She didn't go into specific details, but she mentioned that it was something they had been struggling with for a while. I got the impression it was related to their relationship, maybe some unresolved issues or tension between them," says Jess.

Reilly raised an eyebrow, "That is surprising indeed. Mark never mentioned the argument when we spoke to him earlier. It's crucial that we speak to him again and find out more about this disagreement."

"Mark's emotional state and connection to Carol make him a person of interest. We cannot rule out the involvement of a staff member either. We need to consider all angles," says Moore.

Moore and Reilly make their way to Mark O'Shannessey's location, feeling a sense of urgency to confront him about his omission regarding the argument he had with Nurse Maddison.

They find Mark in a small waiting area, his eyes swollen from crying and his face filled with grief. Reilly takes a moment to empathize with his emotional state before speaking.

"Mark, we need to talk about something important. It has come to our attention that you had an argument with Nurse Maddison before she went missing. Can you tell us more about what happened?" says, Moore. Mark looks up, his gaze meeting Moore's stern eyes. He takes a deep breath, attempting to compose himself before answering.

"Carol wanted to start a family, but I was not ready for that commitment yet. I have been focused on my career as a graphic designer for an advertising agency, and I wanted to establish myself before taking such a big step. We disagreed on the timing, and it escalated into an intense argument. She was passionate about wanting to become a mother and felt that it was the right time for us to have a baby. I, on the other hand, felt overwhelmed by the responsibility and wanted to focus on advancing my career. It caused a lot of tension between us. We had arguments before, like any couple, but we always managed to work things out. This one felt different, though. It was intense, and she seemed really hurt by my stance," says Mark wiping his watery eye with his finger.

Moore and Reilly step aside to discuss their thoughts on Mark's account of the argument with Carol Maddison. Reilly leans into Moore so Mark could not hear her conversation. "I don't know, Moore. Mark seems genuine about the argument. He doesn't strike me as someone who would resort to violence."

"I agree, Reilly. People have disagreements all the time, especially about big life decisions like starting a family and I don't sense any deception from him at all either," says, Moore.

The detectives walk back to the nurse station situated in the middle of the corridor.

"Hi, what is your name?" asks Moore. "My name is Brenda; how can I help you?" Moore replies, "My name is Detective Moore, I have a quick question for you. Can you tell me where Nurse Maddison actually worked in the hospital? I need to gather some information about her work background and times." Brenda, looking up from her desk, meets Detective Moore's gaze with a serious yet cooperative expression.

"Of course, Detective Moore. Nurse Maddison worked primarily in the Trauma ward and close observation ward."

"Thank you, Brenda. Did she have any specific shifts or a regular schedule that she followed?" asks Reilly. Brenda consults the duty roster on her desk, scanning through the information.

"Nurse Maddison had a rotating schedule, which included both day and night. The specific shifts varied from week to week," mumbles Brenda.

"Thanks, Brenda for your help," says Moore as he walks away from the counter.

Moore's agitation is starting to escalate again, and he realises that he needs a moment to compose himself. He looks over at Reilly and says, "I need to use the restroom. I'll be right back." With that, he walks away, making his way to the nearest restroom. Once inside a cubicle, Moore shuts the door behind him, seeking a moment of solace. He reaches into his pocket retrieves the familiar flask containing whiskey and indulges in a drink.

Next, Moore takes out a small pill bottle from his pocket. He pops open the lid and carefully removes a couple of tablets. He swallows them, hoping that they will dull the shakes. Feeling slightly more composed, Moore takes a few moments to collect himself before returning to the investigation. He washes his hands, splashing cold water on his face to further shake off the lingering unease. He exits the restroom and re-joins Reilly who has been waiting patiently for him in the corridor.

Moore and Reilly return to the underground car park to the crime scene, where Allison Lord and her forensic team are still carefully examining the area for any potential clues. They approach Allison, who looks up from her work as they approach.

"Allison, any significant findings so far?" asks Moore. "We have found some fingerprints; we can compare these with the ones at the other murder scenes which can tell us if it's the same person as before. However, without a record, it still does not give us much," comments Allison.

"Keep me informed of any developments. We need to determine if Mark, Nurse Maddison's boyfriend, was involved in her death, we need to get his fingerprints as well." Moore says rubbing the back of his neck as if he has a pain developing.

Reilly says to Moore, "I might go and have a look upstairs in the close observation ward, see what's there, and ask some more questions."

Moore acknowledges her plan with a nod. "Sounds like a plan. We need to leave no stone unturned I will stay here for a bit and join you soon," says Moore.

Reilly makes her way to the elevator, determined to explore the ward and gather any relevant information that might shed light on the case. Reilly walks briskly along the corridor, her gaze fixed on the signs hanging on the walls indicating the various departments and wards. She scans the area, searching for any sign directing her to the Close Observation Ward. After a few moments, she spots a sign with the words "Close Observation and Rehabilitation Wards" accompanied by an arrow pointing to the right.

Following the arrow, Reilly makes her way down the corridor, passing by nurses and doctors attending to their duties. Reilly can hear the sounds of laughter and the occasional cry fill the air, a reminder of the delicate balance between joy and pain within the walls of the hospital. Reaching the entrance to the Rehabilitation Ward. Reilly approaches the nursing station, where Nurse Johnston is diligently going through paperwork. She approaches the nurse with a polite smile. "Excuse me, I'm Detective Reilly," she introduces herself, flashing her badge. "I'm investigating a case. Is there someone in charge I could speak to?"

Nurse Johnston looks up from her work, her eyes reflecting curiosity and concern. "I'm Nurse Johnston, and I'm in charge of this Rehabilitation ward," she responds, her voice calm and professional.

"Nurse Johnston," Reilly asks, "do you happen to know where the Close Observation Ward is and where Nurse Maddison was working recently?"

Nurse Johnston considers the question for a moment before responding. "Yes, Nurse Maddison was stationed a little further down the hall," she explains, gesturing in the direction. "She was assigned to the Close observation ward, just a few rooms away from here and you can call me Shelley."

Reilly nods, appreciating the information. "Thank you, Shelley," Reilly says.

Reilly walks down the hallway, following Shelley's directions. As she reaches the next ward, she is surprised to find the area filled with boxes, timber, and sheets of plaster leaning against the walls. It resembles a storage area rather than an active ward. Perplexed, Reilly retraces her steps and returns to Nurse Johnston.

"Excuse me, Shelley," Reilly addresses her, "I notice that the Close Observation Ward down the hall appears to be used for storage. Can you shed some light on this?"

Shelley nods and replies, "Oh, yes, Detective Reilly. We are in the process of converting that ward into office space. It is part of the hospital's renovation plan to accommodate administrative needs. The boxes and construction materials are temporary until the conversion is complete."

Reilly takes in the information, realising that Carol Maddison may not have been assigned to the storage area after all. "I see," she responds. "Thank you for clarifying that, Shelley."

"Due to recent changes, the patients were moved to other areas, and Nurse Maddison's role shifted to assisting with clearing the rooms of hospital equipment and other items."

"As we are short-staffed, her duties primarily involved managing the rooms when they were occupied by patients," Shelley elaborates. "However, with the recent relocation of patients to other areas, her tasks have mainly revolved around preparing the rooms for the renovation process. This includes organizing the clearing out of hospital equipment, furniture, and other materials."

Reilly inquires about the patients that Nurse Maddison was responsible for in her ward. Shelley informs her that there were three patients under Nurse Maddison's care: an elderly woman, a teenage boy, and an older man.

"Can you provide any information about the people Nurse Maddison was looking after?" Reilly asks Nurse Johnston.

Nurse Johnston pauses for a moment and goes through some paperwork she pulls out of the metal cabinet, to recall the details. "Certainly, Detective. The first patient was an elderly woman in her late 70s Mardi Boyle. She was admitted with a respiratory condition and required close monitoring and respiratory support."

Reilly takes notes, focusing on the elderly woman's condition. "And the second patient?" she inquires.

Nurse Johnston flipping the pages of the paperwork continues, "The second patient was a teenage boy, Peter Davis, around 16 years old. He was admitted for a severe fractured arm due to a sports injury. Nurse Maddison was responsible for his post-operative care and ensuring his comfort during his stay."

Reilly jots down the information about the teenage boy. "And the third patient?" she asks, eager to gather as much information as possible.

Reilly listens intently as Shelley provides more details about the third patient under Nurse Maddison's care. She learns that the third patient is in his mid-30s, has been hit by a car, and suffering from internal injuries. Due to the severity of his condition, he was allocated a room of his own for closer monitoring and specialised treatment under the care of Nurse Maddison but then was moved to another room, sharing with another patient, as the hospital needed the other room.

Reilly asks Shelley, "What is this area and these rooms?" and she continues her exploration of the ward near Shelley. Shelley speaks loudly, "Rehabilitation Ward."

While walking down the corridor and peering into the rooms, she approaches the end of the hallway, Reilly sees a room with the door slightly ajar. She hesitates for a moment before pushing the door open and peering inside. The room is dimly lit, and she can make out a figure lying on the bed near the door. Reilly notices a man looking at her.

"Excuse me," Reilly addresses the man, "I'm Detective Reilly. I am just looking around."

Reilly noticing the man's pale skin and thin frame. "What are you in for?" she asks "If you don't mind me asking?"

The man winces as he shifts in the bed. "I got hit by a car," he says, his voice strained.

Reilly nods sympathetically. "That must have been a shock," she says. "Do you remember anything about the accident?"

The man shakes his head. "No, not really," he replies. "It's all a blur. I just remember waking up here." Reilly senses she knows this man somehow, but in an instant, that feeling is gone.

"Well, I hope you feel better soon," she says, and Reilly heads back to Nurse Johnston.

She approaches Nurse Johnston with a curious expression on her face.

"Shelley, I just spoke with a patient down the hall who mentioned being hit by a car," Reilly begins. "Is he the same patient that Nurse Maddison was looking after in the other ward the Close Observation Ward?"

"Yes, that's right," she replies. "The other two patients were discharged after their recovery. Daniel Nash is the only remaining patient from that ward, and he is sharing a room with an elderly man called George. But George is currently away at physiotherapy."

Reilly's eyebrows furrow in thought. "Do you know if Nurse Maddison had any particular interactions or concerns regarding the patients she was looking after at the time?" she asks.

"No not that I know of," says Shelley.

"I couldn't help but notice that Daniel looks quite pale. How serious are his injuries from the car accident?" Asks Reilly.

Shelley sighs, her expression reflecting concern. "Daniel's injuries were quite severe," she explains. "He suffered multiple internal injuries, including internal bleeding, and underwent surgery to stabilise his condition. It was touch-and-go for a while, but he managed to pull through. However, his recovery has been slow, and he's still dealing with the effects of the accident."

"You mentioned that Daniel's recovery has been slow. Can you provide some insight into his current mobility? How far is he able to walk?" asks Reilly.

Shelley ponders for a moment before responding, "Daniel's mobility is quite limited at the moment. He's still in the early stages of rehabilitation and regaining strength. Currently, he can only manage to walk a couple of metres, if that. His endurance is quite low, and he requires assistance and support during any physical activity."

Reilly expresses her gratitude. "Thank you, Nurse Johnston. Your assistance in providing these details is invaluable." Reilly smiles at Nurse Johnston and walks back down the corridor to the nearest elevator and works her way back to Moore.

As she wanders through the dimly lit area or the underground car park, her eyes scan the surroundings, hoping to catch a glimpse of her colleague.

Her heart sinks as she spots Moore in a secluded corner near the bins, his face shadowed by the darkness. The glimmer of a whiskey flask in his hand confirms her worst fears. She approaches him cautiously, her voice laced with a mix of worry and disappointment.

"Moore, what are you doing? I've been looking for you everywhere. You can't be drinking on the job."

Moore's eyes flicker with guilt as he quickly conceals the flask behind his back. "Reilly, I... I just need something to numb the pain."

Reilly's voice softens as she takes a step closer. "I understand that you're going through a difficult time, but this isn't the way to cope, Moore. We're a team, me and you I need you focused and sober."

Moore's voice cracks as he confesses, "Reilly, I've been struggling ever since my wife's attempted suicide. The guilt, the v isions... They haunt me. I thought a few drinks would help me forget, but I know it's only making things worse." Reilly's voice hardens as she takes a step closer, her eyes piercing through

Moore's facade. "This is not just about today, Moore. We all have our demons, but that doesn't give you the right to drown them in alcohol. You're compromising our investigation and putting lives at risk."

Moore's voice trembles as he confesses, his words slurring slightly. "Reilly, you don't understand... My wife died, she wanted to kill herself... It tears me apart. I can't escape the guilt and the damn visions of her... They're driving me insane."

Reilly's anger intensifies, and her face flushes with frustration. "I've had enough, Moore! Go back to your damn hotel, sober up, and don't you dare show up here until you are fit for duty. If you can't get yourself together, I'll personally report you to Chief Dwyer, and you can deal with the consequences."

Moore's defensive stance falters as he tries to defend himself. "Reilly, you don't understand what I'm going through. I can't just switch off the pain. I need... I need something to numb it, even if it's just for a little while."

Reilly's eyes narrow, her voice filled with concern. "Moore, I get it. I do. But this is not the way to deal with your pain. You're jeopardising your career, and more importantly, you're putting yourself and others in danger. Moore's voice carries a hint of defiance as he tests the waters. "You won't run me in, Reilly. I'm a damn good detective, and you know it."

Reilly's anger surges forth, her voice sharp and filled with frustration. "Don't you dare try to use your reputation as a shield, Moore! Being a good detective doesn't give you a free pass to break the rules and risk everyone's safety. If you can't see that, then maybe you're not as good as you think you are!"

Her words hang in the air, a tense silence engulfing the dimly lit car park. Reilly's gaze shifts behind her, catching sight of a group of police officers watching them from a distance. She quickly realises that their conversation has drawn unwanted attention. Her anger subsides momentarily, replaced by a sense of urgency and professionalism.

With a composed yet determined expression, Reilly addresses Moore in a lower tone. "We'll continue this discussion later, Moore. Right now, we have an audience, and it's not doing either of us any favours. Go back to your hotel, sober up, and sort yourself out. We'll talk when you're in a better state of mind." Moore, now aware of the scrutiny they face, nods reluctantly and steps back, his defensiveness giving way to a mix of shame and resignation. As they part ways, Reilly's gaze lingers on the watching officers, "What are you looking at? Get back to work," growls Reilly, the police officers scatter and continue on what they were doing.

***

The next cold morning, Reilly strides up to Moore's hotel room and raps on the door. She knows that confronting the issue of Moore's drinking on the job is essential for the sake of their partnership and the integrity of their work. After a brief silence, the door opens, revealing Moore, looking more collected than the day before. He locks eyes with Reilly, understanding the gravity of this conversation. "Morning, Reilly," Moore greets her, his voice steady yet expectant.

"Morning, Moore," Reilly replies, stepping into the room. "We need to talk about yesterday, about the drinking." Moore nods, his expression serious. "I know, Reilly. I have crossed a line, and I apologise for compromising our investigation. It won't happen again." Reilly takes a moment to assess Moore's sincerity. She recognises the burden of his personal struggles and how they weigh on him.

Reilly's gaze shifts to the sight of the empty whiskey bottles scattered around Moore's hotel room. She cannot help but feel a mix of disappointment and concern rise within her. It is evident that Moore's struggle with alcohol is getting worse. Her voice softens, tinged with a hint of worry. "What's with all the empty bottles?" Moore's eyes drop to the floor, a flicker of shame crossing his face. "Reilly, I... I cannot resist. The pain... it overwhelms me at times." Reilly takes a deep breath, trying to find the right words. "Moore, I know it's not easy for you, but turning to alcohol won't solve anything. It only exacerbates the pain and clouds your judgment." Moore's shoulders slump, his voice filled with a mix of regret and frustration. "I know, Reilly. I'm trying, but it's just... so damn hard." Reilly steps closer to Moore, her concern evident in her eyes. She takes a deep breath, preparing herself to share a part of her past with Moore. She locks into his gaze and meets his stare.

"Moore, I understand more than you might think. My father was an alcoholic too."

"I'm not an alcoholic Reilly," growls Moore."

"You're on the way to becoming one!" snaps Reilly." He used to drink excessively, and it had a profound impact on our family," says, Reilly.

Moore's eyes widen with surprise and curiosity on his face.

"I had no idea. I'm sorry to hear that."   "It's something I don't talk about often. Growing up, my father's drinking led to anger and violence. I witnessed things that no child should see." Moore's expression softens, "I'm so sorry you had to go through that, Reilly." Reilly offers a small, appreciative smile. "Thank you. It was a difficult time, but it taught me the destructive power of alcohol."

Moore looks at Reilly. "I appreciate your support and understanding, Reilly. I do not want my personal struggles to affect the case or put anyone in danger. I'm ready to make a fresh start, to leave the alcohol behind and focus on our investigation."

Reilly speaks, "One step at a time, Moore. I know it won't be easy." Reilly extends her hand, and Moore firmly grasps it. They exchange a firm handshake, and they walk out of the hotel room.

21

Patients Are A Virtue

Daniel lies in his hospital bed, his breathing laboured and choppy, his heart pounding against his chest. The encounter with Detective Reilly has left him reeling, *why does she have to come in here and ask questions?*

His mind races with anticipation as the voices in his head grow louder, demanding for him to act, to protect himself no matter the cost. They taunt him, their insidious whispers echoing in his ears as they urge him to take a life and revel in the power that it brings. The line between reality and delusion blurs as Daniel battles against his own internal demons.

As the day stretches on, Daniel's paranoia intensifies. Every footstep on the floor, every distant whisper, fuels his growing sense of unease.

Daniel's gaze flicks to the door, his senses heighten, as he strains to listen for any sound outside. The police are getting closer; he can feel it. He has to be careful not to attract any unwanted attention. The hospital room feels oppressive and suffocating as if it conspires with the darkness to amplify his inner turmoil.

Beads of sweat form on Daniel's forehead, and his trembling hands clutch the edge of the bed sheets. He wishes he could escape to a place where no one knows him or his past. A place where he can start over anew. But most importantly, he needs to stay alive now and keep out of sight until this all blows over.

Nurse Johnston strides into Daniel's room, a tray of medication cradled in her hands. Her shoes clack against the unforgiving floor as she approaches his bedside. "Good afternoon, Daniel," she greets him with a warm smile, unaware of the darkness that lingers around him. "It's time for your medication."

Daniel's hands shake slightly as he reaches for the cup and tablets. He wraps his fingers around the cool plastic, taking solace from its fleeting embrace. He lifts it to his lips and swallows the pills quickly, before placing the cup back onto the tray.

Nurse Johnston's eyes drift to the scratch on his face with concern. "How's the scratch going, Daniel, is it healing properly?" A spark of anger flashes in Daniel's gaze as he stares at Nurse Johnston. To him, this is a minor problem compared to the turmoil inside of him. She cannot help him there.

"It's fine," Daniel replies curtly, his voice laced with indifference. "Just a scratch. Accidentally scratched it with a broken fingernail."

Nurse Johnston nods her expression sympathetic. "I'm sorry to hear that. It is important to be careful. If you need any ointment or further assistance, let me know."

Daniel simply nods, his mind drifting back to the sinister thoughts that consume him. The scratch on his face is a reminder of the power he holds, the control he exerts over those who dare to oppose him. Nurse Maddison's attempt to harm him had backfired, and he revels in the satisfaction of delivering his own form of justice.

Nurse Johnston smiles, her attention focused on the tray in her hands. Oblivious to the storm brewing within Daniel's mind, she carries on with her duties seemingly unaware of the danger that lurks beneath the surface. As Nurse Johnston moves the plastic cup on the tray, Daniel's gaze redirects to the nearby table where a pair of scissors rest innocently.

The voices in his head grow louder, urging him to seize the opportunity, to take control. He knows he must act quickly, catch her by surprise. "*Ram the scissors in her throat*" the voices scream at him. "*Cut the fuckin bitch.*"

Suddenly, Nurse Johnston's tear-streaked face catches Daniel's attention. He ignores the voices in his head for a moment and inquires, "What's wrong?"

Nurse Johnston takes a deep breath before answering, her voice trembling with emotion. "It's about Nurse Maddison, who was looking after you in the ICU and the close observation room. Well, she's been murdered in the car park here at the hospital."

Daniel's expression remains stoic, unmoved by the news of Nurse Maddison's murder, he did commit the act himself, after all. Nevertheless, a part of him feels a twinge of guilt and remorse, a fleeting moment of clarity amidst the chaos in his mind.

"I'm sorry to hear that," he says, his voice still flat and devoid of emotion.

Nurse Johnston looks at him with a mix of sadness and suspicion but doesn't press the issue. Instead, she fishes out a pamphlet on grief counselling from her pocket and hands it to him.

Daniel nods, accepting the pamphlet with a small smile. He knows he won't be seeking any counselling. As Nurse Johnston sobbingly leaves the room, he can feel the voices in his head getting louder and more insistent, urging him to act, to take another life.

Old George Dorta enters the room, his footsteps slow and unsteady. Daniel's eyes narrow as he watches him approach, his mind consumed by a twisted desire for violence. To Daniel, old George is nothing, an irritating piece of meat.

"Hey there," old George says, his voice frail and trembling. "How are you doing today? I just came back from physio; her hands are magical!"

Daniel's lips curl into a sinister smile, his gaze fixed on old George's vulnerable form. "Fine," he replies, his tone chillingly calm.

As old George moves closer, oblivious to the impending danger, Daniel's hands clench into fists, his muscles tensing with anticipation. The voices in his head scream with blood lust, urging him to strike, to satisfy his insatiable cravings.

But just as Daniel is about to unleash his madness upon old George, a sudden commotion erupts outside the room.

A public announcement blasts in the corridors over the speakers "CODE BLUE CODE BLUE - WARD 5A." The sound of hurried footsteps and voices fills the air.

Nurse Johnston re-enters the room, her eyes red and puffy from crying. She moves toward old George, concern etched on her face. Daniel's gaze follows her, curiosity mingling with his darker thoughts.

"George, are you okay?" Nurse Johnston asks, her voice filled with genuine worry.

Old George Dorta looks up at Nurse Johnston, his expression weary. "I'm fine, dear," he replies weakly. "Just an old man trying to get by."

Nurse Johnston places a gentle hand on George's shoulder, her touch filled with compassion. "Do you need anything? Don't hesitate to ask."

Daniel watches their interaction with detached interest, his mind still swirling with violent fantasies.

***

Night has descended, casting the hospital ward into a dimly lit silence. Old George lies sound asleep in his bed, oblivious to the evil that lurks beside him.

Daniel, consumed by the voices in his head, sits on the edge of the bed. The lack of footsteps and the vacant nurse station only intensify the urgency within him.

The voices, relentless and insistent, demand another victim. Their twisted whispers coil around Daniel's thoughts, fuelling his desire to quench their bloodlust.

He scans the room, his eyes fixating on the slumbering form of old George. Daniel's grip tightens, his fingers twitching to carry out the gruesome act that the voices command.

In the stillness of the room, Daniel contemplates the twisted satisfaction that awaits him. The voices, a chorus of malevolence, urge him closer to the edge of his sanity. Their whispers taunt him, promising respite from the torment that engulfs his mind.

As he strides closer to old George's bed, Daniel's heart pounds in his chest, each beat a crescendo of exhilaration. The desire to

unleash his inner darkness pulses through his veins, overpowering any lingering hint of morality.

But as Daniel's hand hovers over the slumbering man, a flicker
of recognition stirs within him. Images of past victims flash
before his eyes, their faces indelibly etched in his memory.

With a devilish smile, Daniel leans in closer to old George's
sleeping form. The scent of fear thickens the air, mingling with
the anticipation that hums within him. His fingers tighten
around the pillow that he is holding with zeal as he prepares to
unleash the darkness that hides deep within his soul.

In a single motion, Daniel strikes, his hands pushing down
the pillow onto old George's face. As he tightens his grip on
the cloth, a strange combination of delight and fear washes over
him. Gasping noises and feeble attempts to get away are muffled
beneath the pillow. The room is deathly still as Daniel presses
upon George's body with cold resolve. His fingers tighten, cutting off the old man's air supply until there's nothing left but an
eerie silence. Old George's final desperate movements cease, and
his body stills as Daniel grins wickedly in triumph.

Stepping away from the corpse, he calmly places the pillow
back on his bed, now wet and stained with saliva. Climbing
into bed himself, he savours the feel of the mattress beneath
him—his mind alive with sinister thoughts. He's content in
knowing that his dark desires have been fulfilled.

***

The PA System calls for a doctor which awakens Daniel from his fitful sleep. It is morning, as he stirs, Nurse Johnston stands in the doorway, looking saddened by the news she carries. Her puffy and red eyes speak volumes as she quietly says to him, "Daniel, I'm afraid George has passed away during the night."

Daniel sits up and takes it in. "What happened?" he asks weakly. Nurse Johnston explains that his heart gave out, despite getting a pacemaker recently.

"That's unfortunate," Daniel comments, feigning sympathy. Nurse Johnston looks at him for signs of distress, but his expression remains unchanged. He silently keeps his real thoughts hidden. Then calmly adds, "It's simply a reminder of how fleeting life can be."

Nurse Johnston's voice shakes with sadness as she speaks of her close relationship with Old George. Tears glisten in her eyes, conveying the depth of her feelings. "I had grown to care for him during his stay," she says gently. "He was such a gentle soul, and it's heartbreaking not to have him here."

Daniel nods sympathetically, all the while hiding his true motives behind a mask of empathy. "I can only imagine how hard this must be for you," he replies, compassion ringing through his voice. "Saying goodbye to someone you've formed an attachment with is never easy."

He watches as Nurse Johnston wipes away a tear, her despair present in every action. "It's been a difficult week," she continues, her words faltering. "To lose both a colleague and a wonderful patient so suddenly... It's too much." He feigns compassion for Nurse Johnston's struggles, although inside he takes pleasure in the chaos he has caused. His voice is honeyed with false sympathy as he remarks, "It must be tough. But life isn't always kind, is it?"

The nurse nods solemnly, her gaze cast downward. Daniel takes a long look at her, studying the sorrow that radiates from her body. He enjoys the sorrow of others, finding it almost intoxicating in its intensity. The conversation ends, and Daniel is left alone with his thoughts. As he looks around the room, his gaze falls upon old George's empty bed. After a few moments of silence, he smiles to himself in satisfaction—his mission is complete. He knows that the voices within him have been silenced for now. But it won't be long before they return and demand another kill.

22

THE NEWS

As the sirens blare outside, Reilly and Moore rush through the entrance doors of the hospital. The sliding doors shut behind them, muffling the noise. Reilly shares her findings with Moore as they hurry through the halls. Nurse Johnston's story about Nurse Maddison's patients intrigues Reilly. She believes that the man who was hit by a car could provide insight into Maddison's final moments. They quickly make their way to the rehabilitation ward to investigate further. Upon reaching the ward, Reilly and Moore spot Nurse Johnston attending to her duties nearby. Reilly approaches her with urgency. "Hi Shelley, we need to speak with the patient who was hit by a car. We believe he might have some insights into Nurse Maddison's activities before her death," Reilly explains. Nurse Johnston asks, "Oh, Daniel Nash you mean?" Reilly confirms, "That's correct."

Shelley acknowledges the Detective's request with a nod, fully aware of its importance. "Certainly, follow me and I'll lead you to him," she says. The detectives trail behind Nurse Johnston as she guides them through the ward, where they see numerous patients undergoing different kinds of rehabilitation. Upon reaching Daniel's bed, Reilly and Moore introduce themselves, causing Daniel to feel uneasy. Moore notices a jagged scratch on Daniel's face.

Detective Moore addresses Daniel, his eyes fixed on him, and points out a scratch on his face. "Nasty wound." Daniel looks back and forth between the detectives before stuttering, "Oh, that? I was hit by a car. I already told your partner. It caused some cuts and bruises." Reilly interrupts with her inquiry, asking if Daniel has a job. "No, I don't. I'm currently between jobs," Daniel replies. Reilly follows up with another question, asking about his previous job. Daniel shifts uncomfortably on the bed and adjusts his sitting position before admitting that he is a self-employed gardener.

Reilly carefully explains their purpose, emphasising their hope that he can provide any information about Nurse Maddison's last interactions.

Daniel takes a moment to collect his thoughts before responding, trying to act calm. "I remember Nurse Maddison," he says. "She was caring for me before I was moved to this ward. She seemed nice and professional. However, when I moved, I did not see her again after that. But one night before I was moved, I do recall something strange." Reilly leans closer, her curiosity heightening. "What is it? Please, tell us everything you remember." "After visiting hours, I heard raised voices coming from outside my room. It was Nurse Maddison arguing with someone. I couldn't make out the words, but the tone... it was heated." says Daniel lying.

"Did you see this person with Nurse Maddison?" asks Moore. "No, I could not see him," explains Daniel.

"So, it was a male?" queries Moore. Daniel nods at the detectives. Reilly and Moore exchange a glance, sensing the significance of Daniel's account. "Thank you for sharing this with us," Reilly says sincerely. A thought suddenly crosses Reilly's mind, she asks, "Daniel, have we met before?" Daniel looks at Reilly, his expression one of surprise. He takes a moment to think before responding, "I'm not sure, Detective. I don't recall ever meeting you until the other day when you poked your head in through the door."

Reilly is trying to recall any possible connection or familiarity. "It's just... there's something about you that feels familiar. Maybe it's just my imagination playing tricks on me." says, Reilly. Daniel offers a reassuring smile. "Well, sometimes people have a way of crossing paths without realising it. Perhaps we did meet at some point." Reilly nods, accepting his response but still feeling a nagging sense of curiosity. "Perhaps. In any case, thank you for your cooperation, Daniel. Your information has been valuable to our investigation," with that, Reilly and Moore leave the ward, leaving the question of their potential connection lingering in the air. Reilly and Moore pass Nurse Johnston in the hallway, Reilly turns and asks, "Did Nurse Maddison's boyfriend Mark ever come up to this ward?"

Nurse Johnston straight away answers, "No, I have never seen him up here Detective."

"Did Nurse Maddison ever have any close relationships with any of her colleagues?" asks Reilly.

"If you mean boyfriend, not that I know of," says Nurse Johnston.

"Thanks, Nurse," mumbles Moore.

Both detectives head back to their vehicle parked out on the main street.

***

Nurse Millwood strides into Daniel's room to relieve Nurse Johnston for an hour. Nurse Millwood is a seasoned nurse with a warm and friendly presence. She has shaved fair hair that frames her face, complemented by her captivating green eyes.

While filling up the water jug, Nurse Millwood gazes at Daniel lying in bed, a flicker of recognition crosses her face. She pauses for an instant, attempting to recall where she has seen him before. Suddenly, it hits her. Daniel is an orderly who works at this hospital.

Nurse Millwood takes a step closer to Daniel cautiously. "Excuse me," she begins her voice shaky. "I'm sorry if this seems odd, but you bear an uncanny resemblance to an orderly who works here sometimes. Are you him?"

Daniel stiffens, but he regains his composure swiftly. He plasters on a casual expression and pretends confusion. "No sorry, must be mistaken identity," he responds calmly. "I have never worked at this hospital or any other. I'm just a patient here."

She contemplates pushing further, but doubt overtakes her. She is not one hundred per cent sure and making false accusations against a patient could have serious ramifications, so she leaves it be. Nurse Millwood continues on her way, not before looking back in confusion, she then leaves the room.

***

As Reilly and Moore settle back into the squad car, Moore breaks the silence with a question. "Reilly, what was that all about? Why did you ask Daniel if you had met before?" "It's hard to explain, Moore. It was just a fleeting feeling, like a sense of familiarity. I can't quite put my finger on it, but something about Daniel struck a chord with me." Moore speaks, "Do you think there's a connection between him and the case?" Reilly sighs, a hint of frustration in her voice. "I don't know, Moore. It could be completely unrelated. I just have a feeling I know him from somewhere." The detectives drive off.

The two detectives take a break from their investigation to grab lunch at a nearby restaurant. They find a cosy table and settle in, discussing the case and enjoying their meal.

As Moore scans the restaurant, his eyes suddenly land on a woman sitting alone at a nearby table. It takes him a moment to recognise her, but then it clicks—it is Hannah, his late wife's best friend. Surprised, he nudges Reilly discreetly, nodding in Hannah's direction. Reilly follows his gaze and notices the woman at the table. She glances back at Moore, a questioning expression on her face.

"Who is that?" asks Reilly. Leaning closer, he explains to Reilly that the woman at the table is Hannah Blencowe, his late wife's best friend. Hannah Blencowe is a beautiful woman with long lush brunette hair, like a lion's mane, falls over her shoulders and down her back. Her eyes are a sea blue, highlighted with dark makeup, a hint of mascara, and eyeliner. Her mouth is scarlet red like an apple grown in the sun, 5"9 tall, and has a body straight out of a fashion magazine and she is a smart businesswoman.

Moore rises from the table, explaining to Reilly that he needs to speak with Hannah for a moment. He strides over to her table, his heart thumping with uneasiness. As he approaches, he tosses her a hesitant smile. Hannah looks back at him with surprise.

Moore commences the conversation by demanding why she was not present at his wife's funeral, voicing his confusion and hurt over her absence. Hannah's eyes widen, and a pained expression spreads across her face. She informs him that she had been overseas during that time and had no knowledge of Kate's passing until she returned from her trip. Moore grabs a seat next to Hannah, his heart heavy with regret and sorrow. He bares his soul to her, divulging the depths of his pain and the guilt that has oppressed him since his wife's attempted suicide. With a quavering voice, he admits how he believes his affair and betrayal led to her tragic end, unable to absolve himself for the destruction he had caused.

As he finishes speaking, Moore expects Hannah's confirmation of his guilt, prepared to bear the weight of her words. However, Hannah's expression morphs into compassion and profound sadness. She takes his hand in hers, her touch offering a sense of comfort and understanding.

Hannah's voice trembles as she speaks, her words filled with love. "David, you must know that Kate's decision was not because of your mistake. She loved you deeply, and she told me she forgave you. Her reasons for her actions are far beyond what you can control."

Moore's eyes widen in disbelief, his mind struggling to comprehend Hannah's words. He gazes at her, searching for clarity and understanding in her eyes. And then, with a trembling voice, Hannah reveals the truth that is haunting her.

"David, I need to share something with you. Something Kate confided in me," she begins, her voice filled with anguish. "She was diagnosed with brain cancer. It was a secret she chose to keep from everyone, including you. Kate confided in me and said she was going to leave a note explaining everything, but that must have burnt up in the fire. She insisted I not tell you, but now I have no choice, seeing you like this. She didn't want you to go through the pain and suffering she knew would follow."

Moore's world comes crashing down, the weight of the truth pressing upon him like an insurmountable burden. Mixed emotions swirl within him—relief that his actions didn't lead to her demise, grief for the loss of his wife, and anger that he was unaware of her struggle and Hannah kept it from him.

Hannah continues, her voice quivering with sorrow. "Kate loved you fiercely, David. She understood your flaws and mistakes, and she forgave you. Her decision to end her life was driven by her pain obviously and the desire to spare you from the anguish of witnessing her deterioration."

Overwhelmed by a flood of emotions and the weight of this revelation, Moore's strength crumbles. He tries to flee from

Hannah Blencowe and her news but collapses and drops to the floor, tears coursing down his face as he succumbs to the depths of his grief. Reilly, witnessing the scene unravel, rushes to his side, her voice filled with concern and compassion.

Reilly's voice booms as she glares at Hannah, barking out, "What did you say to him?"

Hannah quivers a bit, as she replies, "Something I should have said half a year ago".

She bursts out sobbing to Moore, "I had no idea she would actually go through with it. I'm sorry."

The restaurant is totally still, all eyes on Moore as he lay on the floor. Reilly notices everyone staring and barks out an order for them to get back to their own business while she helps him up. She gets him onto his feet and walks him carefully to the squad car to take him away.

As they settle into the vehicle, the door closes behind them, Reilly remains steadfast, determined to help her partner navigate through this turbulent time. With a sigh, she starts the engine; the sound fills the air, symbolising their retreat from the prying eyes and judgment of the outside world. Reilly's firm grip on the steering wheel guides the squad car through the city streets, the steady hum of the engine provides a backdrop to the silence that envelopes the vehicle. The journey back to Moore's hotel room is marked by an unspoken understanding, a mutual acknowledgment of the emotional turmoil he was experiencing.

Moore views the familiar surroundings of the hotel looming ahead. Reilly parks the car and turns off the engine with a soft click. She turns towards her colleague, "We're here, Moore."

Moore nods, his eyes still clouded with the weight of his grief. Opening the car door, he steps out, feeling the cool air embrace him. Reilly followed suit, standing by his side, a pillar of strength amidst his darkness. Together, they make their way to the hotel entrance. The corridor leading to Moore's room feels longer than usual.

As they make their way down the dim hallway, the shadows seem to stretch and ripple around them. The thick carpeting muffles the sound of their footsteps, but every step still seems to echo loudly in the silence.

Reilly walks next to him, her understanding evident in her eyes.

As they reach the door of Moore's room, his fingers tremble as he reaches for his key card, struggling to insert it into the lock. The door swings open, revealing the dimly lit interior of the room. Moore steps inside, and Reilly follows, crossing the threshold into his temporary sanctuary. She takes in the room, the place is a mess, and the smell of stale beer and rotten food lingers through the room.

"Take all the time you need, Moore," Reilly says softly, her voice carrying a gentle reassurance. "Do you want me to stay?"

"No, I want to be left alone for a while," mumbles Moore. As he slumps down on the sofa of dirty clothes.

As Reilly turns to leave, she says, "I will tell Chief Dwyer you are unwell."

Moore nods and begins to lie on his side.

Reilly felt useless, she did not know what to say. "I will come back later," she says quietly as she closes the door.

***

Reilly returns to the station, the chaotic energy of the afternoon shift in full effect. Colleagues brush past her, intent and driven, as they go about their duties. She strides directly to her desk, taking a moment to regroup and clear her mind. The events of the day linger heavily on Reilly's consciousness. Reilly sits at her desk and examines the case files, studying the evidence amassed so far, which is minimal. All she has are fingerprints on the car trunk that match those from an abandoned house and Faye Campbell's home, plus an inverted cross-carved into the vehicle's trunk. Her frustration heightens when she realises that if this criminal had any history of criminality, they would have apprehended him already.

Reilly studies the nurse's accounts, searching for any inconsistencies. The afternoon passes and her concentration never wavers, despite the exhaustion that comes with the need to solve this case quickly. Chief Dwyer scans the office looking for Detective Moore.

"Reilly," he says, his voice tinged with eagerness, "Do you know where Moore is?"

Reilly takes a moment to consider what to tell him. She decides to protect Moore's privacy and lies about his whereabouts.

"Chief, I took him back to the hotel. He's come down with a stomach bug and won't be able to continue working today," she says with a hint of worry in her voice. Chief Dwyer appears disappointed but nods in understanding.

"Let him rest up—we expect him back on duty as soon as possible."

Guilt rises within Reilly at her dishonesty, but she nods in agreement, nonetheless. "Of course, Chief. I'll let him know and we'll manage here without him."

Dwyer gives a final nod before walking away, leaving Allison Lord standing before Reilly with a file in hand and an expression of focus.

"Reilly, have you seen Detective Moore anywhere? I need to talk about Nurse Maddison's file urgently," Allison, asks, eyes scanning the room for any sign of Moore.

Reilly internally groans, knowing she'd have to come up with another excuse for Moore's absence. She straightens her back and responds, "Moore is downtown. Is there something specific you need?"

Allison replies. "Ah, I see. Well, we've found some new evidence relating to the case. Moore needs to be alerted right away."

Reilly nods, "I'll let Moore know about it right away. In the meantime, can you tell me quickly what you've found? It may help us progress with the inquiry."

Allison gives an affirmative nod and opens the folder in her hands. The two of them lean in closer; Reilly wanting to know more. Allison discloses that they have found skin tissue beneath one of Nurse Maddison's fingernails on her right hand; implying that she might have scratched someone in self-defence. Reilly takes in the information but appears overwhelmed by what Allison has just stated. "It's a major piece of the puzzle, Reilly. It could take us directly to the perpetrator." Allison comments with a hint of a smile on her face.

Reilly gazes at Allison like someone who has been stunned dumb, bewildered, and stupefied.

Allison yells at Reilly, "Pay attention! If there are scratches caused by her, then there should be marks left behind on the killer's face or arms."

Reilly's mind was a tumult of thoughts as she contemplates the repercussions of Nurse Maddison's injuries on the culprit. Could this person work at the hospital and have noticeable marks from their skirmish with the nurse?

Reilly beaming a big smile to Allison, grateful for her help. "Thank you, Allison," she says, nodding. "This could be a great piece of evidence for us."

Allison smiles back, pleased that she is being useful. "My pleasure, Reilly. I'm still looking into it and I'll let you know if I find anything else important."

Reilly takes her keys and hurries away, more determined than ever to bring good news to Detective Moore in his current state of distress. She drives to his hotel, her thoughts filled with how this breakthrough could cheer him up and give him comfort.

Arriving at the hotel, Reilly makes her way to Moore's room and knocks gently on the door, hoping he will be open to her presence. After a moment, the door opens, revealing Moore's weary face.

"Moore, I have something to share with you," Reilly begins, her voice filled with genuine warmth. "Allison found skin tissue under Nurse Madison's fingernail. It could be evidence of a scratch inflicted on the killer during the struggle. This brings us closer to identifying the person responsible."

Moore's eyes flicker with relief and intrigue shines through his sorrow. "That's... that's great news, Reilly," he stammers his voice a mix of gratitude and determination. "Maybe we're finally getting closer to finding out who did this."

Reilly nods, a small smile gracing her lips. "That's right, Moore."

Reilly glances at her watch and realises the time. She knows it is time to wrap up for the day and prepare for the tasks ahead.

"Moore," she says, her voice tinged with a hint of exhaustion, "It's getting late, and I need some rest. I'm going home and will get to the hospital first thing in the morning, how are you feeling? "

Moore nods, appreciating Reilly's concern for his well-being. "Thank you for everything today."

Reilly gives him an encouraging smile. "We're in this together, and we are making progress," she reassures him. "See you tomorrow," she adds, hoping Moore will accept her invitation.

23

MISHAP

Daniel is filled with a strange sensation of power and excitement. His dark thoughts yearn for the sight and taste of blood as if it is a sign of his command and authority. The lack of bloody combat leaves an empty feeling inside him, one only satisfied by the red liquid that contains life.

He sits in his wheelchair but is still able to think freely, letting his mind wander until he can almost feel the cold steel against warm skin and hear gasps of panic and muffled screaming.

The dark side of him longs for release through violence. The voices inside Daniel's head howl and rumble, feeding his fixation and driving him deeper into the shadows. The lack of bloodshed only makes them louder, strengthening his cravings and refining his wicked intent.

Daniel is aware that deep down, his demons are driven by a hunger for the thrill of their desires. He feels in control now, but it is just an appetiser to the bloody opera they yearn to conduct.

Daniel, concealed in his wheelchair, fights back a grin as he notices the benefit of pretending to be unable to walk far. His seemingly limited ability is nothing more than a trick, an ingeniously crafted cover that protects him from being held accountable for the dreadful deeds he commits.

As the Nurse guides him through the hospital halls, Daniel notices people looking at him with kindness and sorrow. He acts as if he is weak and helpless, but in reality, his brain is sharp and calculating, searching for chances to quench his dark desires.

As he kills more people, his disability becomes a key part of his cover. It makes him seem like an innocent person who could not be capable of such violence, helping him avoid suspicion. Even though his killings apart from Nurse Maddison have been put down as natural or complications of their illness by the medical staff.

Returning to the ward from physiotherapy, Nurse Johnston assists Daniel up into bed. She remarks on how much progress he has been making and that he will be mobile soon.

Daniel puts on a thankful smile as Nurse Johnston speaks, pretending to be grateful for her words. He understands how important it is to maintain the appearance of improvement and healing. Her praise only has him more motivated in his mission to create the illusion that he cannot move well and back up his false story. Once Nurse Johnston finishes her work, Daniel offers a feeble grin to thank her. He realises the significance of developing relationships with the hospital personnel, presenting an attitude of appreciation and cooperation to prevent coming under suspicion. Nurse Johnston's face has an expression of concern as she scans the table and floor, her eyes darting back and forth in search of something she seems to have misplaced. "What seems to be the matter, Nurse Johnston?" Daniel asks his voice laced with concern. "Is everything alright?"

Nurse Johnston sighs. "I can't seem to find my pen. It is a special one that I have been using for years. It has sentimental value, you know. I must have dropped it or left it somewhere."

"Oh, I'm sorry to hear that," Daniel replies, "I hope you find it. I would get down and help you, but I can't, I'm not much help am I?"

"Oh well, it will show up," says Nurse Johnston as she saunters out of the room.

Nurses and doctors, clad in their scrubs, move about with a certain weariness, their minds consumed by their own thoughts and the weight of the long hours ahead. The distant sound of beeping machines and hushed conversations create a haunting symphony that resonates through the halls.

In the nurse's station, the TV plays in the background, displaying a cooking show with an overly enthusiastic chef. His voice booms through the room, bouncing off the walls and merging with the ambient noises. The contrast between the cheerful banter on the screen and the sombre reality of the hospital creates an uncanny contrast, adding to the unsettling ambience.

As the clock strikes ten o'clock, the transition between shifts becomes tangible. Daytime staff start to filter out, their footsteps fading into the distance, while the night shift personnel arrive. They exchange brief greetings, acknowledging the passing of the torch from one group to another.

In the midst of this nocturnal transition, the hospital takes on a different energy.

Daniel lies in his hospital bed, his gaze fixated on the small crack in the door. It serves as a minuscule window into the world beyond, offering him a glimpse of the activity taking place outside his confined space. His eyes trace the jagged line of the crack, his mind wandering as he wonders what awaits beyond the door. Through that narrow opening, he catches fragments of movement and muffled sounds. The soft shuffling of footsteps, the occasional murmur of voices, the squeak of a gurney wheel. Each sound, each fleeting glimpse feeds his curiosity and stirs a mix of anticipation and anxiety within him.

Daniel strains his ears to catch the sound of the conversation happening just outside his room. The hushed voices of Nurse Johnston and Nurse Briggs seep through the crack in the door, carrying with them snippets of information.

Nurse Johnston's voice, warm and reassuring, blends with Nurse Briggs' brisk and efficient tone. They exchange updates, discussing vital signs, medication schedules, and any noteworthy changes in patient's conditions. Daniel's heart quickens as he catches snippets of his own name in their conversation. As the handover nears its end, the voices gradually fade away, replaced by the hum of the hospital's ambient sounds.

Daniel can hear footsteps heading towards his door, the light from the crack disappears, and someone is coming. Nurse Briggs cautiously peeks through the partially open door; her eyes fixate on Daniel lying peacefully in his bed, seemingly fast asleep. The room is dimly lit, with only a faint glow from the corridor seeping in, casting long shadows across the floor. Nurse Briggs then slowly retreats away from the door.

Daniel sits up slowly sliding off the bed he stands, his legs stiff, and sneaks to the door, his body still adjusting to the sensation of not standing and walking for a long period of time. Reaching the door, he peeks outside, scanning the area for any signs of movement or potential witnesses. The coast appears clear, and he seizes the opportunity to venture further into the unknown. Daniel's senses remain heightened, his instincts finely tuned to detect any unexpected encounters or unwelcome surprises. With every step, Daniel inches closer to the culmination of his dark desires, his mind consumed by the twisted satisfaction that awaits him. The corridors stretch out before him, a web of possibilities and opportunities, as he continues his stealthy journey toward his next act of violence.

The volume of the voices in his head is rising, demanding another kill. Daniel's footsteps are careful and deliberate as he moves along the tiled corridor. The cold tiles beneath his bare feet absorb the sound, muting his footfalls to a near-silent whisper. Each step he takes is calculated as if he's trying to blend into the very essence of the hospital's sterile atmosphere.

He notices the door is slightly open, enough not to make much noise. Approaching the door to the room, His hand trembles slightly as he reaches out to grasp the doorknob, his fingertips brushing against the cool metal. With a slow and deliberate push, the door eases open.

Daniel enters the room, his steps muffled by the cold tiles beneath his feet. The city lights filtering through the half-closed blinds cast haunting shadows on the figure lying motionless in the bed. The silence in the room is heavy, each breath he takes reverberating in his ears.

His heart pounds, its rhythm echoing through his chest, as he inches closer to his unsuspecting prey. A thin sheen of sweat coats his forehead, a testament to the nerve-wracking anticipation that courses through his veins.

The room is suffocating, the air thick with tension as he nears the bedside. He reaches for the firm pillow that is placed on the shelf under the bedside table. The rhythmic rise and fall of the sleeping form taunt him, a reminder of the fleeting moments that separate life from death.

Time slows, stretching the seconds into eternity as he prepares for the final act. His breath catches his senses on high alert. The slumbering figure stirs, a faint murmur escaping their lips, but it's too late to retreat.

He tightens his grip on the pillow, and a sudden movement catches his eye. The man on the bed stirs, his eyes fluttering open. Fear grips Daniel's heart as he realises his plan has been foiled. Daniel's mind races, desperately searching for a way to subdue the man without raising an alarm. With a surge of adrenaline, he lunges forward, covering the man's mouth with one hand, muffling any potential cries for help.

The struggle is fierce, the man fighting to break free from Daniel's grasp. Each second feels like an eternity as Daniel wrestles to maintain control, his breath quickening with the exertion. The room is filled with the sounds of their heavy breathing, a symphony of terror and survival.

In a desperate act to immobilise the man, Daniel's eyes dart to the nearby table, searching for a makeshift weapon. His gaze lands on a stylish blue pen, a glimmer of hope in the darkness.

He seizes it, his fingers trembling as he aims for a quick, decisive strike. With a forceful thrust, the pen plunges into the pillow beside the man's neck, missing its mark by mere centimetres.

The man's eyes widen in terror, their struggle intensifying. Daniel's mind races, realising he must act swiftly to complete his dark mission. The voices in his head grow more insistent, pushing him to unleash the final, fatal blow.

The man's eyes swell in fear as he struggles to take a breath. His gaze latches onto Daniel's face, begging for mercy that is swallowed by the pressure of Daniel's grip. Torment radiates from Daniel's eyes, a cruel reflection of the pain coursing through the man's veins. Without hesitation, Daniel places the pen on his neck and stares deeply into the man's eyes with a satisfied smirk. He pushes it through the skin with force, creating an ear-piercing shriek muffled under his hand that clamps down on the man's mouth.

A fountain of blood erupts from the puncture wound inflicted by the pen, Daniel's hand covers his victim's mouth muffling his gurgled screams. Completely entranced, Daniel stares into the man's eyes for what seems like an eternity as he pushes down relentlessly on his mouth. The bed is drenched in a crimson sea of blood and drips onto the floor creating an undeniable metallic taste that lingers in the air. The constant flow of vital fluid coming out of the man's neck shows no signs of stopping.

Daniel's hand shakes like a leaf in a hurricane as he gazes at the lifeless man lying on the bed, blood pooling around his head. Daniel's breathing becomes laboured, and his heart thuds against his chest like a battering ram. As Daniel releases his grip on the victim, he stands up slowly, his body trembling with shock and adrenaline. He stares at the corpse for a few moments in a daze before turning away, feeling sick to his stomach and unable to let go of what he had just done.

He takes one last look at the body, memorising every detail-gazing at the wound inflicted by him - before making his way to the door. Dry heaving, he struggles to hold back the bile that threatens to choke him. As he exits the room, he forces himself not to look back at what is now nothing more than a shell of human flesh.

He staggers out into the hallway, his hand and arm dripping with an oozing red syrup that coats his skin like a thick oil. He sprints towards the nearest restroom with dawning terror in his eyes, Daniel paints a bloodied cross on the mirror before frantically laying his appendage in the sink and switching on the tap. With trembling hands, he scrubs at his arm desperately, as if trying to claw back his life from the depths of hell itself, while each moment is stained a lighter diluted shade of crimson by the water. A discarded paper towel soon turns to pulp as he continues to scrub in a desperate attempt to rid himself of the cursed blood.

Satisfied with his appearance, he takes one last look in the mirror before leaving the restroom. Daniel takes hurried steps, his heart pounding in his chest with each step through the labyrinth of corridors. His every movement seems to take an eternity, but he persists despite an ever-growing chorus of voices demanding death within his head. He grits his teeth and clenches his fists as he pushes forward, desperate to reach the safety of his ward. Daniel gasps as he passes through the door, trembling with a primal terror that grips his body and refuses to let go.

***

It is 4.37 am and the silence of the hospital is shattered by a bloodcurdling scream echoing through the corridors. Nurses and doctors rush to the source, their faces etched with shock and horror as they discover the lifeless body of the victim. Patients stick their heads out of their rooms looking around to see what the commotion is all about. Word quickly spreads, and the hospital is thrown into chaos. Word spreads like wildfire through the hospital, the news of the murder sending shockwaves through its halls. Patients and staff alike exchange fearful glances, uncertain of who can be capable of such a heinous act. Panic and suspicion begin to seep into the once-sterile environment. Blood is scattered and splashed across the hallway leading away from the room and working its way into the restroom. Security guards rush around shouting telling people to go back to their rooms. The hospital goes into lockdown.

As the news of the murder ripples through the hospital, a palpable tension settles over the facility. Patients cling to their loved ones, and their sense of security is shattered. The hospital administration administers strict security measures, implementing stronger surveillance and tightening access controls. The walls seemed to close in, and fear creeps into every corner of the building.

Within the hospital's corridors, an unsettling silence settles in the wake of the heinous murder. The news spreads like wildfire, whispered among the staff and patients alike. Fear clings to the air, tightening its grip on everyone within the hospital's walls. Patients, already burdened by illness and vulnerability, now find themselves enveloped in a cloud of unease.

Nurse Johnston is still reeling from the shock of the murder as she navigates this tense new landscape. Her footsteps echo in the hollow silence, and the once-familiar walls seem to close in, casting long shadows that play tricks on her mind.

As Nurse Johnston tends to her patients, she senses their heightened anxiety. The once-safe haven of the hospital has become a place of uncertainty and fear. She provides reassurance with comforting words and a gentle touch to those in need. She is determined to bring back some sense of normalcy, even as the weight of the murder weighs heavily on her shoulders. One by one, Nurse Johnston enters the rooms, offering comfort and support to her patients. She listens attentively to their concerns, their fears about the recent tragedy that has unfolded within the hospital's walls. With a gentle touch, she reassures them, providing a soothing presence amidst the chaos. As she reaches Daniel's room, Nurse Johnston takes a moment to gather herself. She enters the room and approaches his bedside. Daniel, still unaware of the unfolding events, looks up at her with questioning eyes.

"Nurse Johnston, what's going on?" he asks, sensing the gravity of the situation from the atmosphere in the hospital.

Nurse Johnston's voice is steady, though her heart races within her chest. "Daniel, there's been an incident in the hospital," she begins her words carefully and measured. "A patient was found... murdered."

"Really?" Daniel stammers, his voice filled with disbelief.

Nurse Johnston observes Daniel's reaction carefully, her sympathetic smile fading slightly as she notices his lack of visible response to the news of the nearby murder. It surprises her, as most people would exhibit some degree of shock or concern upon hearing such unsettling information. Concerned about his seemingly detached demeanour, Nurse Johnston decides to address the issue directly.

"Daniel, I can sense that this news may have left you feeling unsettled," Nurse Johnston begins, her gaze locked with his. "It's perfectly normal to have various emotions in a situation like this. We all react differently to such events. If you need someone to talk to or if there's anything on your mind, please know that I am here to listen and support you."

"I'm fine," snaps Daniel.

Nurse Johnston is taken aback by Daniel's abrupt response, her eyes widening momentarily. She quickly regains her composure, understanding that his frustration may stem from the overwhelming situation rather than a personal attack. She takes a step back, giving him space, and offers a small nod and she leaves the room.

24

UNVEILING SHADOWS

Detective Reilly stands outside Moore's hotel room, her mind reeling from unexpected events. She anticipates Moore will take some time off to mourn the news of his wife, retreat into solitude, and find solace in his grief. However, Moore calls Reilly this morning, telling her he is ready to go. The door opens, revealing Moore standing there, his eyes reflecting determination with a touch of sorrow. Reilly notices the fatigue etched on his face, more than usual. Nevertheless, there is also a fire within him, a renewed sense of purpose that sends a shiver down Reilly's spine. "Reilly, come in," Moore greets her urgently. Reilly enters the room, scanning it with her gaze. She notices the whiskey and beer bottles have been cleared away, and the room looks remarkably fresh. "What's happening here?" she questions with confusion.

"A general clean up, Reilly, I can't believe I made such a mess," Moore declares.

She sits down and looks into Moore's eyes, trying to decipher what is going on. "I'm astonished by your strength, Moore," Reilly comments with a worried tone. "I expected you to take

some time to heal, to process everything that's happened."
Moore inhales deeply, his voice trembling yet determined. "Reilly, hearing the news from Hannah really knocked me for a loop.
I laid here last night, wondering what I have been doing --
downing drinks and pills to try to muffle the guilt. However,
her words gave me some kind of solace, ya know? I won't deny
Hannah's news hit me bloody hard."

Reilly nods, understanding the depths of Moore's resolve.

"Just remember, Moore, we are in this together," Reilly says.

Moore lifts his gaze to Reilly, full of appreciation.

The air hangs heavy in the silence until Moore finally gives a
nod and pushes himself up from the chair. "Let's go, Reilly," he
says picking a bouquet of fresh flowers from a vase.

"Where'd you get those?" inquires Reilly.

"I had the hotel supply them for me for a fee," Moore asserts,
marching ahead.

"Take me to the cemetery," says Moore.

Reilly observes Moore's actions, intrigued by his request to
visit the cemetery.

Without hesitation, she follows him as they make their way
out of the hotel room and towards the car.

The drive to the cemetery is filled with tense silence. Reilly
steals glances at Moore, wondering if Moore is all right.

They approach the cemetery, the atmosphere thick with despair and sorrow. The scent of freshly cut flowers floats on the breeze, its pleasant scent carries with it the poignant reminder of the reason for his visit.

Moore strides ahead, and Reilly follows closely behind.

As they near a particular gravestone, Moore stops, his fingers tenderly tracing the carved letters. Reilly notices the name on the tombstone and comprehends its significance. It is the name of Moore's beloved wife, Kate now departed.

Moore gently sets the fragrant flowers he brought on the grave, an act of love and remembrance. Reilly stands at a respectful distance as Moore pays his respects in silence.

Moore shifts his gaze to Reilly, the intensity unwavering. "Thank you, Reilly, I needed that," he says, his voice heavy with anguish.

Leaving the cemetery, Moore and Reilly return to their car. As they drive away, the wind whispers through the open windows, revealing the sounds of passing cars on the busy main street.

While driving down the busy main street, a radio call comes over the car speaker, VKT to Charlie 32 come in over. Moore grabs the mic and replies, "This is Charlie 32, go ahead." On the other end of the mic is the police station, "VKT to Charlie 32, your presence is needed at St Francis hospital immediately, someone has reported another murder over".

Reilly's grip on the steering wheel tightens as she listens to the urgent call coming through the car speaker. The news of another murder sent a shiver down her spine.

Without hesitation, Moore responds to the mic, his voice steady and resolute.

"Copy that, VKT. We are en route to St. Francis Hospital," Moore replies, his eyes meeting Reilly's for a brief moment, both detectives sharing a silent understanding of the gravity of the situation.

They immediately change their course; Moore places the blue police light on the dash.

Their car speeds towards the hospital with sirens blaring.

Reilly and Moore hurry to the hospital, a thick blanket of dread engulfing them. They hurry through the ER, their badges shining in the light of morning. Nurses and Doctors turn their heads, instantly recognising the detectives and sensing the gravity of the situation. They are directed to a room where a small group of officers and hospital staff are gathered. Reilly recognises the stern face of the officer in charge, Sergeant Flanagan.

"Hi, Sergeant Flanagan, what do we know so far?" Reilly asks, her eyes scanning the area for any additional information.

Sgt Flanagan begins his briefing, his voice low but authoritative. "We have a male victim, mid-40s, identified as Doug Lyell. He is a patient in this room, admitted for a respiratory condition. Cause of death appears to be blunt force trauma to the neck," he explains, his gaze shifting to the lifeless body lying on the hospital bed.

Reilly's eyes widen as she takes in the sight. The bed sheets are stained with blood, and medical equipment is lying on the floor. There is so much blood.

"The victim's personal belongings and medical records seem undisturbed," comments Sgt Flanagan. Reilly's mind races, her instincts sharpening. She looks around, searching for any potential clues.

Reilly's eyes widen as she follows the trail of blood. She steps carefully, her every movement deliberate as she approaches the restroom. The door stands slightly ajar. Sgt Flanagan's voice breaks through her thoughts, "The attacker went in there to wash the blood off, it's all over the basin and mirror, and an upside down cross is smeared on the mirror also detectives."

"Thanks, Flanagan," Reilly acknowledges, her voice laced with a sense of urgency. "We need to process that restroom thoroughly. Every trace of evidence matters."

Moore, always attentive to the logistical details, interjects with a question that aligns with Reilly's thoughts. "Is Allison Lord and her forensic team on the way?" he asks.

Sgt Flanagan nods, his expression serious. "Yes, sir," he affirms. "Allison and her team have been notified and should be arriving soon."

They realise that the killer is intentionally leaving behind these disturbing signs as a twisted signature. "Our killer is in this hospital," says Moore.

Reilly nods in agreement, her expression growing more serious. The realisation that the killer is among them, hiding in plain sight within the hospital's walls, sends a chill down their spines.

"We must exercise extreme caution and keep a close eye on everyone that works here. The killer could be a staff member," says Moore in a quiet voice.

Moore focuses as he directs his question to Sgt Flanagan, seeking any possible leads that could shed light on the mysterious events. Flanagan scanning through the notes he had gathered from the initial interviews conducted at the hospital. "I've spoken to a few nurses so far," Flanagan replies. "Most didn't report witnessing anything unusual last night or this morning."

"Oh, for fucks sake," growls Moore, "Are we ever gunna get a fucking break or what?"

Reilly winces at Moore's choice of words, finding them vulgar and unprofessional. She glances at Moore.

"Moore, we need to stay focused," Reilly interjects, her voice calm. "We can't let frustration get the better of us."

Reilly's eyes scan the corridor, observing the nurses gathered around with their curious gazes fixed on the ongoing investigation. Among them, she spots Nurse Johnston, whose presence catches her attention. Reilly wonders why Nurse Johnston, who works in a different ward, is among the onlookers. She mentally notes this observation, making a mental reminder to speak with Nurse Johnston later to satisfy her curiosity.

Suddenly, the door swings open on the elevator, and out walks Allison Lord, accompanied is her forensic team. Dressed in their white lab coats.

The area becomes electric with anticipation as they set up their equipment and get to work. Her photographer immediately starts taking photos of the Metz flash blinding onlookers. Allison, with her piercing gaze and razor-sharp intellect, commands the area, barking orders to her team. Reilly and Moore stand at the edge of the crime scene, their eyes lingering on Allison and her team as they work diligently. They exchange a few words in hushed tones. Both detectives are eager to see what Allison will uncover from the evidence they have gathered.

Reilly leans against a nearby wall, her arms crossed, and watches Allison's photographer capture every detail of the crime scene. They remain there for a while, silently observing the

forensic team's meticulous work. The atmosphere is charged
with the weight of the investigation.

Allison Lord walks out of the room, holding a plastic bag
with a clear window that reveals the contents within—a blue,
fancy pen. Reilly and Moore's attention is immediately drawn
to the item, their curiosity aroused. Allison approaches them,
"Detectives, take a look at this," she says, holding up the bag with
the pen inside. "This was the weapon that they used, in the neck
of the victim. Hitting the jugular vein, the poor guy did not have
a chance."

Reilly and Moore quickly look at each other in surprise, their
interest growing. Reilly steps forward, her eyes fixated on the
pen. "Any significance to it?" she asks, her voice filled with anticipation. Allison nods. "It's not just any ordinary pen. It is
a high-end brand, often associated with executives and profes-
sionals, but we do have a name on it, engraved in gold, Shelley
Johnston

Reilly's eyes flicker, and a sense of intrigue fills the air. She
leans in closer, her voice dropping to a hushed tone. "Shelley
Johnston? That's Nurse Johnston's pen."

Reilly and Moore exchange glances, their minds racing with
questions. *Could Nurse Johnston be connected to the murder in
some way?*

Moore comments, "I don't think Nurse Johnston would murder someone with her own pen, especially not with her name engraved on it, and then leave it at the crime scene."

Reilly nods in agreement, considering Moore's point. "You're right, it does seem unlikely. However, we cannot ignore the connection between Nurse Johnston and the pen."

Moore and Reilly make their way to the Rehabilitation Ward to interview Nurse Johnston about the incident that occurred.

Nurse Johnston slouches in the chair, her eyes flickering with caution as Reilly and Moore approach the nurse's station. Her body language reveals a subtle tension as if she is bracing herself for the upcoming conversation. Reilly takes a step forward, maintaining a professional demeanour. "Shelley, we'd like to speak with you regarding the recent incident. It's important that we gather all the information we can to assist in our investigation."

Shelley straightens up slightly, her expression turning more attentive. "Of course, Detective. How can I help you?"

Moore joins the conversation, his tone measured. "We're interested in understanding if you have any knowledge or insights related to the murder that took place. Any information, no matter how small, could be valuable in helping us solve the case."

"I've been busy attending to my patients. I haven't seen or heard anything out of the ordinary."

"Well, that is not entirely true is it Shelley? I noticed you standing with the other nurses in the corridor, at the murder scene, which is not anywhere near your ward looking after patients," says Reilly with a stern look on her face. Reilly observes Shelley closely, noting her initial reaction. She decides to press further, wanting to gouge her responses. "Are you familiar with a pen that goes by the name Shelley Johnston?"

Shelley's eyes light up, and she exclaims, "That's my pen! I've been looking for it everywhere! It was given to me by my father when I became a nurse," her voice carries a sense of relief as she explains, "It went missing a few days ago, and I've been trying to locate it. But I can assure you, it has nothing to do with the murder."

"Shelley, the pen was found lodged in the victim's neck in the very room in that corridor where you were standing earlier. That raises some serious questions." Says Moore.

Shelley's face pales, and she stammers, "I... I do not understand. How could my pen be involved in such a horrific incident? I swear, I have no knowledge or involvement in this, it is not even my work area"

"Can anyone verify this?" says Reilly.

"Yes, I do recall mentioning it to Daniel yesterday. I was searching for the pen around his table, and he offered to help me find it."

Reilly raises an eyebrow, intrigued by Shelley's response.

Reilly and Moore look at each other, Reilly speaks, "Where can we find Daniel at this moment?"

"Daniel should be in his room." Replies Shelley.

"How is his mobility nurse?" Asks Reilly.

"Daniel's mobility is limited due to his condition. He needs assistance to move around, and he uses a wheelchair for most of his activities. However, he can manage a very short distance with the help of a walking aid." Replies Shelley.

"How short?" asks Moore.

"A few metres, that is all," replies Shelley.

"Thank you, Nurse Johnston."

Shelley nods and guides Reilly and Moore towards Daniel's room. The hallway is filled with the sounds of bustling activity, but Nurse Johnston maintains her composure as they approach the door. She opens the door and steps aside to let the detectives enter first. Inside the room, Daniel sits on his bed, his gaze fixed on the floor. The room is dimly lit. "Hi Daniel, we are back for more questions if that's alright?" asks Reilly.

Daniel looking annoyed, "Do I have a choice detective?"

"No not really Daniel, just being polite," says Moore with a cheeky smile.

"Nurse Johnston mentioned that she lost a pen and was searching for it. Did she happen to ask you about it or mention it in your interactions?" Asks Reilly opening her notepad.

"Yes, Nurse Johnston did mention the missing pen to me. She was looking for it around my table and on the floor, and I offered to help her search for it. I explained to her I could not be much help though," replies Daniel.

Moore asks Daniel his question, "Did Nurse Johnston seem particularly concerned or upset about the missing pen?

Daniel hesitates before responding, his gaze shifting to Nurse Johnston standing at the door. "Well, she did seem a bit frustrated and mentioned that it was an important pen to her. But she didn't seem overly worried or distressed," mentions Daniel.

"Thank you for your cooperation, Daniel. We appreciate your assistance in this matter," says Reilly.

Reilly notices the scratch on Daniel's face, which appears redder and more pronounced than before. "Your scratch on your face Daniel" Reilly pointing to his cheek, "It's not healing?"

Nurse Johnston quickly interrupts the interview, "I have been monitoring Daniel's scratch, and it does appear to be getting more inflamed and weeping a bit also. I've been treating it with antiseptic ointment, but it hasn't improved as expected."

Moore butts in, "How did you get it again?"

Daniel with an annoyed expression, Look, Detectives, it is not a big deal. It was from when I was hit by the car, I mentioned that before."

"Oh, that's right, you did say that. Our mistake, replies Reilly.

"Thank you for your cooperation, Daniel. We appreciate your assistance in this matter," says Moore.

Daniel tries to get comfortable on his bed, "Am I a suspect?" he asks.

"Not at all Daniel, just getting information that can help in the case," says Reilly. With that, Reilly and Moore conclude their interview with Daniel, and they exit the room.

Reilly and Moore bid farewell to Nurse Johnston and make their way down the corridor, ready to delve deeper into the twisted puzzle that surrounds the hospital murders.

Reilly and Moore make their way back to the murder scene, where Allison Lord, the forensic expert, awaits their return. As they enter the room, they find Allison meticulously examining the area, her attention focused on every detail.

Allison Lord, the forensic expert, shares her findings with Reilly and Moore. "The evidence and injuries suggest it was a botched attempt at smothering," she explains. "The fight between the victim and the attacker leads to a pen being used as a weapon, resulting in a deadly plunge into the neck."

Moore is inquisitive. "You mean the killer was going to suffo-cate him with a pillow, how do you know that?" he asks Allison.

Allison interjects, "A nurse told me that all the spare pillows are usually kept under the table on a tight-fitting shelf. The fact that the contents of the table have remained undisturbed while the pillow is now on the floor strongly suggests it was pulled out. The pillow was torn during the scuffle and ink around the hole in the cushion on the ripped opening further supports the theory of forceful impact and perhaps even a pen being stabbed into it, but I could be wrong."

Reilly cuts in, "Could the killer have done this to more peo-ple?"

Reilly's question hangs in the air, filling the room with a sense of unease. Allison pauses for a moment, "It's certainly a disturbing thought," she says, her voice tinged with concern. "If the killer has targeted this victim in such a way, it raises the possibility that they could be doing it again or have done it before."

Moore inquires, "But if the killer suffocated them, why wasn't it reported?" Allison murmurs, "It could have been deemed natural death, considering their ailments. That's what I would rule."

Allison's observation sparks a realisation in Reilly and Moore. "You're right," Reilly says, her voice filled with understanding.

"Given the victims medical conditions, their deaths could be attributed to natural causes without arousing suspicion."

"Holy Shit," exclaims Moore in disbelief.

Reilly queries Moore, "What do you think about the Daniel guy?" Moore looks at Reilly and says, "He uses a wheelchair, Reilly. Focus on someone who can walk or run, Reilly. Judging by how they get around, I'd say it's definitely a staff member."

"You are right, Moore. It does seem impossible that someone in a wheelchair could maneuver unnoticed. There is just something about that guy I cannot get out of my head." says Reilly.

Moore emphasises, "We should concentrate our efforts on people who have the ability to move around without suspicion, like doctors and nurses."

"Excuse me, Detective Reilly, can I speak with you?" Shouts Shelley from a distance.

Reilly raises an eyebrow at Nurse Johnston's urgent request. She strolls casually over to Shelley standing at the police tape stretching across the corridor, marking the boundaries of the crime scene.

Shelley's face has a worrying look on it. She lowers her voice, her words filled with apprehension. "Detective Reilly, I need to tell you something about Daniel,"

Reilly's curiosity awakens, her attention fully focused on Nurse Johnston. "Go ahead, Shelley. What is it?"

Shelley takes a deep breath, her hands trembling slightly. "The scratch on Daniel's face... it wasn't caused by the car accident. He lied about it. The truth is, he got that scratch around the same time as Nurse Maddison's murder. He told me he scratched it with a broken fingernail on his hand."

A look of concern washes over Reilly. She leans in closer, ensuring their conversation remains confidential. "Are you certain about this, Shelley? Could it be a coincidence?"

Shelley shakes her head; her eyes fill with worry. "I've been treating that scratch, it only showed up after he arrived here. He lied about it, Detective."

Reilly's wrinkles are more prominent on her brow, contemplating Nurse Johnston's words. The puzzle pieces seem to clash, creating a sense of confusion. She leans in closer to Shelley, lowering her voice to a whisper. "I understand your concern, Shelley, but how could Daniel be responsible for Nurse Maddison's murder or this murder here with Doug Lyell? He's in a wheelchair, after all."

Shelley's eyes dart nervously around the corridor before focusing on Reilly. "I know it seems unlikely, but there's something off about Daniel."

"I understand your perspective, Shelley," Reilly replies, her voice thoughtful. "However, we need to approach this investigation with an open mind. It's essential to gather more evidence before drawing any conclusions. Just because there is something off about Daniel, does not make him a killer. You said it yourself he can only walk a couple of metres."

Shelley looks somewhat disappointed but acknowledges Reilly's stance. "I just thought it was worth mentioning, Detective Reilly. I've seen my fair share of things during my time here at the hospital."

"Thank you for bringing this to my attention, Shelley," says Reilly turning away from her and making her way back under the police tape.

Shelley stands there disappointed watching Reilly return to Detective Moore at the crime scene, she then turns and heads back to her ward.

25

THE DILEMMA

Reilly and Moore stand in the hallway of the hospital, surrounded by a complement of Coulson's police force. Officers chatter while processing and investigating the murder scene.

"Moore, I've made up my mind. I'm returning to interrogate Daniel again about the scratch on his face. Nurse Johnston's account has raised some serious suspicions, and I can't ignore them," Reilly declares firmly.

"Reilly, I get your point, but maybe you're getting too caught up in the little things? We have a bigger problem to solve here. Going after Daniel based on a scratch seems like grasping at straws, so make sure you hurry; we have to attend Chief Dwyer's briefing soon," protests Moore.

"I hear you, but sometimes it's the small details that lead us to the greater truth. We can't ignore any possible clues or discrepancies. If Daniel is lying about the scratch, maybe there's something bigger he's keeping silent about." Reilly states.

"Alright then, don't take too long," Moore says.

Reilly steps back under the police tape and strides down the corridor.

Reilly enters Daniel's room, her feet dragging on the ground. Nurse Johnston's disconcerting facts about the scratch on Daniel's face linger in her mind. She knows she must challenge him about this deception.

Reilly strides in, seeing Nurse Johnston attending to a scratch on Daniel's face as she snips away at the gauze with her scissors. Daniel reclines on his bed, glaring up at Reilly with undisguised hostility and resentment.

"What do you want now? Haven't I already answered enough of your damn questions?"

Reilly keeps her composure, her voice controlled yet commanding. "Daniel, we need to talk about this scratch on your face. Nurse Johnston said it wasn't caused by the car accident like you said."

Nurse Johnston apologises to Daniel for divulging the truth.

Daniel shoots Nurse Johnston a venomous stare, making her cower in fear.

"Your lying only generates more questions. We deserve the truth," says Reilly.

The voices in Daniel's head ignite into rage, bellowing at him to slay the intruder.

Daniel stammers, W-Well, I might have gotten confused...It happened when I accidentally scratched myself with a broken fingernail. It was nothing."

Daniel's frustration mounts as his face reddens with anger. "Why don't you believe me?!" he yells, his voice quivering with disbelief and indignation. Every nerve in his body trembles as he struggles to contain the rage that boils inside him.

His eyes, which were formerly tranquil and steady, now smoulder with a fierce intensity, a mirror of the chaos churning within him. The atmosphere grows tensely charged with the unspoken words suspended in the air between them. "I've been cooperative," he snarls through gritted teeth, his hands balling into fists at his sides, "I've answered all your damn questions!"

The weight of his frustration hangs heavy in the room, each word he says bursting with energy. The atmosphere crackles with a fiery intensity, a clash of wills that seems to distort reality. He struggles to keep his mounting emotions at bay, a fight waged on the battleground of his own restraint. His voice, once steady, wavers with the intensity of his feelings, a testament to the storm raging beneath his calm facade. Suddenly, in a flash, Daniel shifts and seizes Nurse Johnston by the arm as he yanks her scissors from her hand and presses them against her neck while standing up and holding her hostage.

Reilly's heart pounds in her chest as she witnesses Daniel's sudden shift in behaviour. Reilly fixates on Daniel as if he has transformed into another person.

Panic and adrenaline surge through her veins, but she remains steadfast, her mind racing to find a solution to diffuse the dangerous situation.

"Nurse Johnston, stay calm," Reilly commands, her voice steady despite the rising tension in the room. Her eyes lock onto Daniel, assessing his every move. "Daniel, listen to me. This is not the way to resolve anything. Let her go and we can figure this out together."

"I know you have a gun detective, take it out slowly and throw it on the bed." Snarls Daniel.

Reilly's heart pounds in her chest as she processes Daniel's demand. She knows that complying with his request might buy them some time and de-escalate the situation, but it also puts her at a disadvantage. Reilly remembers the academy training, never give up your gun. But with a deep breath, she decides to comply for now, hoping to find an opportunity to regain control.

***

Detective Moore stares at the gruesome sight before him, his gaze unwavering. The room is cloaked in an unearthly silence, only to be broken by the sound of his steady inhalations. He carefully scours the scene while having a conversation with one of the officers.

Suddenly, a figure races from the other end of the hallway towards him and he can make out her frantic strides. The nurse is panting heavily and it's evident that she ran all the way here. Her terror-stricken expression and shaking hands make her fear palpable.

"Detective Moore!" she cries out in a trembling voice as she extends her palms for support. "You have to come now! It's Nurse Johnston and Detective Reilly."

***

Reilly keeps her gaze fixed on Daniel as she slowly reaches for her holster, moving with precision and control. She retrieves her firearm and places it on the bed, making sure it is within reach but not in immediate danger. "Daniel," Reilly says in a calm and measured voice, "I've left the gun on the bed. Now please release Nurse Johnston. We can discuss this and find a solution that doesn't harm anyone." Though Daniel holds onto Nurse Johnston tightly, his eyes betray a hint of uncertainty. His voice shakes with fury as he speaks, "You think I'm a monster, don't you? Do you believe I enjoy hurting others? But you don't know what I've been through."

Reilly remains composed and speaks with compassion, "Daniel, we want to understand. We want to help you. However, keeping Nurse Johnston captive won't resolve anything. Please release her, and we can address your pain." Nurse Johnston, her face pale with fear, also pleads with Daniel, "Please, Daniel, listen to Detective Reilly. They're here to help. Let me go," she begs while struggling to free herself from his grip. "We all battle our own demons, Daniel," Reilly says, her voice delicate.

"Demons! What the fuck do you know about demons? I am Legion, for I am many," he roars, tightening his hold on her.

Time seems to stretch as Daniel deliberates, his grip on Nurse Johnston loosening ever so slightly. It is a fragile moment, a pivotal juncture where lives hang in the balance. Reilly holds her breath, her gaze locked with Daniel's, willing him to make the right choice.

Reilly takes a step forward, Daniel notices it, and he shouts, "Get back bitch or else." Reilly freezes in her tracks, her heart pounding in her chest. She knows that any sudden movement could escalate the situation further. With a calm but firm voice, she responds, "Daniel, let us talk this through. There is no need for anyone else to get hurt. We can find a way to resolve this peacefully."

Daniel's eyes dart between Reilly and Nurse Johnston, his grip tightening once more. "I said, stay back! Don't test me!"

His voice trembles with anger and fear. The sharp edge of the scissors slices into Nurse Johnston's delicate skin. A cry of pain escapes her lips, and blood begins to trickle from the deep laceration on her neck. Reilly's heart sinks, a surge of adrenaline coursing through her veins. Blood continues to seep from Nurse Johnston's wound, staining her uniform as she trembles in pain and fear.

Daniel now knows he holds a dangerous advantage, with the sharp blade of the scissors pressing against Nurse Johnston's vulnerable neck. The weight of the situation bears down on him, but he also senses the fragility of his own position. Detective Reilly's revolver, a symbol of authority and control, lies tantalisingly close to the bed in front of him. It is a tempting temptation, a potential means of escape or defence.

The room hangs in suspense, the air thick with uncertainty. Reilly's eyes remain fixed on Daniel, trying to gauge his next move, searching for any signs of wavering or vulnerability. Daniel with Nurse Johnston close to him and scissors still to her neck rushes for the revolver on the bed.

Nurse Johnston screams a deathly scream that echoes through the room as the scissors pierce her neck deep, blood splattering the pristine white floor. The sight sends a shock wave of horror through Reilly, fuelling her determination to subdue the dangerous assailant. As Nurse Johnston grips her neck she falls to the floor, Reilly's heart pounds in her chest as she lunges at Daniel, her instincts taking over. With a surge of adrenaline, she tackles him just as his fingers brush against the revolver on the bed knocking the gun over near the wall. The two of them crash to the ground, grappling with each other in a desperate struggle for control. Reilly's mind races amidst the chaos of their struggle, her muscles straining against Daniel's desperate resistance. However, amidst the intensity of the moment, a flicker of recognition ignites within her. As their eyes lock, a rush of memories floods Reilly's mind.

She is transported back to that fateful day in the dark pine forest, where she was attacked. The piercing gaze that had haunted her dreams now finds its way to Daniel's eyes. It is he, the attacker she can see him now. A chilling realisation takes hold of Reilly's thoughts. The resemblance is unnerving—the same chill, the same predatory glint. The pieces start to fit together, and a sinister truth starts to take shape, she is face-to-face with the very person responsible for her own suffering. Daniel's grip tightens around Reilly's neck, cutting off her air supply. She resists the encroaching darkness, determined not to succumb to the stifling pressure. Every fibre of Reilly's being is focused on survival. Her instincts kick in and she musters every ounce of force within her to break free from Daniel's stifling hold. With a surge of energy, she swings her elbow into Daniel's side, attempting to weaken his hold, but it does not seem to make any difference.

Daniel, fuelled by desperation and the need to regain control, grabs the bloody scissors from the floor. With a menacing gleam in his eyes, he pushes the cold metal blades against Reilly's neck. The razor-sharp points dig into her skin, triggering a sharp intake of breath from her. A wave of fear washes over Reilly, but she refuses to let it overpower her. Her mind races desperately, searching for an escape from this perilous predicament. She knows one wrong move could cost her life. They stand locked in place as Daniel has her by the waist and scissors at the neck, Reilly's eyes drop involuntarily, and her gaze falls on the still body of Nurse Johnston sprawled on the floor. The sight of her motionless frame and blood streaming across the floor like an ocean of red paint.

Daniel yanks Reilly out into the corridor, the scene playing out before the horrified onlookers. Nurses, doctors, and security guards stand back, their faces etched with fear and confusion. The gravity of the situation hangs in the air, keeping them immobile and unable to do anything but watch.

Reilly knows she is running out of time as each second brings her closer to a devastating outcome. Her eyes frantically search for a glimmer of assistance among the anxious faces, her heart pounding with desperation.

Daniel's back presses against the cold corridor wall, his body tense with anxiety. With every step he takes, he inches closer to an exit, searching the surroundings for any sign of potential interference. His voice booms through the hallway as he orders them all to keep their distance and stay away. Voices rumble in Daniel's head, loud whispers urging him to do bad things. He struggles against the darkness inside, trying hard not to give in. But it is a losing battle, as the voices keep coming, pushing him to unleash violence.

Amidst the deafening chaos, his grip on reality slips further. Reilly is his lifeline, a fragile tether to his fading humanity. She is the only barrier shielding him from the abyss, a delicate shield standing between his uncontrollable urges and the innocent lives surrounding him. His trembling hands tighten their grip on the chilling scissors, their icy touch grazing against Reilly's vulnerable neck. The weight of his survival rests heavily on his shoulders as he contemplates his only chance of escape.

The onlookers, their faces etched with terror, reluctantly part like a sea, granting Daniel a path forward. Each step he takes is a treacherous journey through the depths of his fractured mind. It is a battlefield where competing voices wage war, tearing at his sanity with relentless fervour. The clamour of the voices intensifies, drowning out all reason and sanity. Their power suffocates him as if his mind were a pressure cooker about to detonate.

His muscles and joints ache with tension, the strain of resisting their insidious influence coursing through his veins. Every movement is a struggle, as if invisible chains bind him, constricting his freedom and suffocating his will. He pushes backward through an exit door, and Daniel's desperate escape leads him through the dimly lit stairwell, his steps reverberating off the cold, concrete walls. The voices in his head relentlessly bombard him, climaxing with each downward step. His descent is a gruelling battle against time, and Daniel's breath grows heavy. Sweat beads upon his forehead, mingling with the cries of his tortured thoughts. The scissors pressed against Reilly's neck serve as a constant reminder of his tenuous control. The stairs seem to stretch on forever.

As Daniel reaches the ground floor, he pushes open the exit door and returns into another corridor, he drags Reilly with him heading for the way out. He scans the surroundings, searching for any sign of escape or possible refuge. As Reilly and Daniel stand in the ground floor corridor, consumed by the intensity of their struggle, a distant voice slices through the chaotic haze. "Reilly!" the voice calls out. Reilly recognises the familiar tone—it is Moore. Her eyes dart towards the source of the voice, and there, emerging from the bustling crowd, is Moore, gun in hand, sprinting towards them. The weight of relief washes over Reilly, knowing that she is not alone in this harrowing ordeal. Screams of onlookers fill the corridor.

Moore's eyes lock onto Reilly, as he navigates through the flurry of people, his focus unwavering. Each stride brings him closer, his presence a beacon of hope amid the darkness that engulfs them.

Daniel's gaze shifts between Reilly and the approaching detective, his mind racing with calculations and decisions that could alter the course of their fate. Moore closes the distance, and his voice rings out once again, commanding and resolute. "Let her go! It is over! Drop the weapon!"

For Daniel, the corridor becomes a stage of blurred movements and heightened tension. As Moore reaches the scene, his footsteps falter for a split second, his eyes scanning the intense standoff before him. His grip on the revolver tightens.

His knuckles turn white, as he squares his shoulders and raises the weapon, aiming it directly at Daniel and Reilly. "It's over! Release her and drop the scissors!" Moore's voice reverberates through the corridor, a commanding tone laced with a sense of urgency.

Leaning against the wall, Daniel's breath is ragged and uneven and steals a fleeting glance at Moore. The glint of scissors pressed against Reilly's neck remains a chilling reminder of the perilous situation they're trapped in. In this heart-pounding standoff, the corridor reverberates with the hushed gasps of onlookers, the air saturated with electrifying tension. Every eye is locked on the trio, hearts racing in unison, as they collectively hold their breath, teetering on the edge of the unknown.

Moore's finger hovers over the trigger of his revolver, his unwavering gaze locked onto Daniel's. The weight of an impending decision bears down on him, the gravity of the outcome clear in his mind. One misstep could unleash a cascade of catastrophic events.

A stark realisation washes over Daniel. The illusion of control he clung to is crumbling, his power dissolving like smoke in the wind. He's ensnared within the confines of his own making, a prisoner of his desperate choices.

Then, like a lightning strike, Reilly summons an adrenaline-fueled surge of determination. In a burst of energy, she wrenches herself free from Daniel's grip, narrowly evading the deadly arc of the scissors. The air is thick with the tension of split seconds, the entire confrontation hanging in precarious balance.

With a desperate lunge, Daniel's hand stretches out, the scissors aimed to strike with lethal precision. Moore's training takes over, his senses honed to a razor's edge. He's been watching, calculating, anticipating. His finger tightens on the trigger of his revolver, muscles responding to the urgent call of duty. A sharp crack shatters the tense air as gunfire erupts through the corridor.

Time fractures into fragments as the bullet hurtles through space, finding its target with chilling accuracy. A suspended moment follows the trajectory of the bullet intersecting with Daniel's shoulder, a fraction of an inch from disaster. The impact jolts him, the searing pain merging with a disorienting rush.

The scissors slip from Daniel's grasp, their clatter against the ground a dissonant echo in the chaos. Gravity tugs at him as his balance falters his grip on reality slipping. The corridor becomes a battleground of wills, a crucible of fate, and in the midst of it all, Daniel stands on the precipice of a life-altering outcome.

As Reilly darts agilely out of harm's reach, Moore stands resolute, his unwavering focus riveted on Daniel. His grip on the weapon is unyielding, his senses heightened to an acute awareness, prepared for the next perilous move. The corridor trembles with tension, the very air fraught with the weight of imminent consequences, the crescendo of this pivotal clash.

In a desperate, frenzied bid for freedom, Daniel's hand lunges out like a striking viper, seizing a nearby nurse in his grasp. His fingers coil around her arm like a vice, desperation in his eyes as he clings to the last threads of hope. The nurse's wide eyes mirror her terror, her body paralysed by the nightmare unfolding before her. The corridor transforms into a crucible of raw emotions.

Within the breathless hush of the corridor, the scene shatters into pandemonium. Onlookers gasp in horror, their faces contorted with shock at the sudden twist of fate. The innocent nurse's cries pierce the air, an anguished melody that reverberates through the chaos. Moore's heart pounds in his chest, as he comprehends the urgency of the situation.

With unwavering resolve, Moore's finger once again finds the trigger, the world around him narrowing into a singular focus. The deafening roar of gunfire drowns out the frantic cries, momentarily silencing the turmoil. The bullet streaks through the corridor like a deadly comet, its path unfaltering, its aim true.

Time slows, and the bullet finds its mark with chilling accuracy. It strikes Daniel's chest. His grip on the nurse slackens, his eyes wide with shock and disbelief. The corridor seems to hold its breath, a suspended moment in which fates are sealed.

As the wounded Daniel staggers back, the nurse freed from his grasp dashes to the closest helping arm reaching out. The atmosphere crackles with the aftermath of violence, a stark reminder that within the span of heartbeats, lives can irrevocably change.

Daniel's body slumps and slides down against the wall, blood pooling beneath him, as life slowly ebbs away. Moore, his duty fulfilled, lowers his weapon, the gravity of the situation etched upon his face. He approaches the freed nurse, his steps are measured and deliberate, focusing on providing any assistance he can in the aftermath of the chaos.

Reilly stands nearby, her eyes filled with relief. She had hoped for a different outcome.

Reilly takes a moment to compose herself, her breathing slowly returning to normal as the adrenaline subsides.

Reilly races back to the ward, desperately hoping to find Nurse Johnston alive and well. The corridors blur around her as she pushes through the bustling hospital staff. The weight of regret and sorrow hangs heavy on her shoulders. However, as Reilly reaches the ward, her worst fears are realised. Nurse Johnston's lifeless body lies still, surrounded by medical personnel who tried in vain to save her. The room is filled with an overwhelming sense of loss and grief, and Reilly's eyes well up with tears.

At that moment, Reilly realises the magnitude of the tragedy that has unfolded. She feels an immense responsibility for Shelley's fate, haunted by the belief that she could have done more to prevent it. Guilt washes over her, threatening to consume her.

Reilly takes a trembling step forward, her hand reaching out to touch Shelley's cold, lifeless face. She whispers a heartfelt apology, her voice choked with emotion.

Moore rushes to Reilly's side, his presence a comforting anchor amidst the storm of emotions that engulf her. He places a
gentle hand on her shoulder, offering silent support and understanding. The chaos has brought them closer, forging a bond
that transcends words.

Together, they stand in the presence of Nurse Johnston's
lifeless body, their hearts heavy with grief. Moore, too, feels
the weight of responsibility for what has transpired. Moore's
thoughts turn introspective as he reflects on his personal struggles with alcohol addiction and the impact it had on his ability
to fully engage in the investigation. He acknowledges that his
intoxication and reliance on pills clouded his judgment and
hindered his capacity to be present and attentive to the details.

Back at the scene of the shooting, Reilly and Moore return, standing and looking at the body of Daniel under the
blood-stained sheet that has been laid over him.

Chief Dwyer arrives. He surveys the aftermath of the intense
confrontation, his eyes lingering on the covered body of Daniel,
the man who had caused so much chaos and devastation. Moore
and Reilly, standing nearby, meet Chief Dwyer's gaze, their expressions a reflection of the toll this case has taken on them.
Dwyer approaches them with a sombre mood.

"I'm sorry you both had to go through this," Chief Dwyer
says, his tone heavy with genuine empathy. "You did what you

had to do to protect yourselves and others. It's a tragic outcome, but sometimes, there is no other choice." Moore nods, his eyes weary yet determined. "We did what we had to do," he responds, his voice carrying a hint of sadness. "But it doesn't make it any easier."

Reilly, her emotions still raw, looks to Chief Dwyer for guidance. "What happens next, Chief?" she asks.

Chief Dwyer sighs, his look shifting to the surrounding officers who are securing the scene. "We'll conduct a thorough investigation, as we always do," he explains. "We'll piece together what led to this moment, gather witness testimonies, and ensure that all the necessary protocols are followed."

He pauses for a moment, his view turning back to Moore and Reilly. "You both will be debriefed, and we'll provide you with any support you may need during this time." Moore and Reilly nod, grateful for the support offered by their Chief.

"You've proved yourselves as capable and resilient officers." With that, Chief Dwyer turns and walks over to Allison Lord and talks to her.

Moore and Reilly remain where they are, sharing a quiet moment of reflection amidst the controlled chaos.

Reilly mentions to Moore that while Daniel had Nurse Johnston hostage, he mentioned that he was Legion, for we are many. Moore's eyes widen as Reilly mentions Daniel's claim of being

"Legion" memories of his own research on the subject flood his mind. "You're right," Moore replies, his voice tinged with realisation. "I remember reading that out aloud to you about the Gerasene demoniac and the concept of "Legion" in the New Testament. It is often associated with demonic possession."

He pauses, contemplating the implications of this revelation. "Schizophrenia," he continues thoughtfully. "It's possible that Daniel was suffering from schizophrenia, which could explain his delusions and erratic behaviour."

Chief Dwyer walks back to both detectives, "Start heading back to the station for your debriefings." Chief Dwyer's voice breaks the solemn silence that envelops the scene. Moore and Reilly turn their attention towards him, acknowledging him with a nod.

"Yes, Chief," Moore responds, his voice steady despite the whirlwind of emotions swirling within him. He takes one last glance at the covered body of Daniel, a reminder of the darkness they had faced. Reilly, too, gathers her composure, ready to face the debriefing and share their account of the events. She knows that this is just the beginning of the process, as the incident will be thoroughly examined and analysed. As the two of them start making their way back to the station, the reality of the situation sinks in.

Upon reaching the station, Moore and Reilly prepare themselves for the debriefing, knowing that the road to closure and healing will be long. They will need to share their accounts, provide insights, and face the tough questions that arise. As they enter the station, their resolve remains unshaken.

***

A few days later, Moore and Reilly receive the news later in the day. The weight of uncertainty and self-doubt that had been lingering is lifted. Knowing that their actions were justified and within the bounds of their duty.

In the following days, Moore began attending AA meetings, determined to address his personal struggles with addiction head-on. Reilly, on the other hand, seeks professional counselling to help navigate the complex emotions that have surfaced during this ordeal.

Together, Moore and Reilly attend Nurse Johnston's funeral, standing alongside her grieving family and friends. It is a solemn occasion, a time for them to pay their respects to the dedicated nurse who tragically lost her life. They find solace in the collective support and remembrance of a woman who dedicated herself to caring for others.

As Moore reflects on his journey alongside Reilly, a deep sense of gratitude fills his heart. He recognises that his initial resistance to having a partner, especially a female one, was rooted in his own biases and preconceived notions. However, working alongside Reilly has shattered those stereotypes and proved to him the immense value of collaboration and trust.

Moore acknowledges that without Reilly's quick thinking, bravery, and unwavering support during their encounter with Daniel, the outcome could have been much different. Moore has learned the importance of relying on others, embracing diversity, and acknowledging the strengths that individuals bring to the table.

At that moment, Moore feels a deep sense of respect and admiration for Reilly. He realises that his career and, quite possibly, his life have been greatly enriched by having Reilly by his side.

A week has passed, and a few small cases have been resolved.

Moore is taken aback when he discovers that Reilly has been approached by her old station in Hobart with an offer to return. Mixed emotions flood his mind as he grapples with the realization that their partnership, which had grown into a deep bond, might be ending.

Part of him feels a sense of pride for Reilly, knowing that her skills and dedication have been recognized by her former colleagues. He understands that returning to her old station could offer her familiarity, a chance to work in a familiar environment, and perhaps even more opportunities for career advancement.

Whatever Reilly decides, Moore is determined to cherish the time they have shared and the memories they have created. Their partnership has made an indelible mark on his career and personal growth, and he will forever be grateful for the experiences they have had together.

As Moore awaits Reilly's decision, he prepares himself for the possibility of facing new challenges on his own or with a new partner. He knows that change is inevitable in the ever-evolving world of law enforcement.

Reilly's announcement that she will stay brings a sense of relief to Moore. He listens attentively as she outlines the rules of agreement, a mixture of lightheartedness and sincerity in her voice.

First, Reilly suggests that she take over driving duties, as she has noticed Moore's less-than-stellar driving skills. They share a light-hearted chuckle, recognizing the need for a safer and more efficient mode of transportation during their investigations.

Next, Reilly gently brings up the topic of personal hygiene, playfully mentioning that Moore could benefit from wearing deodorant more often. She emphasises the importance of maintaining a professional image and minimizing any potential distractions. Moore, though slightly embarrassed, agrees to make a conscious effort to address this matter.

Finally, Reilly expresses her genuine concern for Moore's well-being. She emphasises the importance of open communication and trust between partners, encouraging him to confide in her if he is struggling with anything, be it personal or professional. She reassures him that she is there to support him through thick and thin.

Moore listens to Reilly's conditions with a mix of gratitude and amusement. He appreciates her straightforwardness and the underlying message of care and camaraderie in her requests. He agrees wholeheartedly to the terms, recognizing that their partnership is based on mutual respect and understanding.

With their rules of agreement in place, Moore and Reilly share a renewed sense of commitment to their partnership. They know that challenges will arise, but they are determined to face them together, supporting each other every step of the way.

Together, they navigate the complexities of their cases, relying on each other's strengths and unwavering support.

Reilly and Moore sit at a large window of their favourite local pub, a quiet respite from the chaos of their demanding lives. The air was thick with the scent of nostalgia and the weight of unspoken words. As they sipped their drinks, their eyes met a silent understanding passing between them.

"You know, Reilly, when we first started working together, never thought we would make it this far. I had my doubts about having a partner, especially a female one. But you proved me wrong, I am grateful to have had you by my side. You saved my career, maybe even my life," says Moore.

A mixture of emotions swirled within Reilly's gaze. "You saved me too, Moore."

Moore sitting by the window looks out at the city's skyline as the sun begins to set. Reilly's eyes caught Moore's reflection in the glass. Reilly took a seat closer, her voice softening. "You know, there's something about the way we work together. We make a good team, Moore."

Moore's eyes meet hers; his eyes fill with gratitude and some-thing more. "We do, Reilly. I couldn't have asked for a better partner."

As the last rays of sunlight cast a warm glow in the room, they sit together, their shared experiences etched in their minds. The future was uncertain, but one thing was clear - their journey was far from over. A new beginning loomed on the horizon, hint-ing at a future where their partnership, and perhaps something more, would continue to evolve.